This book is dedicated to my Late Grandmother,
Elizabeth Taylor Wilson
'Lily'
Thank you fo

GW00726741

BOOK NAME: SAINTS, SINNERS AND TV DINNERS
AUTHOR NAME: LISA MAJURY
TRAFFORD NUMBER: 06-0433
ISBN NUMBER: 141208677-9

Note for Librarians: A cataloguing record for this book is available from Library and Archives Canada at www.collectionscanada.ca/amicus/index-e.html
ISBN 1-4120-8677-9

Printed in Victoria, BC, Canada. Printed on paper with minimum 30% recycled fibre. Trafford's print shop runs on "green energy" from solar, wind and other environmentally-friendly power sources.

TRAFFORD
PUBLISHING™
Offices in Canada, USA, Ireland and UK

Book sales for North America and international:
Trafford Publishing, 6E–2333 Government St.,
Victoria, BC V8T 4P4 CANADA
phone 250 383 6864 (toll-free 1 888 232 4444)
fax 250 383 6804; email to orders@trafford.com
Book sales in Europe:
Trafford Publishing (UK) Limited, 9 Park End Street, 2nd Floor
Oxford, UK OX1 1HH UNITED KINGDOM
phone 44 (0)1865 722 113 (local rate 0845 230 9601)
facsimile 44 (0)1865 722 868; info.uk@trafford.com
Order online at:
trafford.com/06-0433

10 9 8 7 6 5 4 3

Saints, Sinners & TV Dinners

Lisa Majury

CHAPTER ONE

"We're going to Dublin!" cried Pauline at the top of her voice. Analeise wasn't in the mood to hear her bubbly but very dear friend feeling and sounding so jolly! She was parked outside a Beauty Salon in the Arsehole of nowhere and wondered what kind of clientele would frequent such an establishment! She was having a bit of a shit day and wished she had thrown a 'sickie'.

Pauline had been Analeise's best friend for years, she was always happy, always bubbly, and to everyone's annoyance, probably the nicest person in the world, was never negative, even whenever things were rock bottom. She was the type of friend that everyone would call for advice. Her words of wisdom were a mere drop in the ocean in comparison to her very big, generous heart. Pauline always put her friends and her family first, which is why she always looked like she had been pulled through a hedge backwards. She didn't give fiddlers what she looked like! She was relatively attractive but didn't believe in hairbrushes, clothes brushes and sometimes toothbrushes! "Couldn't be arsed!" she would say when people told her to make more of an effort on herself. She would often get dressed under the duvet on very cold mornings, be known famously for wearing the same make-up 2 days in a row, and cut her hair with kitchen scissors when it wasn't behaving itself! These are just a handful of her terrible habits, but on the whole she was a diamond, and looked like a princess when 'she *could* be arsed!'

" Where are you today baby? " Pauline asked, realising that it might not be a good time to talk to her lovable, but very moody friend.

" Outside a salon in Ballyclare staring at a couple of sheep, life doesn't get much more exciting than this! " Analeise replied as she pouted to herself in the rear view mirror.

" Never mind that, we're going to Dublin next weekend so make sure you clear it with Martin, its all booked and organised, gotta go byee!"

She hung up.

That one-minute phone call was enough to cheer her up for the rest of the day. She was in a marriage, which was going nowhere. Analeise thought whenever she married Martin two years ago things would get better. They had been together for a total of ten years, which deteriorated year upon year. Analeise loved him dearly even though his selfish ways made her life a misery. He never used to be selfish, in fact whenever she met him things were very different.

She met him whenever she was working temporary for a vending company in Belfast. They started dating and were head over heels in love. He was Analiese's first and only love. At the time she was a part time model for a top model agency. She loved it and got a lot of work. Martin didn't really like the idea of this, so she gave it all up for him. He also didn't like the fact that Analeise had lots of friends who might have been a 'bad influence' on her.

So she ditched them too.

For years Martin was the only thing in Analeise's life. He was a plain old ordinary Sales Rep whenever they met, but he wanted to further his career. They went on a holiday to Florida where Martin started messing around with a camera, and then he became more and more interested in photography.

Analeise helped him and supported him all the way. They would have spent night after night in his makeshift darkroom.

That was Analeise's only outlet in life; she became very dependant on Martin because he was all she had!

The more interested he became in photography the less interested he was in his devoted girlfriend.

He would get invited to special bar openings and premiers and leave Analeise behind most weekends.

She couldn't imagine her life without him, and told no one about how she was treated.

Her new career was the only thing that kept her sane. She was very lucky to land the position as Regional Sales Developer with a prosperous company such as 'Dermarome' a French Skincare Company where she was in full control of business in Ireland. It involved travelling in her company car to various Beauty Salons around all corners of the Island. Some small towns wouldn't be the most glamorous, quite dingy to be frank! Analeise loved it anyway. It was a good excuse to get away from her bog standard role as housewife, or 'general dogs body' as she would prefer to describe it.

"I'm going to Dublin with Pauline and Jenny next weekend!" Analeise announced to Martin as he walked through the door of the flat that evening, he was clutched to yet another Dolce and Gabanna carrier bag. (Analeise was convinced he was on 'first name terms' with the designing Duo!)

Ignoring her comment he sailed into the small kitchen and looked at what is best described as ' Death by Chicken Stir-fry'. She wasn't exactly Gordon Ramsey standard, although liked to think she was!

" What the hell is that in the pan?" he asked as he stared down at the sorry sight, which lay before him.

" It will be chicken fajitas, " she proudly announced as she stirred (a little too rapidly!) Spilling sauce all over the place.

She tried so hard to be adventurous at cooking, but the long and the short of it was; she was a terrible cook. She would spend hours in the kitchen destroying perfectly good food.

" Why, what did it used to be?" he laughed.

Analeise looked at her pan of mush trying really hard to be positive!

She was hurt; she'd spent ages trying to make something special for tea.

" Why don't you just get yourself a takeaway then you ungrateful bastard".

"Think I will" he screwed up his nose "I might get food poisoning!"

He then walked in to the lounge, sat down on the uncomfortable sofa and unravelled his perfectly folded Blue Designer Shirt.

She was sick of him always ridiculing her, no matter how hard she tried. He would never offer to help as housework was completely below him. She would spend all her spare time ironing, cooking, cleaning and picking up his socks and cacks! His shirts just *had* to be ironed to perfection! (Just the way his Mum would do them!) Analeise was as good at ironing as she was at cooking! She remembers burning lots of Designer clothes in failed attempts at 'ironing to perfection!' Anyway, he had far too many important things to do like photographing Beautiful Women for the front cover of Magazines. Martin Moran was a good-looking, arrogant brilliant photographer and knew it. He had become so cocky and confident in the last few years. He was rude, aggressive and headstrong to everyone in his life. This included Analeise's friends and family who he just refused to tolerate. He would never listen to anyone's advice because he always knew better. His phone would never stop with Women just begging to spend studio time with him.

Even so- Analeise loved him unconditionally.

The week dragged in for Analeise and Saturday couldn't have came quickly enough. It had been a long time since she had been on a night out. Pauline was such a star for organising the weekend. She knew Martin was a bit of a wanker towards Analeise and knew she needed to get away from him for a night. The further the better! Of course Martin didn't give one if she was away or not. She kissed him excitedly as she left the flat at 5.30 that evening with her little modest overnight bag.

He wiped his face and raised his arm as he stared at his computer screen without looking up. He was delighted to get rid of her for a night out so he could spend quality time with his 'Beautiful People'.

At 6.00 that evening Pauline and her mixed up friend Jenny stood and waited at Belfast city hall for Analeise.

"I wonder should I go to the loo now? Oh my nerves are wrecked!" Jenny kept repeating while she bounced up and down. It was obvious that she hasn't had a night out without Colin, her overprotective husband in some time. Pauline and Jenny worked together in the department store selling cosmetics. Sometimes Analeise wondered how Pauline ever got employment in the Beauty Industry. The truth is that she was Personality Plus and everyone loved her, scruffy or not! That is where she originally met Analeise 6 years ago and took her under her wing. She taught her a load of 'Tricks of the Trade' like how to apply make-up under the counter so that nobody could see! When somebody wanted to know the price of a bottle of perfume (this worked especially well with men!) always, always quote the most expensive bottle and to tell him or her that is much better value! She taught her how to wrap gifts to perfection by using the smallest sheet of paper!

They remained friends ever since.

Jenny Sharpe. 5'8 inches, long blonde, straight and shiny hair, always a full face of make up, nails always polished, totally immaculate and incredibly intimidating! She could sell anything. Pauline would stand and watch bewildered, confused housewives leave the store with bagfuls of beauty products in the hope of eternal youth, and wonder how the hell Jenny slept in her bed at night!

Jenny and Pauline were like chalk and cheese. Complete opposites!

"Oh my god, I wish Analeise would hurry up" she cried, doing an Indian rain dance in the street.

She arrived within minutes.

Four hours later after about 10 piss- stops, and a Mc Donald's on the way down, they finally arrived in Dublin. They were staying in a rented, two-bedroom penthouse apartment for the evening, which overlooked the popular Temple Bar area, which at weekends is full to the brim of party animals!

"Happy days!" shouted Pauline as she bounced on the bed wrecking Jenny's carefully laid out clothes.

"What are you wearing?" Analeise asked Pauline as she wiggled into her dress.

"This" she said pointing at herself like first prize in a raffle.

Pauline wasn't prepared to change from the clothes she travelled in.

"Jeans and a vest top?" Jenny stopped and looked at her with disgust.

"And trendy boots!" she pointed at her chosen footwear as if it made a huge difference! "I can't help being naturally stunning!!"

She laughed.

The others looked at each other and shrugged.

"There is just no hope for you my dear friend!" Analeise said as she jumped on top of Pauline. The two of them wrestled on top of Jenny's dress.

"Just hurry up and get ready, its nearly 11.00. We're missing good drinking time." said Jenny as she rolled the two of them off the bed to retrieve her no longer perfectly ironed garment.

CHAPTER TWO

Whenever they eventually got ready it was 11.45, so they hit the first bar they came to and started drinking wine. It was a bit of a scruffy drinking mans bar, but they didn't care they stayed there until around 1.30am.

"Lets go to Zoo!" A famous nightclub in Dublin, which has been host to many musicians and movie stars.

"We'll never get in," said Jenny as she fumbled into her bag in search of some lippy.

"Just keep your mouths shut, and I will get us in.," announced Pauline.

The walk to Zoo nightclub seemed short for everyone except Analeise, who at this stage had a matching pair of blisters on each heel.

"Hi there" Pauline said in her best Texan accent to a sober looking doorman.

"Oh my good god!" mumbled Analeise.

"Are you members?" asked one of the curious looking men.

"No" she continued (The accent was becoming more exaggerated!)

"You see we are all stewardesses from Virgin airlines, we've just flown in from Miami, and would just love to go dancing in your club."

The men looked at each other in sheer disbelief.

"It is members only, but seeing its quiet tonight you can go on in"

No one spoke; Analeise and Jenny prayed that no one on the door would ask them a question. All they were capable of was a very large Texan smile.

The nightclub was a sea of beautiful people wearing designer clothes. The dance floor when it was eventually found was a mere postage stamp full to the brim of people trying really hard to impress.

"Stuff this," said Analeise "I want to sit down somewhere, my feet are really starting to hurt now"

Analeise walked (like she was constipated!) over to a couple of very elegant chairs in the corner of the room and found her space for the rest of the evening.

"Ana, you're such a fader!" Pauline announced as she handed her a glass of wine.

"Twenty four fucking Euro for three drinks!" she said as she drank her eight Euros worth down in one.

"Excuse me" A very elegant man wearing an expensive suit, looking like Kevin Costner from The Bodyguard was standing opposite Analeise.

"You can't sit there"

Analeise was disappointed for two reasons. One being that she dreaded standing up again, and the second reason was Kevin Bodyguard didn't actually fancy her. He just wanted her to get off the seats!

"Why?" She asked.

"You need to be a regular to sit here" he replied.

"That's ok, I'm as regular as clockwork!" Analeise laughed.

Kevin didn't.

"I'm up!" Analeise sheepishly got up, only to find Jenny and Pauline engrossed in conversation with a weird bald headed guy who was inviting the girls back to his privileged seats.

"C'mon with us, we're going into the VIP room!" Jenny whispered to Analeise.

"Anything for a seat!" she groaned.

When they got behind the velvet curtain there were two young men, one a slick Italian whose eyes were stripping everyone naked. He was a hairdresser. The other guy, who was well built, wearing a 'spray-on' T-shirt had the hairiest arms known to mankind happened to be a record producer by the name of Paul.

The guys ordered champagne all night. Eventually the slick Italian took himself off after a few attemps to get into Jenny's knickers. Analeise was having the time of her life, she even temporarily forgot about her blisters. It had been a long time since she felt this good. Analeise *was* beautiful although in the last few years had lost a lot of interest in herself. She managed to keep her youthful looks with the help of a very strict skincare regime! She certainly didn't look 33 years old! Martin had stripped her of any kind of confidence; she didn't believe anyone who told her that she was attractive.

"Party in Parnell Square!" cried Pauline. "Lets go".

Jenny looked at her watch. It was 3.30am and she was delighted to be still standing upright!

Everyone followed Pauline and weird bald headed guy to an apartment block.

Through a door, which opened to another door, four flights of stairs, and one more door to find the most amazing state of the art apartment. It had floor to ceiling windows the whole way around, and the most amazing white leather sofa in the shape of a doughnut in the centre of the room. There were fabulous sculptures all around. This led into another room, which had an enormous mixing desk, and all kinds of digital technology.

"Don't touch anything" shouted Paul as Jenny had started to sing Blue moon of Kentucky.

Paul had taken a fancy to Analeise although she had no idea. She was far too fascinated by the fabulous apartment. She was like a child on its first visit to Disneyland.

"You're very beautiful." He said.

"Why thank you." She blushed. "But your apartment is much more beautiful" She was flattered.

Analeise looked incredible in her black halter neck dress; it showed her curves off to perfection. She had natural 34E boobs – something she wasn't really proud of. She constantly tried to hide them!. Her hair was long, dark and curly. According to Martin, she was fat and ugly! Analeise believed every word.

"Can we sit down?" Analeise asked as she pointed to the inviting white leather sofa.

" Of course, your feet have been bothering you all night haven't they?" he said as he slipped off one of her shoes.

"Would you like a foot massage?" he asked, and without waiting for an answer he started to rub Analeise's tired, worn feet.

It felt weird for her, as her husband wouldn't even touch her feet, never mind massage them! It also felt great. He treated her like a queen and she wished that Martin would do the same thing from time to time.

"IF YOU GO TO SAN FRANSISCO, BE SURE TO WEAR SOME FLOWERS IN YOUR HAIR............"

The sound coming from the next room would curdle milk, as Jenny and Pauline tried to impress weird bald guy.

"Don't give up your day jobs girls," he shouted as he walked into the kitchen to refill their glasses with wine.

Meanwhile in the lounge Analeise was having the best foot massage ever!

"Wow, that was amazing, you're good at that. I give a great back massage you know."

She felt she needed to repay him in some way.

"Ok then, do you mind?" he asked delighted.

"No, its fine, I need the practise!" she replied.

Paul was away like a 'rat up a drainpipe' to retrieve some massage oil.

It seemed pretty harmless to her, as it was part of her job to train some of her clients on the technique. After all, it was only a back massage. What harm would it do? The guy seemed pretty genuine.

Then he came back into the room and Analeise's mouth dropped to the floor...

"Oh my god, I'm only massaging your back! You've got the wrong idea." She was horrified, shocked and mortified all rolled into one!

Paul was standing in front of her completely bollock naked!

"Its ok, I just want to be comfortable" he replied as he lay on his front on the floor.

"I'm not doing anything else you know!" Analeise was a little bit shaken.

Ever confident he continued to lie on his front showing his big hairy arse for the world to see!

She hadn't seen a naked man except Martin for nearly ten years. Even at that, she hardly had seen him naked, as they hadn't had sex for a few months.

She was very uncomfortable with the whole situation, but decided to start massaging his shoulders, just then Pauline walked into the room.

"JESUS!" she cried. "I'll be back in an hour, say no more" she touched her nose twice, giggled and disappeared into the other room again.

Analeise was disgraced; she stopped and sat on the sofa.

"MMMMM, don't stop Analeise" Paul started to groan, sat up and started to play with himself in the most obscene way! "You feel so good!"

"NO!" She shouted "THIS IS WRONG!"

She ran into the others in the next room.

"WE'RE GOING!" She screamed at Jenny and Pauline who looked very comfortable in a couple of armchairs watching MTV guzzling on another bottle of wine.

"Keep your hair on drama queen" said Jenny as she stumbled to find her shoes.

"Where is my bag?" Pauline asked weird bald guy who had passed out on the floor.

"Just hurry up, I want to get out of here NOW!" Shouted Analeise again.

As the three girls got to the door, Paul, still naked stopped them.

"Hey big boy!!" Pauline laughed as she looked down at Paul's manhood (Which had shrivelled into a peanut by now!)

"Analeise, don't go, finish me off…. Please! Come with me to London. I want you."

"Let us out!" She shouted.

He did, reluctantly.

It was 7am, and they arrived back at the apartment, exhausted.

Analeise felt really guilty; it was as though she had been unfaithful to Martin although nothing happened. She couldn't stop thinking about it.

Two hours sleep later Pauline was shouting out the window "GOOD MORNING DUBLIN!"

She bounced on Analeise's bed.

"Well, dish the dirt? What was your game last night?"

She kept her head under the duvet.

"Nothing" she replied.

"It didn't look like nothing to me!" said Pauline said as she tried to pull the bedclothes off her. "There was a mouse in the house and it wanted to play!"

Analeise jumped out of bed. "It was nothing I said! I only offered him a back massage, and he got carried away, that's all. I want no more talk about it. I feel shit."

Pauline and Jenny got the message. No more was said. They made a full Irish breakfast, and got ready for drinking spree part two!

Bar Twenty-One seemed to be the place where everyone would congregate on a Sunday for a spot of 'hair of the dog'. It was buzzing full of locals discussing the night before. Mostly English stag and hen parties would finish their 'lets drink Ireland dry Weekends' here. They took over the majority of the bar. No one was listening to the two guys playing 'Whiskey in the Jar' on the Penny Whistle in the corner who were paid to create an Irish aura about the place.

Analeise's face meanwhile was looking very irish and traditional! It was a whiter shade of green as she sat nursing an orange juice, which was all her delicate stomach could take after throwing up her breakfast. Pauline and Jenny instantly got wired into beers.

"Would you like to join us for a drink ladies?" asked an elegant young man in a golfing jumper.

Before anyone could open their mouths. "YES," shouted Jenny "We'd love to"

She then wiggled over to the feisty bunch of Londoners who were on a stag golfing weekend.

"What would you like to drink?" He asked.

"Three beers please" answered Jenny.

"Make mine another orange juice please," announced Analeise.

"BORE!" Shouted Pauline.

Analeise didn't care, all she wanted to do was to go home to her normal life, and be a good wife to her grumpy husband who preferred the company of his friends. He didn't even care that she was away for an evening with *her* friends. It was probably a good opportunity to go clubbing with his pretentious click.

Pauline seemed to be hitting it off nicely with a very pleasant and funny member of the golfing bunch named Clive. Jenny was strangely attracted to James, a banker from south London who loved to hear himself speak. The whole thing was completely boring for Analeise who didn't participate in any conversation; it was too much hard work.

"Cat got yer tongue luv?" Asked Rob; a nice but dim creature that looked like he was straight off the front of a knitting pattern.

Analeise knew it would be a long and exhausting day.

On the journey home Pauline was very excited about meeting this wonderful Clive. Jenny was deciding whether or not to have an affair with a middle-aged banker with a very large wallet. Analeise couldn't wait to see Martin again who she hoped would be sitting waiting for her in anticipation.

He wasn't.

CHAPTER THREE

*T*wo weeks had passed since the Dublin night out, and Analeise was starting to wish that she had gone to London with Paul. Pervert or not!

Martin was becoming more and more difficult to live with. She had sat him down one night, and asked why he won't take her anywhere, and why he preferred his friends company to hers.

"Ok then, if that's what you want, we'll go out Friday night for a meal" was his answer. Analeise was delighted, she couldn't wait, and it had been months since she'd been out with him.

In fact, she couldn't remember the last time they stepped out together in public! He hadn't seen her dressed up properly for a very long time.

She had hated the way he was acting over the last lot of months. He would go and play pool with his friends after work most evenings and maybe not show his face until eight or nine o'clock most of the time. By then Analeise was exhausted and would be sitting in her pyjama's with all of her make-up off. She didn't even care; she was past caring at this stage as physical contact was completely off the agenda. It was probably her cooking that he dreaded coming home to *most* of the time. She knew she had faults too. She became numb in the relationship. She was going to have to try harder to win her man back.

That Friday evening as Analeise was putting the final touches of make up on, Martin walked into the apartment sporting another pair of new shoes.

" What do you think? I got them with 20 percent discount, aren't they cool as fuck?"

He asked, completely oblivious of his beautiful wife who had spent the best of two hours getting ready.

" Just what you need, another pair of shoes to add to your collection" Analeise replied angrily "You could start up your own shoe shop, you've probably got more pairs than the fucking shop you bought them in"

Martin stormed into the kitchen, unhappy with the response.

" Oh, by the way" he shouted "Danny and Sarah are meeting us in the restaurant at about eight"

Danny was Martins very annoying work colleague, who thinks he is Gods gift to Women and his girlfriend Sarah was nothing but a pain in the ass. The last time Analeise met them was at a photographer's function.

Danny tried it on with every woman in the place while Sarah flirted unsuccessfully with every man! (Including an 82-year-old war veteran). Analeise hated them. They were pretentious; they talked shit and were full of their own self-importance!

"Do they have to come Martin? I thought it was going to be just us, I really wanted to spend the evening with you." Analeise said, disappointed.

She longed to spend time alone with her husband, as she wanted to sort out a lot of problems.

Martin poked his head into the bedroom, where she was putting on her shoes (old ones!) " You have a choice, they come or you can have a 'Marksies' meal for one on your own!" He replied with a grin.

He would have done anything to avoid spending one hundred percent of the time with her.

"Oooooh, long time no see, hee hee hee, where have you been? I've been to the opening of that new bar H2o. Did I see you there, or maybe Martin was on his own without you, blah blah blah!!" Was Sarah's opening line.

Analeise sighed, how could she be able to cope with 4 more hours of this?

All of a sudden the Ready cooked meal for one seemed very appealing.

The more Analeise drank, the more sober she became. She spent the majority of the meal staring at Sarah's hair, wondering if she put it up herself. She couldn't work it out, was it supposed to look like a birds nest? Maybe it was a wig? She had absolutely no taste whatsoever! Oh god, what did she do to deserve this! All she wanted was a meal out with her husband to try and sort things out. She was so unhappy as she watched Martin talking to Danny she realized that her marriage was on a slippery slope. Where was her life going? They were living in a rented apartment above an alcoholic in a housing estate. Analeise knew she could do better, they were both earning good money. Martin had no interest in buying a house; he seemed to want to spend all his money on clothes, shoes, and anything that made him look better. It was like being married to a child. " He must be going through the change of life," her mum would say. "Thirty three is a funny old age for men". Analeise was the same age.

The difference was, she acted it.

"C'mon we'll go to that new bar in town," Analeise suggested after the meal. She might as well make the most of the evening while she could.

"No!" said Martin " Its crap"

"You didn't say that last week mate" Danny nudged Martin with a wry smile.

It made Analeise more determined to go.

"Its three against one" she said.

H2o was a hive of people who'd finished work for the week, out for that well deserved pint. The noise of the bar was intense, everybody very excited due to the fact that it was Friday, and they were off work the next day.

The décor was magnificent; a waterfall trickled down the wall behind the bar. Glass bricks gave the effect of ice cubes, which made nice little nooks all over the room. Danny found a great spot just at the fountain in the centre of the room. As Analeise looked around in admiration she realised in the excitement of it all she'd mislaid Martin.

"Danny, have you seen Martin?" she asked.

"Yes, he's gone to the loo."

Twenty minutes later had passed, still no sign of Martin.

"That's one mighty long pee! I'm away to find him," she said to Sarah.

Analeise searched all 3 floors for him. By the time she'd got back downstairs they were shouting last orders.

She was out of her mind with worry.

Another frantic twenty minutes later, the doormen were starting to kick people to the front door. "DRINK UP NOW FOLKS!" one doorman shouted at a very worried Analeise who was being comforted by Sarah.

"Where would he go Danny? Its just not like him, I'm gonna stay here and wait for him." Analeise said.

"Now Ana you're coming with us, maybe Martin can leave you in a bar on your own, but we wont." Sarah put her arms around her and escorted her outside. Analeise didn't really like Sarah that much, but under these circumstances she needed to be around someone.

"Did you definitely look outside Danny?" Sarah asked as Danny tried to flag a taxi down.

"Yes, all over the place, he's probably gone home." He replied, uninterested in the whole ordeal. If the truth were told, Danny was generally uninterested in everything that didn't concern him! He used people (including Martin) to get what he wanted. It frustrated Analeise that Martin, an intelligent person just couldn't see it.

"He's got no keys," Analeise said, crying.

They all got a taxi back to Sarah's apartment, which was in an exclusive new property development in south Belfast.

Danny went straight to bed and left Analeise in hysterics clutching to Sarah.

"I'm outta here, I'm sure there is a simple explanation to all of this" he yawned.

"He's your friend you wanker, how can you be so insensitive you heartless bastard!" squealed Sarah. "Any sign of trouble and he fucks off!"

She was right.

"His mobile phone, house keys and car keys are in the apartment, so he cant have gone home. He wouldn't get in."

Analeise phoned every one of his friends, no one knew where he was. Or at least that's what they said to her.

"I'd better get home, maybe he's trying to get in, or maybe he's trying to contact me."

"Don't fool yourself Analeise." said Sarah " I know if it were me he did this to, he'd get a right kick in the balls!"

But it wasn't Sarah he did it to, it was Analeise, and she was distraught.

CHAPTER FOUR

*A*naleise couldn't sleep a wink all what was left of the night. She had taken enough crap and this was the last straw.

The next day she packed every piece of clothing belonging to her into bags, she couldn't see anything for tears in her eyes. She wondered what she was doing and what exactly she was packing. Where is he? Was going through her mind constantly over and over again. Who will she call? Where will she live? Her life had come to a complete standstill.

Eventually she carried all her old bags into her car.

"Compose yourself" she looked in the rear view mirror at herself. She looked awful. In the last 24 hours she looked like she'd aged at least 10 years. Was she a widow? Or had she been abandoned? She wishes she had answers for all the questions in her mind.

"You look a mess Analeise, what's wrong?" asked her mum as she stood in the doorway.

She broke down immediately and couldn't speak. She cried like a small child.

"What am I gonna do?" was all she could say.

"Tell me please, please pet?" her mum asked again.

"M-Martin has gone, he's left me, or at least I think he has… I can't take anymore, what am I going to do Mum?"

Analeise's Mum had no idea of how troubled she had been, she didn't tell anyone. Didn't want anyone worrying. Whenever Analeise told her the whole story, she was completely shocked. She was also as broken hearted as Analeise. She was the most thoughtful, kind woman and would do anything for her family. There had been lots of family incidents in the past and she held it together every time. Analeise called her 'Frog'. It was a term of endearment of course, as she loved frogs and anything cute and funny.

Frog managed to calm her down slightly!!

Analeise couldn't just sit around; it was as if her husband had just fallen off the face of the earth! She phoned his mother who thought the whole thing was 'blown out of proportion'

"Never worry dear, he's probably at his friends house"

She had no idea what her precious son had put her through.

"Just go back to the apartment, he'll show up soon. You know what he's like."

All the woman could think about was herself, she was the complete opposite of her own mother.

Mags was as self-centred as her son! Analeise couldn't bare her. She meant well, but she never ever made Analeise feel like part of the family. She always seemed to look down her nose at her. It was as though Analeise just wasn't good enough for her wonderful son. She knew it would be a bad idea calling her, but she was desperate for some answers.

She would have hated the idea of her son breaking up with his wife. What will the neighbours think? Analeise was sorry she called. "Insensitive bitch" she thought.

Analeise spent the next two nights at her Mums house; she couldn't bare the thought of going back to the apartment. She was out of her mind with worry.

There was no sign of Martin until Monday evening. She was out with Pauline walking in the park trying to make sense of it all when she received the phone call.

"I need your keys to get in to the apartment" were the only words that he said to her.

They agreed to meet at the flat in twenty minutes.

She said her goodbyes to Pauline who hugged her and said " Take no shit, I'm here if you need me". Analeise didn't know what she'd have done the last few days without her.

As Analeise walked into the vacant apartment, memories, good and bad came flooding into her mind. It felt like the end of an era. She was exhausted, and couldn't think how the next few days would be like, never mind the rest of her life. She heard him walking into the hall. Analeise couldn't look at him, she was afraid that she might cry.

"Where the hell were you, I thought you were dead. You just don't care anymore, isn't that right?" She said as she stared out the window.

"I've got somewhere to stay, you can live here until you get yourself sorted" was his only reply.

"I've moved my stuff to Mum's, I don't think I can live here on my own." Analeise still couldn't look at him. Her stomach was in knots.

" I can't live with you anymore Ana, you drive me insane. You're too clingy, and you just turn me off. I have met someone else, and I'm moving in with her"

Martin said the words as if he were ordering a pizza. It meant nothing.

"Suppose that's were you were all weekend?" she asked.

She turned around, afraid of what he might say.

His look answered her question.

For some reason, Analeise didn't get angry. She was too sad to be angry. She was weary, and it didn't matter what she said because it wouldn't have made any difference.

Analeise went back to her parent's house while Martin carefully packed his belongings into suitcases. She couldn't stand to be there and watch as her husband took everything that he owned to his new live-in girlfriend.

Analeise stayed with her folks for the rest of the week; she couldn't bear to go back so soon after Martin had gone. Meanwhile Pauline and Jenny organised another Dublin trip for the following weekend.

"It'll do you the world of good babe, just what you need!" Pauline explained that Thursday evening while she was standing in work, filing her nails, ignoring customers so she could speak to her dear friend. (Much more important!)

Analeise was in the centre of town for some retail therapy. She had treated herself to a whole load of things, Tops, Trousers, skirts for work, a couple of dresses, and of course shoes!

"You did ok girlfriend!" Pauline said as she pointed down to the abundance of bags.

"I did!" Analeise said proudly.

"So, this weekend chicken!!" Pauline winked "We'll have a good one!"

"I don't know, everything is so fresh, my life is upside down. I'm going to have to move back to the apartment sooner or later." She hesitated.

" Ok, move back after the weekend" Pauline pleaded " You need cheered up!"

"Alright then, but if I'm a miserable bitch, its not my fault" Analeise replied.

" Sure you're a miserable bitch anyway" Pauline laughed. " Treat yourself to a nice new lipstick! Cock-sucking red!"

"Dirty bitch!" Analeise laughed.

The following night Analeise drove to Dublin on her own, she'd meet up with the others on the Saturday evening, as they had to work. She decided to take advantage of the offer to stay with her dear friend and work colleague Pamela. Who was always there for her in times of disaster (which was often).

She worked in the head office in Dublin. She processed all of Analeise's sales and always kept her right. Sometimes when Analeise would be stuck in Ballygobackward with a nightmare client. ' At least she knew that Pamela would be there to keep her sane'. She was a great help to her whenever she just started, she would have warned her of clients from hell and helped give directions when she was lost in the wilderness!

"What a complete bastard!" she said after Analeise told her every detail. "How did you work last week? Were you not demented?"

"Another bottle of wine in here Des" she shouted into the kitchen where her very loving husband was doing the dishes. " Urgent supplies needed immediately in lounge!"

"What kind of wanker leaves his wife in a bar?" Des asked as he carefully carried two bottles of white wine into the lounge as instructed. "He will be very sorry, you mark my words Ana! You deserve so much better!"

Somehow Analiese found the negative things so much easier to believe.

She smiled and shrugged as if dismissing it. She was trying desperately hard to forget what happened.

The three of them laughed all night, Analeise was enjoying being away from the doom and gloom of normality.

She eventually got to bed at 3.15!

The following day after a long lie-in and a big Irish Breakfast cooked by Des, Analeise said farewell to her good friend Pamela.

She picked Pauline and Jenny from the train station at 4.00pm.

It felt quite exciting.

Jenny came running over to her and hugged her.

"I'm so sorry, what a dickhead, you didn't deserve that" she said with compassion.

" Its ok" replied Analeise "I'm here for a good time, not to think of him".

"That's the spirit I like," said Pauline as she got into the front seat of her car.

"Drive to the University of Dublin babe, that's our home for the night!"

Analeise realised that this would be her first night out as a single girl in ten years. She thought she would never be in this position.

Age 33.

Status. Separated.

It felt weird. She had no choice; just take it day by day she thought.

When they arrived in their room at the University the three of them were silent.

"Is this it?" asked Jenny

"Not even a picture on the wall?" said Analeise.

The dormitory was very basic; it was designed for students to stay during term. In the summer the dorms are open for the general public to stay at a very attractive rate. It was very handy, as it stood in the centre of Dublin, just minutes from restaurants, pubs and nightclubs.

"Its cheap!" answered Pauline, who organised it. "What do you want for 30 Euros each, Dublin fucking castle?"

"YES!" said Analeise and Jenny at the same time, laughing.

"Shut up you silly cows it's only somewhere to lay our lazy heads tonight, that's if we don't get lucky!" said Pauline, who claims to be in love with Clive from London her very amusing new beau. She talks about him non-stop. Has been over to visit him 3 times since they met.

"I'm the only singleton here!" said Analeise, it didn't feel normal to say it, but it was true.

Ignoring her comment Jenny shouted, "Lippy on lets hit the bars!"

"At this time? Its only 4.30 in the afternoon."

Analeise wasn't used to this, drinking at this time was only ever done on Christmas day. But hey, this is her new life now!

The first pub they ventured there were at least 20 blokes sitting around the bar.

"This will do for starters," said Jenny under her breath.

The girls got a great welcome from the friendly Londoners who were on a stag weekend.

To Analeise's left she seen the most stunning, beautiful creature she had ever seen in real life sitting amongst the rowdy bunch.

From nowhere she pushed through the two girls and sat down beside him.

"So what's your name then?" he asked.

"Analeise, but you can call me Ana!" she replied, her eyes were like saucers.

"I'm James," he said, holding out his hand.

"Well James, are you the unlucky one getting married?" Analeise said with a smile.

"God, no!" he cried.

The relief on her face was very obvious. The two of them started laughing. They really started to hit it off.

"Ana, did you take your wedding ring off for the weekend or what?" James said as he picked up her left hand examining her third finger.

Analeise drew her hand away immediately "Jesus, can you really notice that I'd a ring on?" There was a welt across her finger, it was quite obvious.

"I've been branded for life!" she then told him that she had been separated for only a week. They talked for a while and enjoyed a few drinks together. The more Analeise drank, the more she fancied this beautiful man.

"Where are you going later?" he asked.

"Probably Aussies across the road to start, will I see you later on?" she replied.

"I'll make a point of it," he said, staring deep into her eyes with his big brown 'come to bed' eyes.

Analeise felt sick to the pit of her stomach with nerves, as she turned round to tell the girls, she found Jenny doing an Irish dance with a fag hanging out of her mouth. Pauline meanwhile was singing Randy Crawford in the wrong note. "YOU MIGHT NEED SOMEBODY TOOOO!" She pointed to Analeise and gave a big wink.

"Oh my god, total carnage!" she laughed.

"Time for a burger, what do you say chicks?" Analeise suggested as she got the girls to finish their drinks and say their goodbyes to the boys.

"MMMMM! I don't feel well," said Jenny.

"Is it any bloody wonder? Even Michael Flatley couldn't do the River Dance in that state!" Analeise said, helping her dear friend gather her belongings.

They all said goodbye to the boys and agreed to see them all later.

"Oh my nerves!" cried Analeise when they got outside. "I'm meeting James later, what am I gonna do?"

She felt like she was 17 all over again. It had been years since those fluffy butterflies visited her tummy.

"Which one did you fancy?" Jenny asked Pauline.

"None, I just fancy a cheeseburger!" she replied, then ran down the street in search of a fast food joint… the faster the better!

"I like freckly face, he's quite sexy" Jenny said to Analeise as she put her arm around her.

"Who is freckly face?" she asked.

"You wouldn't know, you were too interested in pretty boy, he's gorgeous. You cow" she smiled.

After their carbohydrate filled fast food meals they all ventured back to their very basic room again

Jenny always took the longest to get ready, so she was first in the bathroom. Meanwhile Analeise was taking a panic attack, kindly assisted by Pauline.

"DEEP BREATHS" said Pauline as she held her hands.

"Water, yea, that's what you need…?" Pauline was nearly taking a panic attack herself! "Oh Analeise, don't die, not here, you deserve to die somewhere nicer!" Pauline was making her worse!

"PAPER BAG!" Analeise shouted, as she pointed to a brown Burger King bag.

She slowly breathed into the bag, and started feeling better within 5 minutes.

"Hurry up you smelly bitch" shouted Pauline into the bathroom. "Ana's taking palpitations out here!"

"I'm ok, I'm just a little nervous," said Analeise.

" By the way, bathroom is flooded, shower curtain is too short – it's like the sinking Titanic in there." Jenny said as she walked over to Analeise, who was sitting on one of the beds.

"J-E-S-U-S! I don't need a shower, I could just sit on the fucking floor and have a bath in here!" shouted Pauline from the bathroom.

"Are you ok babe?" Jenny put her arms around Analeise and gave her a big hug.

"What am I gonna do? It's been so long since I've been with anyone. I'm so out of practise" said Analeise.

"You don't have to if you don't want to" Jenny replied with real compassion "It's your life now, just be yourself. It might be too early to jump someones bones."

By the time it was Analeise's turn for the bathroom, she needed a rowing boat to get to the sink!

High heels and glad rags on, they all looked stunning.

Aussies bar was full to the brim with shiny, happy people. It was buzzing with a great atmosphere.

Analeise was having problems composing herself.

"Will you just calm down, you're doing my head in!" said Pauline.

She could see James and his friends over at the other side of the busy bar.

"Oh my god, there he is – I feel sick!" Analeise was shaking like a leaf!

"Maybe he's changed his mind, he isn't coming over, that's it, I'm going back to the room." Analeise was beside herself with nerves!

"Will you just take it easy baby, you're going to take another palpitation! Then you'll look really cool!" shouted Jenny at the top of her voice.

"Shut up" replied Analeise. "He probably heard that, you two are like my fucking parents." She was acting like a 13 year old at the school disco. Trying to be cool, but looking like a complete idiot!

Pauline could take no more; she walked across the room towards James and his buddies.

"Fuck, what is she doing?" Analeise asked Jenny, who was doubled over with laughter.

Within seconds James was standing in front of Analeise.

"Hi there, where were you? Have you just arrived? I didn't see you when we came in." she lied.

Pauline and Jenny could not believe that this was the quivering wreck they had to deal with all evening!

They all stayed for a few drinks, then moved downstairs to the nightclub. It was hiving. The music was great! They danced to the Bee Gee's, Abba and Madonna. It was quite cheesy but great fun.

Analeise couldn't keep her eyes off James all night. He was so handsome. His little turned up nose, perfect lips, chiselled cheekbones and that cheeky cockney smile really turned her on.

"Where do you want to go next?" she asked as James came back from the bar with handfuls of drinks.

"Where do you think?" he replied with a cute grin.

More butterflies were set loose in the pit of her stomach.

Analeise walked over to Jenny who was completely bedazzled by freckle face.

"I think I'm going to shag him," Jenny announced, as she whispered very loudly.

"You're married, you can't!" Analeise was horrified.

"Love them, then leave them! That's my motto!" she replied.

"Well, I'm single, and I'm going back with James!" Analeise said proudly.

"Go girl!" Jenny said, as she raised her drink, not able to stand straight.

Jenny was drunk; maybe Pauline would bring her round to her senses Analeise thought.

Until she saw her dancing on one of the speakers! She beckoned her down.

"I'm going now!" she shouted into Pauline's ear. "Look after Jenny, wont you?"

"Go you crazy kids, enjoy yourselves!" she said as she bounced back up onto the speaker again totally oblivious as to what was going on.

"Lets go" Analeise whispered into James ear.

It was a short walk back to James modest hotel.

"Room 324" he asked the receptionist.

"There you go," he said, as he handed James the key. "The lady can't go with you sir, she isn't a resident." He looked at Analeise disapprovingly.

All of a sudden, Analeise felt like a total prostitute!!

"Oh my god" she thought "He knows we are going to have sex, I feel like a tart!"

She walked away as James tried to persuade the guy to let her up.

"No, sorry sir, that is a single room, and there are two of you" he said as he looked under his eyes at Analeise.

They both walked outside.

"I have a plan" he suggested "I'll go swap rooms with one of the lads, some of them have twin rooms."

They walked back towards the nightclub. By the time they got there they found Pauline and George (one of James uglier friends) standing outside contemplating going to the hotel.

"Do me a favour mate," James asked him. "Lend us your room?"

"No way! Me and Pauline are going back" he replied

"NO WE'RE NOT!" Pauline was disgusted.

"Where did he come from?" Analeise whispered to Pauline.

"I have no idea! He's a fucking cling on!" They both looked at him with complete pity, he definitely was at the back of the queue when the handsome pills were being handed out! He was 5ft 4 with a limp, a broken nose and a face that resembled a bulldog chewing a wasp!

"Ok, Ana and George, go to reception, pretend you're staying in the hotel, then I'll meet you upstairs." James plan sounded good in theory, but in practise it was a disaster!

Analeise and George went to reception.

"Room 411 please" George asked, smiling as he held her hand. (A little too tightly she thought)

The receptionist glanced at Analeise again, bemused.

"Yes sir, you can go, but the lady stays here" he looked under his eyes at Analeise again.

She stormed out.

"I feel like a bloody hooker, he thinks I'm on the fucking game, I'll never show my face around here again. I'M MORTIFIED!"

James, Pauline and George were on the pavement laughing so hard much to Analeise's disgust!

"Where is Jenny?" Analeise asked Pauline, just to stop her from laughing.

"Away with the freckly guy" she replied, still giggling.

"You were supposed to look after her!" Analeise said, soberly.

"Can you do me a favour, lend me the key of our room?"

"Do you want me to spend time with Quassie while you shag Brad Pitt look-alike?"

Pauline said as she pointed over to George who decided to take a piss up against the wall.

"Please?" Analeise begged. " I really fancy James"

"Its only because I love you!" Pauline said " Go, enjoy yourself, I'll go to another club with gorgeous George!"

"You're the best" Analeise hugged Pauline. "I'm really nervous"

She felt like she was going to lose her virginity all over again.

"What am I doing?" she kept asking herself.

They sailed through the gates of the University no problem, as they were walking towards the bedroom Analeise suddenly realised that it was a mess and ever so slightly flooded!

As they got to the door she announced " The room is a bit of a tip, please excuse it"

"No worries babe, it'll be fine" he assured her.

Analeise opened the door, and James went into the bathroom.

"JESUS CHRIST! You must have had a leak in here or something!"

"Oh, I forgot to say, the bathroom is flooded" Analeise shouted as she franticly tried to tidy away pant liners, false tan, rollers and make up from the bed.

"I think I've wrecked my shoes now" he moaned as he paddled out of the bathroom.

He took off his clothes and got into the sheets of one of the single beds as Analeise stood there like a statue!

"We don't have to, its ok" James said as he held out his arms.

"No, I want to" Analeise's heart was throbbing. She was so nervous that she had forgotten to undo her skirt. Then when she was eventually in bed undressed, she broke James necklace!

The whole thing was a complete disaster. The sex didn't last very long, but it was enough for Analeise.

They lay together, staring into each other's eyes. She felt great; she had missed this intimacy, which actually involved foreplay. Sex with Martin was merely he getting off, and Analeise was left feeling like a blow up doll! James made her feel like a real woman again, until.............

"I hope you enjoyed that sweetheart, now what you want to do is lose a bit of weight and go on a few sun beds."

Analeise was devastated as she looked down the bed and seen the moon reflecting off her white arse!

James started to dress.

"Don't go, why don't you stay with me?" Analeise pleaded.

"No luv, gotta go, but I'll call you – yeah?"

She put on her old faithful saggy 'Tweetie Pie' pyjamas and they exchanged telephone numbers.

When James left, Analeise went to the mirror. "I must be a fat, white cow!" she thought to herself, then burst out crying. At around 5.30 she called Pauline.

"Paulies brothel, how can I help you!"?

"Its me"

"Jesus Ana where are you? Where is James?" Pauline asked.

"He's gone" she sobbed, "I feel like an ugly whore!"

"We are on our way round" Pauline hung up.

Analeise lay on the bed wondering if this was the shape of things to come forever. Maybe it was too soon? How will she ever get over being rejected by her husband?

What do single people do nowadays?

At around 7.15 Pauline and Jenny arrived back with 5 cans of coke, 3 breakfast rolls and 3 plastic cups full of Luke-warm tea.

"Thought you might be hungry after your wild night of passion!" Jenny handed Analeise a breakfast roll.

"Hope you didn't do it with those efforts on" Pauline said as she pointed to her old, but comfortable pyjamas.

"Well I had to wear something as he left!" Analeise replied angrily.

"Why did he go so soon?" asked Jenny as she stuffed half a roll into her mouth.

"Because I'm fat and white – that's why!" Analeise was upset.

"Did he say that you were fat and white? Cheeky Bastard!" Jenny said as she spat crumbs all over the place.

"He might as well have. I was advised to take sun beds and lose weight. Am I that bad?" Analeise asked the girls who were really enjoying their breakfast.

Pauline was still joking, "You are a stunner in those pyjama's!"

Analeise started to cry again.

"Don't worry, I'm sure you'll see him again, wont you? Has he your number?" asked Jenny.

"Yes" Analeise replied, drying her eyes on a napkin.

"I am going to burn those 'Tweetie Pies' in the furnace" laughed Pauline.

"Not the sexiest thing to wear on your first night of passion!" agreed Jenny.

Analeise was so used to being round Martin, and not caring how unattractive she may have looked. It was time to start wearing clothes that flattered her, time to start caring for herself again.

"Where did you go hussy?" Analeise asked Jenny.

"Just walking, then we met up with HER, and her gorgeous date!" she laughed as she pointed to Pauline.

"Wings Night Club! We were two very respectable girlies, we sent them off with their stiffies in their trousers!"

They all laughed.

The journey home to Belfast the next day seemed endless to Analeise, the two girls slept the whole way. Analeise Moran was going to have to change, she'd no choice – she had become a shadow of Martin, always his wife....but never herself. She would have to find her true self again. "This isn't going to be easy, but I'm going to give it a damn good try" she thought.

CHAPTER FIVE

After the weekend in Dublin, Analeise hadn't really let it sink in that she was separated from her husband. She knew it was time to move back into the flat. Her Mum had been great, but she wanted to stand on her own two feet again. Also, she didn't like the thought of being in her thirties and living at home, it seemed so naff!

So that Monday night she packed all her wrinkled clothes back into her bags, and set sail back to Crows field Park.

"Are you sure I can't give you a hand?" Analeise's Mum asked as she was stuffing her bags into the car.

"I'm fine, honestly. You've been great Frog, I appreciate your help." She replied as she gave her Mum a great big hug.

She found it hard to hold back the tears, but for her Mums sake she did.

When she arrived back to the flat, after unpacking, it felt like she had been on a very weird holiday and things would be back to normal any minute now.

She had to keep telling herself to stop looking back, and to concentrate on the future!

Over the next few days she had scrubbed the apartment from top to toe, changed some furniture around, and bought new bed linen. She wanted the flat to start feeling like hers. The transformation from married to single seemed to be going flawless; it was like Analeise had brushed everything under the carpet, until she took her very first trip to the supermarket on her own. She was lifting things like fresh chicken breasts and fresh stir fry vegetables. Martin wouldn't tolerate any thing 'pre-packed'.

"Jesus" she thought to herself. "What do I like? I hate chicken breasts! And I can't cook stir-fry vegetables! What the fuck am I do-ing!!"?

She started sobbing, walking around the store like a lost child, wondering what to buy. For the last two years, she always ate what Martin liked, just for an easy life. She couldn't be bothered making separate dinners; it was hard enough for her to concentrate on one, let alone two!!

Two hours later, after a few weird stares from security men, her basket was full of ready-made lasagne, low calorie spaghetti Bolognese, and tins of macaroni cheese. 'Easy to cook, no hassle food at long last!' She thought.

It made her feel happy, maybe in a way selfish, but now she only had herself to worry about, and it felt good!

CHAPTER SIX

A few weeks had passed now since the Dublin weekend, and Analeise was feeling pretty happy with her new life. She went on a shopping spree, spent money on herself like never before! She started exercising most evenings, took some sun beds (as advised!) She totally indulged by taking a trip to Alan at Toni & Guy for a whole new hair restyle. He cut it, conditioned it and colored it; she looked totally amazing. It had more body, looked shinier and he put some blond highlights in at the front to give it the wow factor!

"You look great!" Alan said as she was leaving "Takes years off you!"

He was a fantastic stylist and she promised herself she would go back. It was definatly money well spent. The extra weight she had been carrying had just fallen off due to stress and she was looking pretty good. She promised herself that the Moon would never reflect off her big white arse again!

She went for a facial and even treated herself to a set of nail extensions!

Her job was keeping her very busy, as this was the launch of the new moisturiser, which meant she had to see as many clients as possible. Which also meant, more driving.

"LIVING LA VIDA LOCA!!" Analeise sang to the radio at the top of her voice, whist driving behind a big smelly tractor on a very rocky road in County Cavan.

Her phone rang, it was Pauline. "Where are you?" she asked.

"Sitting on Ricky Martins face in Miami!" she replied concentrating on the bendy road ahead.

"Only in your wildest dreams love!" Pauline cried, "Do you want to do Lunch tomorrow?" Pauline asked.

"Its probably gonna be the best offer I get all year!" said Analeise "Think I might call James today, what do you think?"

"Why the hell not, at this stage you've nothing to lose but your dignity!" Pauline replied unhappy at the fact that her naive friend met a bit of a bastard a few weeks ago, and didn't need to be hurt again.

This would be Analeise's third attempt. Both times she called him, he kept saying

"Oh hi, it's a bad time, can I call you back?"

She was determined to get at least a 5-minute conversation from him!

The phone rang only once…

"HELLO!"

"Hi James, its Ana calling from sunny Ireland again…"

Before she could say another word.

"Listen, I'm just about to go into a meeting, I'll call you back in about an hour"

"Will you call?" pleaded Analeise " because you didn't the last time, should I call you back?"

"NO! I'll call you – bye!"

The phone call didn't even last a minute.

Analeise didn't understand the expression "DON'T CALL US – WE'LL CALL YOU!!"

She wouldn't let herself believe that she'd been ditched again.

She was hanging by a thread all day, as expected no phone call!!

Analeise loved going to Hungry Hugh's Diner on the Lisburn Road…. It was the sort of place where they served all day breakfast, and evening if desired! They cooked just about anything she liked, and they made their own fresh squeezed orange juice. It was always busy.

Pauline was talking on her mobile phone to Clive when Analeise arrived; she had already ordered 3 glasses of coke for herself.

"How would you like to come to London this weekend with me?" she asked as she beckoned a waitress over.

"Oh, full fry for me, and an orange juice please" Analeise was in the mood for loads of carbs!!

"And me!" said Pauline who still had the phone glued to her ear!!

"Gotta go babe, byee," she announced to an eager Clive on the other end.

"What's this about London?" Analeise asked Pauline curiously.

"Yes, you're coming to Clive's this weekend with me to meet his friend Trevor,"

"No way!!" She shouted. She knew it would only be a matter of time before her friends started setting her up on blind dates like she was some kind of desperado!

"Why not? Or is this the weekend you tie the knot with James!" she said with sarcasm. "What else are you doing?"

"Very funny" Analeise replied, "What does this Trevor look like?"

"Apparently 6 feet, blonde hair and blue eyes" she said with a grin.

"I'm imagining Brad!" Analeise said excitedly.

"I imagined him too!" Pauline rubbed her hands together like some kind of Mad Professor.

"I'll organise it later, you are coming. No arguments!" she insisted.

Analeise never normally believed in blind dates. Any she had heard about in the past had always ended in disaster, but she was open to anything at the moment!

If the truth be told, she was secretly looking forward to going to London that weekend, although was slightly nervous about meeting Trevor. She had spoken to him during the week and he sounded really nice. He had his own building business and seemed a gentle, sensitive, intelligent guy. Analeise must have asked him about 4 times if he was fat!

"No I'm not fat! Why do you keep asking?"

"Oh you sound too good to be true" she would reply. Much to his delight!

On the following Friday, Pauline and Analeise had two vodka and cokes in the airport while waiting to board the plane. Then when they were on board, they had another double each!'

"I'm so nervous!" Analeise cried, " I know he's going to be ugly. I can see him now, a big potato head, and an ugly hairstyle!!"

"Will you shut up!" said Pauline "I told you, Clive said that you'd like him!"

"He seems too perfect to me" Analeise sighed. Just then her mobile phone started to ring to the tuts and moans from the other passengers.

"OH JESUS! I forgot to turn it off!!"

She lifted it out of her handbag, and the sound got louder. As she looked to see who was calling her, a stewardess came dashing over.

"Turn it off please!" she said, pointing to Analeise who felt like a convict!

"I'm sorry," She said as she blushed.

As Analeise was putting her phone back into her bag, she stared at Pauline who was laughing into her magazine.

"It was Martin," she said slowly.

"I wonder what he wanted, the bastard!!" instantly she stopped laughing and put the magazine into the front pouch.

"I don't know" she replied " But I get a really bad vibe about this whole trip!"

Pauline started sniggering again.

When they arrived at Stanstead Airport…. Analeise needed the ladies room.

"Will you just hurry up!" shouted Pauline "They'll be waiting for us!"

She applied the final touches of her lip-gloss, and took a deep breath.

"Stop pouting Analeise, you look like you're trying too hard!" Pauline said as they walked towards arrivals.

Analeise couldn't remember what Clive looked like from the first time she saw him in Dublin as she was beside herself with bad images of the night before.

She stared at a sea of faces hoping to recognise a tall, blonde, handsome Brad Pitt look-alike!!

Pauline started to run towards a dark, curly haired Clive.

"Hi gorgeous, good to see you" she said and started to kiss him. Meanwhile Analeise stood like a blind man waiting to cross the road!

"Come on!" shouted Pauline. She beckoned her over to the bar where Trevor sat eagerly.

"OH GOD!" Analeise thought, as she got closer. "Please don't let it be him!"

All of her dreams of Brad Pitt had been shattered into smithereens!!

The dream was slowly turning into a nightmare as she approached Trevor very slowly!

He stood up and shook her hand. "You must be Analeise" he said "Pleased to meet you at last"

Her face was expressionless as she said "And you." Trying really hard not to look disappointed.

Trevor and Clive went to the bar to get the girls a drink.

"You seem pleased with yourself mate!" Clive said to Trevor.

"I sure am, she's gorgeous," he replied as he looked over to a very stern Analeise

"I'm gonna knock your head in!" Analeise whispered to Pauline who couldn't stop giggling.

"Its not my fault he's like the back of a bus!" she replied.

"Back of a bus? He's got an arse like the Grand Canyon, and a face like one of the reptiles that lives on it!" Analeise was really angry.

"Clive obviously thought you wouldn't be that fussy," Pauline said as she tried to pacify her friend.

"I'm not that desperate either!" she snapped.

After their drinks, they drove back to Heldon Hotel in Harlow, East London. The whole journey was exhausting for Analeise. She was stuck in the front with Trevor while he showed all the markings of a good BMW to her, and rattled on about how much money he owned.

Pauline and Clive fondled in the back like a couple of love struck teen-agers.

Analeise was glad to get to the hotel. She wanted a shower and was very hungry. She didn't need to ask Pauline what she wanted!!

"See you guys in a couple of hours" she winked as Clive and her scurried naughtily into the lift.

"A couple of hours!" thought Analeise. "What the hell will I do?"

She looked at Trevor and couldn't believe what she had let herself in for. Its not as if she could just bail out or anything!

"Well, I need to get showered and changed, where are we going later?" she asked him with a very straight face.

"I've a great Chinese restaurant booked. Best in the area! Anyway, I might as well come up to the room too" he replied.

Analeise was horrified!!

As she opened the door to room 512, Trevor asked, " Well, what do you think?"

He held his arms out "Was I what you expected?"

A 'still in shock' Analeise couldn't believe he had the nerve to ask such a stupid question. She had given him no encouragement that she was interested, he bored her the whole way in the car, he must have used a whole tub of brylcreem on his 'yellow over dyed hair' he must have weighed around 20 stone, wore ugly brown trousers her Dad wouldn't even wear, and he looked like a tortoise! "I wish I had half of his confidence," she thought.

"You never answered my question!" Trevor asked as he jumped on the bed as if 'testing it for later'.

Analeise couldn't even speak, she was so angry with this cocky arrogant shithead!!

"If it means anything, I'm really pleased! You are even nicer than I expected!" he shouted into the bathroom where she had dragged all her luggage into, hoping he wouldn't see her getting ready.

"He's got a bloody nerve!" she thought to herself. "Ok, I'm here now, just make the most of a bad situation" she said quietly while looking in the mirror.

Half an hour later she appeared from the bathroom, showered, changed and ready.

"Good to see you again, I thought you'd fallen down the toilet, never to return to civilisation!!" joked Trevor.

"I'm starting to wish I had!" thought Analeise as she tried to appear happy.

"Are you not getting ready?" she asked.

"No" he replied, "I got ready earlier on."

"Mmmmm, ugly and smelly" she mumbled as she picked up her handbag. She couldn't believe that this was the same guy she had been talking to all week. He obviously had lost his personality on the way to the airport!

They went down to the lounge bar and waited for the lovebirds. Analeise felt more comfortable now that they were out of the bedroom situation.

What a relief it was to see Pauline again, who couldn't keep the smile off her face!

Analeise wasn't sure if it was the sex, or the fact that this blind date was very amusing for an onlooker!!

"Right, I'm starving. Lets go!" said Clive, who was deliberately avoiding eye contact with Analeise.

Trevor decided to drive, so of course Analeise had to sit in the front with him while he gassed on AGAIN about how many people that work for him. How much money he earned last week. Now that he realised his looks didn't impress her, maybe his bank balance would!!

His dick might be strung with diamonds, but Analeise didn't care for that!

Sun Palace Chinese restaurant according to Trevor was the best in the area.

"Its empty!"

Pauline moaned as they arrived, everyone was looking around, wondering where the people were!

True enough there wasn't another sinner in this so-called amazing, famous restaurant!

All Analeise could think about was food. She had decided what she was going to order on the journey there!

"At least we'll get good service!" assured Clive as he sniggered.

They had their choice of seats, so they chose a large round table in the centre of the room. They ordered immediately.

Analeise sat with her back to Trevor the whole night. He tried to show off by eating with chopsticks!

"Why don't you just eat with a fork like the rest of us?" asked Pauline who hadn't 'warmed' to him either.

He was losing brownie points with Analeise the more the night went on.

"Glad you booked this Trevor" She said, "We wouldn't have got a seat otherwise"

Everyone started to laugh – Except Trevor.

He decided on the way back from the restaurant he would show everyone around his new apartment (Or 'Love Nest', as he preferred to describe it!)

Analeise was disgusted, she hated it, no matter how hard Trevor tried the worse she became.

She sat the whole way through dinner without saying a word. It was miserable. What the hell was she doing in East London eating in an empty Chinese Restaurant with a complete plonker and two love-birds?

At one point Clive asked her if she was going to leave the pattern on her plate, she was eating so fast!!

Her skin was beginning to crawl whenever he totally insisted that everyone go back to his 'pad' for coffee.

The painting in his lounge of the naked woman (with snake) draped over a motorbike was enough to send her over the edge until she caught a glimpse of his boudoir!

"How Many guys have pink flowery wallpaper in their bedroom?" she asked Clive while Trevor was in the kitchen making coffee.

"He's disgusting! Is he really your friend? And what the hell made you think I'd like him?"

"Dunno, he's a nice guy. He's my mate. He's normally very popular with the ladies. Leave him alone, you have been horrible to him all night Analeise." he replied.

"Get real Clive!" piped Pauline "he's been winding me up all night, let alone Ana What were you thinking babe?" Clive was starting to feel a little bit guilty by now. Analeise had a sneaking suspicion that Clive didn't really like her.

He thought Analeise was a little bit uppity from the first time he met her. He didn't like the way she was treating his friend.

He just didn't realise that the first time he met her she had a terrible incident the night before and was on a guilt trip. And the second meeting with her she was on a blind date from hell!

Pauline turned to Analeise and said " I would feel the same as you if this was happening to me"

Just at that moment, Trevor came into the room wheeling a hostess trolley!!

"Coffee and biscuits"

Analeise couldn't contain herself any longer. She laughed so hard that everyone thought she was crying.

"Are you ok?" asked Pauline.

Analeise was hysterical. She couldn't stop laughing. The tears were rolling down her face.

"Is she ok?" Asked Trevor who didn't understand what was going on.

"Yes mate, lose the trolley for fuck sake!!" Clive said as he blushed.

Pauline started to snigger "My granny used to have one of those!" she pointed to the sad effort that lay before her.

It made Analeise worse! She was creased, she hadn't laughed as hard for years.

Trevor drove everyone back to the Hotel. Analeise was exhausted.

Pauline and Clive got out, said their goodnights, and went back to their room.

Trevor turned to Analeise and attempted to kiss her.

She pulled back.

"I'm sorry I disappointed you" he said "I'm normally a big hit with the ladies!"

"Its ok" she replied as she got out of the car. "I'm sorry too." She felt a bit guilty for being so curt with him all evening.

"Can we do lunch tomorrow?" he asked.

"You don't give up easily do you?" she smiled.

He shrugged, and as he drove away she felt good about herself. Someone actually fancied her, not that she was interested. Nevertheless she was flattered.

When she got back to her room, she suddenly thought about James. Maybe she could meet with him tomorrow seeing as she was in his town!

She picked up the phone and dialled his number.

"Hello?"

"Hi James its Ana, I'm in Londo…"

The phone was put down instantly!

"Oh god, he thinks I'm a psycho stalker!!"

All of a sudden, this wonderful feeling of satisfaction turned into mental torment of rejection again.

As she cried, she tore up James telephone number, and threw it in the bin and promised herself never to be that desperate again!

Analeise tried so hard to forget about the fact that Martin had dumped her, now she was being dumped again by a guy she had a one-night stand with. She realised that she had to learn to deal with rejection, as she would have to kiss a lot of frogs in order to meet her prince. She also temporarily forgot about the weird phone call from Martin earlier.

"What did he want?" she thought.

She lay in bed that night and cried until she fell asleep.

CHAPTER SEVEN

The whole journey home from London Analeise moaned and groaned at Pauline.

"Why did you bloody come?" she shouted back.

Analeise thought all her dreams would come true. She'd meet Prince Charming and live happily ever after. It wasn't going to be just as simple as that. She needed much more time to settle into her new life again. She yearned to be loved and to be held again. That feeling of being a part of something just had to wait.

Apartment 2b Crows field Park was starting to get on her nerves. Analeise wanted a change, there were far too many memories here she thought. As well as that, Martin wanted her to move out shortly as he wanted to give up the apartment and move his life on to the next level.

That's why he had called her on that awful weekend.

"I want a house," she announced, seated at the breakfast bar in her Mums house.

"You're going to have to stop running up and down to Dublin then" her Mum replied as she dished out home made apple pie.

Analeise's Dad was in the next room. A man who feared any kind of risk. Mr sensible, plays it safe kind of guy. She loved him dearly, but she knew he was still living in the last century! She never used to get along with him. They used to fight like cat and dog whenever she lived at home. Since she has moved out she has learned to understand his ways, as her moods were very similar to his. He wanted the best for his children, but worried constantly about them.

"For goodness sake sweetheart, whatever you do, don't tell your Dad! You know what he's like!" her Mum warned.

"I can afford it you know!" Analeise snapped.

"Your Dad will worry!" Her Mum said, but secretly knew that Analeise was doing the right thing.

Analeise had spoken to her boss Kevin, a very shrewd business-man who thought everyone had the same amount of money as him-self. Analiese got on the best with him. She had a lot of respect for him and they got along swimmingly. He created an empire for himself out of absolutely nothing years ago. They were similar in age (Kevin looked 10 years older) but he was the more sensible one with all the clever business moves. His marriage had also broken down, so they had a lot in common.

Whenever Analeise had told him about her marriage, he worried. Not about her, but as to how she would perform as representative of his company. He hoped she wouldn't start moping around and 'piss her career up against the wall!'

She didn't. Instead she through herself into it one hundred percent and her figures over the last couple of months just proved that.

"It's the best investment you'll ever make" he assured her "Just put down ten grand on one of those new developments at the river."

They were having a pub lunch in a very busy place in Dublin.

"Just like that Kevin?" Analeise asked, "I don't have that kind of money"

"Well, whatever you have. You can't go wrong with bricks and mor-tar! I pay you good money, you should have something to show for it" he replied, shovelling 6 chips into his mouth in one go!!

He was right, Analeise thought. She decided from then on she would start saving, and start looking for some property.

Analeise had been healing pretty well over the next couple of weeks. She kept her head down and was concentrating on the more positive things in life. She had spent a few boring weekends sitting in like a complete 'saddo' watching saturday night game shows and sunday matinees and felt the urge to go to Dublin for one more bender. This time they would do it in style. No crappy dormatory this time; they would stay in a five star hotel. No expense spared. Analeise even treated herself to a black designer dress.

On the Saturday afternoon they arrived at the Five Star Hotel, which stood in Grafton Street in the centre of Dublin. They got there early so they could pamper themselves all day. They went to the Gym and then for a swim and sauna. Then afterwards they went to the beauty salon for a facial each.

"Oh, this is the life for me" said Pauline when they got back to the room.

"Say goodbye to this babe when you get a mortgage!"

"I don't care!" shouted Analeise from her deep bubble bath. "At least I'll be working for something!"

"I want to be a kept woman," said Pauline as she started to blow dry her hair.

"No you wouldn't, you'd be controlled by a man. You'd be expected to do the housework, cook, and do whatever he wants. Remember he would be the boss! I'd that life with Martin, and I was miserable!"

"Yes, but you weren't rich" she answered.

Analeise jumped out of the bath in horror and stormed into the bedroom, dripping wet.

"Money means fuck all! If your life is miserable it doesn't matter what you have!!"

"Ok tiger, calm down" Pauline was sorry she upset her. "You're obviously not over Martin yet"

"YES, I SO AM!!" Analeise shouted. " I'm just angry at the way that I was treated!! There is a fine line between love and hate, and I'm standing on the line. I hate him for what he has done." She scurried back into the bathroom.

Pauline felt terrible for upsetting her.

"GOOD!" She shouted, "I'm glad you feel like that, now hurry up and let's grab some action!!"

Pauline put on her killer Gucci heels with a very low cut red dress.

She made a real effort on herself like never before. Analeise was delighted.

"You scrub up well whenever you try!!" She said to Cinderella.

Analeise looked stunning in her new open backed dress. It cost a fortune, but was worth every penny.

They both looked a million dollars each! All heads turned as they walked through reception. They felt great. It was a long time since Analeise felt this special. Things were starting to fall into place. She for the first time would have her own home, her own independence. She even noticed that her personality had slightly changed. She was much more confident and more assertive. Analeise wasn't afraid to make herself heard anymore, before she would have stood in Martins shadow, with very little to say for herself.

Pauline was so proud of how she had become lately.

"You know, I'm waiting for you to crack up or something" she asked her as they were downing their first double vodka in the sophisticated hotel lounge bar.

"I'm not going to crack up!" replied Analeise.

"It's just that you picked yourself up so quickly, remember you've been with Martin for ten years. It's a long time.," said Pauline.

"Yes, and five of them were miserable. I feel like someone has handed me the key to freedom. I was like a bloody prisoner!" Analeise smiled.

Pauline was very protective with her dear and troubled friend; she just thought that Analeise was brushing her real emotions under the carpet.

"Ok, end of serious discussion, lets get pissed" Pauline didn't want to dampen Analeise's high spirits.

They stayed in the hotel bar for a few more because a crowd of English Rugby supporters had paid for their drinks.

The girls wanted to move on, but they felt obliged to stay and be grateful.

"We're wasting our time here, I want to go!" Pauline whispered in Analeise's ear.

"Lets go to the loo, then do a runner," she suggested.

"We're away to the loo!" Pauline announced to the five randy Englishmen who couldn't keep their eyes off Pauline's legs and Analeise's tits!!

"Dirty pervs!!" she whispered to Pauline.

"I think they had ideas on us tonight baby!" she replied.

"I come more expensive than a miserable vodka and coke," laughed Analeise as the two of them legged it towards the toilets and then made a sneaky run for the front doors.

The centre of Dublin was a hive of more rugby mad Englishmen!

"There must have been a game today, the place is crawling with them" said Analeise as they entered onto Talbot street.

Just as they walked towards Aussies bar a very handsome guy was standing on the street corner.

"Hello" he said as the girls passed.

"Hi" Analeise grinned at him.

"Oh my god, did you see him!!" She nudged Pauline's arm as they approached a very large queue outside the bar.

"What do you want to do?" Pauline asked her. "That queue is mad, I'm not standing in it"

"Lets go to Buffalo Bills," suggested Analeise.

"Ok, does that mean we walk past handsome again?" asked Pauline curiously as she raised her eyebrows.

She smiled, and as they walked past again.

"Hello again!" he said to them.

"Hi again" smiled Analeise "I'm Analeise, and this is my friend Pauline."

"My name is Dillon" he replied as he held his hand out. "Would you like to come with us, we're going to Johnston's Bar?" He pointed to his waiting taxicab.

The girls looked at each other and shrugged.

"Yes, why not!" they said, flattered.

Dillon was 6 feet tall, dark curly hair, piercing blue eyes and a smile that would lighten any room. Analeise couldn't keep her eyes off him.

He had been in Dublin to watch England play Ireland.

"Regrettably Ireland won!" he told the girls as they all jumped into a people carrier patiently waiting for the rest of the lads.

"It would have been easier to walk it you know, it's only round the corner." announced Analeise as they were all aboard.

He fascinated her. His life seemed so exciting as he told her about living in Brighton. He travelled a lot with his work, buying and selling property across Europe.

"You'll have to come over to see my apartment before I sell it. Its amazing." He said to Analeise who was completely bedazzled by this stage.

They had a great evening. They stayed for a few in Johnston's bar and then headed to Zoo nightclub where Analeise was looking over her shoulder all night for a 'hairy-armed' naked man!

She danced with Dillon all night. He was a true gentleman. He couldn't have been sweeter to her.

Pauline was having a whale of a time with his friends downing shots at the bar. She left around one, completely pissed!!

"Are you ok?" she staggered over to Analeise who was engrossed in conversation with Dillon.

"I'll look after her, " Dillon answered. "Are *you* ok?"

"Oh yes, going now!" she pointed at Analeise and wiggled her finger. "See you later babe!" Then lost balance and fell in a heap!

"I'll get you a cab!" Dillon insisted

Analeise picked her up and ushered her outside while Dillon hailed down a cab for her.

"Like him!" Pauline slurred and winked as she stepped into the car.

At around 2.30 he left her back to her hotel where Pauline anxiously waited for her.

Dillon kissed Analeise goodnight, and told her he'd call her on Monday night.

"WELL?" Pauline bounced on Analeise like Tigger as she entered the room." Dish the dirt!!"

"No dirt." She proudly announced.

"WHAT! Are you mad? Is it your period or something? Why didn't you shag him? He's lovely!"

Pauline asked in horror as if it were compulsory to 'shag' within hours of meeting a guy.

"I'm not going to shag every one I fancy" Analeise replied, disappointed at her forever-caring friend. "I'm going to see him again, he wants me to visit his apartment."

"Heard that one before!!" Pauline replied. "Glad he didn't see your sexy pyjama's!"

"Don't even go there!!" Analeise shouted angrily. "I'm happy, ok. Don't you dare try to burst my bubble!!"

Pauline apologised. She was scared of her friend getting hurt again. She felt as though she needed some time to play the field and not get involved with any more assholes in her life. Everyone has their own way of dealing with heartbreak, and if getting kicked in the teeth time and time again were Analeise's way, well she'd have to accept it.

Pauline passed out snoring shortly after. It took Analeise a while to get to sleep!

When she woke the next morning Pauline was in the bathroom singing.

"How do you never get hangovers?" Analeise asked curiously as she held her head in her hands.

"Love is in the air!!" Pauline sung at the top of her voice. Analeise laughed at the state of her. Her hair had stuck up like a rooster and her make-up from the night before was all over her face.

"I don't get hangovers, and the ugly monsters don't get you in the middle of the night!" Pauline pointed to Analeise whose eyes were sparkling. "So we're even Princess!"

Monday came round and Dillon called Analeise at 6.30 that evening, just as she was micro waving (Like a true professional!) a low calorie lasagne.

"Oh hi, I was just 'cooking' my tea!" she lied. "Yes, I love cooking, I'm not a bad cook" she lied again!

They arranged a weekend together at his apartment in Brighton the following Friday. Analeise was so excited; she couldn't even eat her so-called home cooked treat when the call was finished!

Analeise Moran wondered where her destiny lay. It had been 8 months since Martin left her. She thought she had been on her own for long enough. She longed to be held and loved. Why could every one else meet someone so fast after a break-up she thought, meanwhile she had to go through all this agony? True enough, everything between Pauline and Clive were wonderful. Pauline was seeing him every two weeks.

She seemed settled lately and didn't want to go out to nightclubs anymore. All of Analeise's workmates had boyfriends, and she was always the single one. She was becoming fed up with it. Maybe Dillon was her destiny? She couldn't wait to see him again.

CHAPTER EIGHT

*A*t Gatwick airport Analeise had a stomach flip as she seen Dillon standing waiting for her at arrivals.

He seemed very pleased to see her.

"Hi, you look gorgeous" he shouted as he lifted her up and kissed her. "I've got a great weekend planned."

As they drove down the motorway they really started to get to know each other. They talked about their families, their careers and their friends. Dillon was such a nice guy; he seemed so down to earth. He was successful, funny, and to top it all of, he was drop dead gorgeous!

Analeise was thrilled.

She was even more thrilled whenever he gave her the 'grand tour' of his amazing penthouse apartment.

"Oh my god, it's fabulous!" she cried as she walked through the marble floored hall and entered the split-level lounge with flat-screened television on the white washed wall. Top of the range Bang and Olfson hi-fi attached to a metal frame on the other end of the room. Two black leather sofas's faced a glass coffee table on a wooden floor. On the lower level a glass dining table sat on a cream Persian rug, complete with 8 stainless steel and glass chairs. This led into a 40 feet by 35 feet kitchen complete with Aga cooker.

"So maybe you'll cook me one of your culinary delights this weekend, eh?" asked Dillon, as Analeise blushed trying to avoid the question with another question.

"Where is your flatmate David?" Hoping that he'd cleared off for the weekend.

"He'll be back from work soon, he's a steward for Virgin Atlantic, he'll probably be shattered and sleep for a few days." He replied.

"Great!" She Thought "I've got this great, intelligent, beautiful man for the whole weekend. All for myself!"

Everything seemed to be going so well when she arrived in Brighton. She hummed in delight as she unpacked her weekend bag. La perla underwear – a real indulgence- but this was a special occasion! She felt so lucky as she hung up her black wraparound dress and new Jimmy Choo shoes for dinner in the best restaurant in town. Dillon told her to pack something for a club on Friday night, dinner on Saturday night, and a pub lunch on Sunday. A perfect weekend she was going to make sure she would enjoy.

"HI DARLING!!" A roar came from the hall. "I'M HOME!"

Dillon laughed and shouted into the bathroom where Analeise was trying to get ready, but seemed more interested in the abundance of 'male grooming products' that were on the market these days! Men's false tan, hand cream, smelly rose scented body lotion, and wondered if he lived with a girl as well!

"Coming!" she shouted back. "I'm just getting ready"

She stepped out of the bathroom, dripping wet with a towel around her.

"Let me introduce you to David, my completely mad flat mate!" he announced as a puddle started to gather round Analeise's feet.

There he was, Analeise should have known better. Air steward, fake tan, soft hands, and stunk of rose. David was as camp as anything she'd seen. She shook his soft hand as the other one tried to hold up her towel.

"Pleased to meet you." She said.

"And you" he replied "Caught you at a bad time?"

"Suppose you could say that" Analeise laughed. She seemed very at ease with him, probably because he was just like another girl!

"I'd better get back and finish what I started! Excuse me." She said as she pointed back to the bathroom.

She spent another half an hour in the bathroom, applied her make-up, and stepped into her satin mini dress and knee length boots. She looked gorgeous.

Meanwhile Dillon and David had been drinking vodka and downing tequila shots to the sounds of Basement Jaxx full blast on the stereo.

"WOW!" Dillon shouted as Analeise entered the room.

"Oh yes girlfriend – work it!!" said David as he drew on a very exotic pastel cigarette.

"Have some tequila and catch up with us. You have to tell me about your skincare product! I'm addicted to them!" he said as he rubbed his hand up and down his very well cared for face!

Dillon took himself off to get ready as Analeise put her business head on for 15 minutes.

"Sold to the queen in the corner!! Can you get me some?" David said pointing at himself.

"Of course!" She laughed.

Dillon eventually appeared back about half an hour later wearing a black T Shirt and a pair of Levi's. His hair was immaculate. He looked amazing thought Analeise as she drunk her third tequila shot.

"Lets hit he town!!" he shouted.

"See you later love's I'm having a bath, and then going to beautify myself!!" said David as he raised his glass.

As they stepped outside, Analeise asked "Is David coming with us?"

"Oh yes, he's great!!" replied Dillon.

She tried not to look disappointed. *As she also tried really hard to walk in a straight line!*

They went to 'The Tree' the first watering hole where they downed a few black russians. Analeise was starting to become numb from the brain downwards and hoped her body would be better behaved when she got up from her seat.

By the time they got to Wonderland Club, they were completely plastered! Earlier they had met with a few of Dillon's friends. Mostly women, which un-nerved Analeise slightly until his friend Sally (who looked like a goldfish staring at her from a bowl) said, " He really likes you, and he thinks you're gorgeous"

Analeise and Dillon had a great night drinking and generally bouncing off the walls.

"Don't go!" he moaned "Its just getting good!"

Dillon didn't feel great, and Analeise was completely pissed! They got home and passed out on the sofa.

7am on Saturday morning they got awakened by David, singing at the top of his voice. " I'M COMING OUT, I WANT THE WORLD TO KNOW, I WANT TO LET IT SHOW!! Dear god, look at the carnage on the sofa!! Get to bed you bores!"

Analeise's head was thumping, she felt sick, and looked around hoping she hadn't thrown up anywhere!

She hobbled into the bathroom. "Oh my god, what a mess!!" she said to herself. Her eye make up was on her cheekbones, and her face was grey.

She crawled into Dillon's very large, comfortable bed and slept until 12.00.

When she woke, Dillon was not beside her, so she got up and looked around the apartment for him, and wondered if he had even slept in his bed at all!

The front door opened, and in bounced Dillon, fresh as a daisy holding a pint of milk and a newspaper.

"Good morning you lazy bitch!!" he said as he waltzed into the kitchen. Analeise felt terrible. There she was, still wearing last night's clothes looking like a bag of tripe and wondered how Dillon managed to look so good!

She went to the bathroom, had a shower and tried to make herself look remotely presentable again. She suddenly realised they didn't have sex last night. At least, she thought so. She was so horny. Dillon looked so damn fine.

Looking like a human being again she walked into the kitchen where she found Dillon sitting reading his newspaper. She walked over and kissed him.

"That's more like it." He said "Would you like some coffee?"

"Yes, that would be nice" she answered " Where did you sleep last night?"

"When that maniac came in" he pointed to David's bedroom "I couldn't get back to sleep, so I'd a shot of tequila and some anadin. Right as rain!"

They spent the rest of the day lazing around the apartment drinking coffee, and watching DVD's. At around 6.30 Analeise started to get ready for their romantic dinner. She carefully put on her new sexy underwear, smothered herself in Chanel body lotion and stepped into her elegant black dress. Dillon walked into the bedroom and blushed.

"You're beautiful," he said

"You didn't say that at 12.00 today!!" Analeise replied.

"It's amazing what a couple of hours can do to a girl!" he laughed.

Analeise held up two pairs of shoes, a comfortable pair of mules in one hand, and a pair of Jimmy Choo's in the other.

"They're sexy," he said as he pointed to the diamante 4-inch stilettos.

"Jimmy it is!!" She was glad as these shoes cost her a week's wages!

"Tonight's the night!" she thought to herself as the mere thought of jumping Dillon's bones was so exciting!

The restaurant was booked for 7.30pm. Dillon wore a black suit and a plain white T-shirt underneath. They made a very handsome couple. The restaurant was very elegant, full of well-dressed bankers. In the corner there were four Americans who watched in awe as the couple walked past. They were given a table just at the front of the restaurant. They ordered a bottle of Chablis. Dillon held Analeise's hand as they stared at each other across the table. The service was excellent; the restaurant was everything that Dillon had described it. They ate monkfish on a bed of fresh salad to start, and fillet steak cooked to perfection for main course.

"I can't believe we ordered the same thing!" said Dillon as he stared into Analeise's eyes, which were sparkling like diamonds. She couldn't have been happier. There she was sitting in front of this charming, funny, sweet guy who couldn't keep his eyes off her all night.

"I got to go to the ladies room, excuse me," She said as she stood up. She asked the waitress to point her in the right direction.

"Just down the stairs, to the left" she replied.

Dillon watched her as she left her seat and wiggled to the top of the stairs.

Just then one of her Jimmy Choo's lost grip on the first step and within seconds she had fallen down 12 more on her arse!! She eventually landed at the bottom of the stairs in a heap. The restaurant fell silent and Analeise couldn't get up with the pain.

"Oh my good god" she mumbled as she looked up – Four faces were staring down at her.

"Are you ok?" asked one of them.

"Oh yes, I'm great, no worries" she jumped up totally mortified.

She then found that the complete contents of her handbag had been scattered down all of the stairs. Make up, mobile phone, purse, hairspray and tampons cluttered the whole stairs, she crawled back up and retrieved them one by one. Her hands were shaking like crazy as she walked into the safety of the ladies loo!! As she was trying to compose herself, the waitress walked in. "You're boyfriend asked me to see if you were ok?" she was very sweet, but Analeise needed to be left alone as she thought she was going to cry.

"I'm just a bit shocked you know, tell him I'll be up in a minute"

She had been in the bathroom for 15 minutes trying to pluck up the courage to face the whole restaurant again. When she eventually got back up there was another silence.

"Hi, I'm ok!!" she said to the couple that stared at her with complete pity.

Dillon was standing waiting for her holding her coat in his arm.

"Are you alright?" he asked.

"Yes, I'm great!" she lied.

They said goodbye to the waitress and left.

"I'm so sorry" Analeise said whenever they got outside. "What must you think"?

They both laughed.

Analeise decided she needed a less intimate environment now so they met with Dillon's friends and went to Escapade nightclub.

"Don't expect me to do much dancing tonight!! My leg is aching." She lifted her dress to show Dillon a huge bruise on her left leg where she landed!

"You're lucky to be alive! You could have gone down head first, those stairs were pretty steep!" he said.

"I know" she replied " Saved by my ass!!"

For Analeise the remainder of the night was spent talking to Sally, one of Dillon's friends. A very overpowering Dental nurse who talked about trying to get off with Roger the Dentist!

"Oh, I don't know if he likes me or not, should I just go for it?" she asked Analeise as she downed a glass of wine. Analeise didn't give a shit; she was more concerned about Dillon's interest in Anna. She was engrossed in a conversation with him about cosmetic surgery.

"Well, if you feel the need" he touched her breasts "Go for it girl!!"

Analeise walked over " Hi there" she politely said to the 'close to perfect' flat chested Anna.

"My leg is aching babe, do you want to go home and kiss it better??" she whispered in his ear.

"In a minute" he replied "I've just got to console Kathy, she's had a fight with Paul"

"What is this?" she said angrily "What about consoling me?"

She was getting pissed off now.

"Ok, hold on" he walked over and said something to Kathy who was bawling her eyes out.

"He's such a bastard. How dare he!! Will you call me tomorrow??" she asked Dillon as she wrapped her arms around his neck.

"Yes" he replied, "Of course I will, go home and get some sleep. It'll be ok"

He kissed her on the cheek and walked back to Analeise who was feeling a bit guilty tearing 'Saint Dillon' away from his troubled friends.

"I'm sorry, I'm in a lot of pain now" she apologised to him.

"I'll put some arnica on it when we get home" he said.

Analeise didn't want arnica! She wanted him to take her home and give her a right good seeing to!! That would definitely make her feel better.

When they closed the door of Dillon's apartment, Analeise started to kiss him passionately. She couldn't remember the last time she had been so horny. At this stage she didn't care about her bruised leg!

His lips were so soft. She couldn't get enough of him, she then pushed off his jacket and put her hands inside his T-shirt, he felt so good! Dillon meanwhile kissed Analeise gently, but his hands remained at his sides. She thought he was teasing her; it was making her hornier! She started to move her hands slowly down to his crotch, where there was completely no movement!

She stopped kissing him and asked, " Are you ok?"

"Yes" he replied "I'd better get you something for that bruise, now let me see."

He scurried into the kitchen.

"Oh Jesus!" thought Analeise. "He either doesn't fancy me, or he's gay... My god, I've been so blind!!"

She followed him into the kitchen.

"There we go, Arnica!" Dillon said as he held up a small jar of very smelly ointment.

"I don't want arnica! What's wrong with you? Don't you want to screw me?"

Analeise was confused; she was really embarrassed after confronting him.

"Its not that" he stuttered, "you're gorgeous! Its just..." he didn't finish.

He blushed and put his head down.

"I understand Dillon, you're confused. Have you got gay tendencies?" She asked.

"I don't know" he replied.

"You must know! You would prefer to rub that stinking stuff onto my bruise" she pointed to the jar of arnica. "Than to fuck my brains out!! I think I would know!"

Analeise was mortified speaking to him so bluntly, but she needed to know for her own sanity.

"Have you been with a man?" she asked confused.

"No" he quickly replied. His head still staring at the floor like a scolded child.

"I really thought you fancied me, why the hell did you invite me over if you weren't sure??" Analeise asked.

"I do fancy you, it's just that I'm not great in the bedroom department, and I don't want to disappoint you. You're so fucking sexy, I thought you might laugh" Dillon was close to tears.

Analeise couldn't believe her ears "What a passion killer" she thought.

"Are you a virgin?" she asked.

"NO! Oh fuck, this is so humiliating!!" Dillon stormed into the lounge and turned on the stereo.

Analeise felt a bit sorry for him; she was convinced he wasn't sure of his sexuality right now. One thing she was sure of was that her chances of getting a shag this weekend were very slender!

She followed him into the lounge and put her arms around him. He kissed her gently on the mouth and they held each other for a while.

"Lets go to bed," said Dillon.

They went to bed and slept soundly all night. Analeise was disappointed in a way, but she decided to enjoy the rest of her weekend with Dillon, a confused bi-sexual, and boil it down to experience!

The next day they went for a drive and stopped for lunch in a quaint little pub in a village called Lindfield, they laughed about the weekend.

"I'll never forget the sound of you tumbling down those stairs!" said Dillon.

"I'm a walking disaster," she laughed as she polished off her second glass of wine.

"I suppose I'd better be heading, can you give me a lift to the airport?"

"It's the least I can do!" Dillon replied.

When they got to Gatwick Airport Dillon gave Analeise a great big bear hug and thanked her for being so understanding. She knew she would never see him again, but would never forget her weekend in Brighton.

On her journey home she decided she would have to stop looking for 'Mr Right'. That he would have to come looking for her when the time is right! She'd have to stop forcing herself upon people, and expecting too much too soon!! That weekend was a lesson she would learn and never forget.

CHAPTER NINE

*A*naleise threw herself back into her work for a few weeks after her interesting weekend in Brighton. She didn't want to go out dancing, she stopped drinking at weekends; she just wanted to focus on other things. She needed to save as much money as possible if she wanted to buy a house!

"So what do you think Thelma, isn't it gorgeous??" she said with delight for the 50th time that month as she gently massaged 'moisture boost' into Thelma's smooth tanned hand.

Analeise was in 'Beauty Works' Beauty Salon in Bangor, Co Down.

Thelma was a long-standing client with the company for many years. She seemed more interested in Analeise than in this wonderful cream!!

"Yes, it is lovely Analeise, but tell me how you've been these days. You've changed, you seem more... Oh I don't know, at ease?" she looked at her with caring, kind eyes.

"My marriage broke up a while ago, I feel a bit better about myself I suppose" Analeise answered.

"I'm sorry!!" Thelma said surprised.

"Don't be" Analeise said. Then she went silent, she didn't really want to go into the gory details, but sooner or later she'd have to start talking about it.

"It's none of my business darling, but if you don't mind me saying you seem different lately."

Analeise looked at her puzzled.

"Happier, more contented with yourself, and you look great!"

"Really?" Analeise was astounded. She couldn't believe that people had actually begun to notice the change in her. She knew herself that she was happier, but didn't realise that it showed!

"Whatever you're doing, keep doing it," said Thelma. "You seem more at ease or something and you are a pleasure to do business with! Just don't force things!" she advised.

"I must have been a miserable old sod before!!" said Analeise

Thelma laughed.

Delighted with her compliment, she skipped out of the salon complete with a very large order in her hand.

That evening she was sitting in the flat, bemused by the sounds of Brian, the alcoholic singing 'Achy Breaky Heart' at the top of his voice downstairs in the bottom flat. He was a harmless sod, always getting himself locked out. He would often bang on the door "Sorry luv, can I use your phone to call my Da?"

Analeise and Martin felt sorry for him and always would help him out. For instance help him find his key, which happened all the time! He would have about 25 keys on his key ring; god only knows what they were for! He spent all of his day in the pub, then come home around 8.30 get wired into a bottle of vodka! Sing at the top of his voice, and then pass out!!

Analeise heard a noise at the front door, and thought it was Brian again, then the door opened and Martin walked in.

"Hi, just in to get a few more things. I'm going on holiday!" he announced.

She was becoming tired of him letting himself come and go whenever it suited him!

"Martin, I could have been doing anything, you just sail in and sail out whenever it suits you. When are you going to give me more privacy?" she was furious.

He kept on packing T-shirts into an old brown rucksack.

"Its still my flat, Its in my name! I can do whatever the hell I want, when I want!!" He said without turning round.

That was the final straw for Analeise; she would start looking for a house that week!

The sooner she broke all ties with Martin, the better. She would feel more independent, and would never have to look at his miserable face again! Anyway she thought, its only going to be a matter of time before Brian burnt the whole place down in one of his drunken attempts to cook chips! Analeise could do much better than Martins crappy flat!

CHAPTER TEN

*T*he following week, surrounded in property guides, Analeise felt the need to contact Pauline.

"Hi babe, what are you doing?" she asked.

"At this moment, or in general?" Pauline asked back.

"I need someone to come with me to view a house?" Analeise asked.

"When?" asked Pauline?

"Tomorrow" she replied, "I've seen this great house in Lisburn, can you come?"

Lisburn was 9 miles south of Belfast centre, and a great location for Analeise's job as it was just off the motorway. Easy access for anywhere she travelled without having to deal with Belfast traffic every day.

"Sorry babe, no can do, I've got to take Mum to the hospital, its her varicose veins!!" Pauline replied. She was an only child and Analeise was like a sister to her, but Pauline's mum Mary ruled with an iron fist!!

"Ok." She thought, " I can do this on my own. I'm a big girl. My decision."

She was very excited about seeing this house. Perfect location, gardens front and rear, it sounded great! At 6.00 as she drew closer to it, it didn't seem just as glamorous as described in the estate agents. They had forgotten to mention the small detail of a very large, very colourful 'red commando' logo on the side of the house. Not forgetting that since the photograph had been taken, the front door had been kicked in!!

'A little bit scary!!' she thought.

Analeise kept driving.

The next day, she called into McCormick & Sutton Estate agents on Railway Street, arranged a few more appointments with other properties around the town.

"No murals on this one? Or maybe it's surrounded by a barbed wire fence?" Analeise joked with Margaret as she soberly smiled and wrote down directions.

When Analeise got back to the car, she had a few missed calls on her phone. One from the office enquiring if 'Butterflies Beauty Salon' paid their bill, one from Pauline wondering how she got on with the house last night! The last caller didn't leave a message. 'Must have been a new salon somewhere' Analeise thought. Just then the same number was calling her again.

"Hello. Is that Analeise Magowan?" the male voice asked.

"Y-Yes, suppose so" Magowan was Analeise's maiden name and hadn't used it for 2 years.

"Its Chris Drummond, how are you?"

Oh my god! She thought!!

Chris was an old flame from around 12 years ago, she went out with him a few times and then he cleared off to South Africa to live with his father who had emigrated there some years ago. She hadn't seen or heard his name mentioned in all these years.

"Jesus, how the hell are you? How did you get my number?" she asked.

"I seen you one day, coming out of a beauty salon, so I went in and asked her for your number!!" he replied.

"That was very forward!!" Analeise joked.

It didn't surprise her one little bit, Chris was a very good-looking arrogant creature. The sort of person Analeise was very attracted to. He was in public relations whenever they dated. He knew everyone, got invited to the right parties, and never had a problem getting a table in the best restaurant with no reservation. Blonde, 6feet tall, he worked out every single day, his body was perfect! His eyes sparkled like diamonds when he smiled, and he made a woman feel that she was the only person in the room whenever he looked at her. A total bastard, and a genuine heartbreaker!

"Would you like to meet for a coffee?" he asked.

"Its years since I've seen you Chris, you've been in South Africa. How did you know I was single?" She was still in shock.

"I didn't!" he replied with confidence. "I know now!"

Analeise laughed, and agreed to meet him that Friday in a coffee shop in Belfast. She wondered what he looked like now. Could he still be as gorgeous? What did he want?

Why was he not married? She was curious, and couldn't wait to catch up with him again for old times sake.

That evening Analeise drove to Lisburn again in hope of finding her dream house!

Number 5 Birch Avenue.

It sounded good she thought as she fumbled with the hand drawn map that Margaret the Smiler from the estate agency drew for her earlier!

When she drove up the tree lined avenue it looked gorgeous.

"This couldn't be it?" she thought. It was so nice, considering the house she had seen before. There it was a modest little semi detached house surrounded in well-kept shrubs, she walked up the driveway and seen a gorgeous hanging basket in the porch.

She rang the bell; her head was spinning around admiring the well-maintained garden that lay before her.

"Hi, you must be Analeise."

A small red haired, middle-aged lady answered the door.

"Yes" she replied "Hi"

"Come in, my name is Ruth, are you on your own?" she quizzed, looking anxiously behind her.

"Afraid so! I'm recently separated, and am looking for a house for myself." Analeise couldn't believe she was explaining herself to a total stranger, who at this stage had a look of pity right across her face!

"I'm sorry" Ruth replied as Analeise curiously looked around.

"I'm not!" she replied quickly as she pointed into the kitchen.

"Oh my manners! I'm sorry, yes this is the kitchen, come on through" Ruth replied as she escorted her into a very large fitted kitchen.

Analeise was very impressed, she could see herself in there attempting to roast a chicken in the brand new oven! It was perfect, very spacious, plenty of cupboard space. It was double the size of the kitchen in Martins flat. The bathroom was quite small, but it was enough for one person.

Upstairs there were 2 small box rooms, and at the front one very large bedroom. Analeise visualised herself again, this time swinging from the ceiling.

"Yes" she thought.

Finally, she viewed the lounge downstairs, it was at the front of the house, and it also was a great size.

"This house has given me 5 great years," said Ruth with a glint in her pale blue eyes as she stared at the marble fireplace.

"Why are you moving?" Analeise asked.

"I'm getting married. We are building a house near Moira. A village about 8 miles away" she replied.

"Nice" replied Analeise "It's a funny old world, there's you moving to get married, and there's me moving to be single!"

They laughed.

They instantly liked each other. Truthfully Analeise was convinced that Ruth felt sorry for her, but she didn't care. She loved the house.

As she drove away, all she could think about was how she would decorate it. What she would do, what furniture she would buy.

The next morning Analeise phoned the estate agents and put an offer in for the house.

CHAPTER ELEVEN

*F*riday morning came round, and Analeise just couldn't decide what to wear for her reunion with Chris.

"Professional" she thought, "Business like, yes, I'm an independent woman, and want to look like one!"

She settled for a black pinstripe trouser suit, and pinned her hair back, she didn't want to look like she had tried too hard!

They had agreed to meet at 3.00 that afternoon at Randall's, a very posh, upmarket patisserie.

Analeise was very anxious, she was so curious.

She arrived at the coffee shop to find that Chris was already there.

"Thank god" she thought.

He hadn't changed a bit, apart from a few extra lines around his eyes. Her heart missed a beat.

He got up and kissed her on the cheek.

"What can I get you?" he asked.

"Coffee" she replied, slightly nervous.

"What kind?" he asked again.

Analeise couldn't think straight.

"Just plain" she shrugged, angry with herself for not being able to compose herself properly.

As he walked over to the counter she couldn't keep her eyes off him. He had kept himself in perfect condition, his body looked just as good as before, and he carried himself so well.

Three cups of very strong coffee later, they were still sitting talking about old times. Analeise was bouncing off the walls!

"So you just decided to come home again, for what?" She asked curiously.

"I missed it here, anyway it was too warm" he replied.

Analeise looked at her watch "Jesus, its 5.30!! My car is on a meter, I'll have a ticket!!"

"Would you like to meet for a drink sometime?" he asked.

She was delighted.

"Yes, I'd like that" she replied as she awkwardly got out of her chair.

"I'll walk you to your car" Chris suggested.

"You haven't changed you know" Analeise said as they stepped outside "You're still a charmer! Will you go back into PR?"

"Its all I know" he replied. "I'm starting with McCallum & Ernest next week"

"Nice one!" She said, secretly delighted.

They stopped at her Car.

"I'm meeting with a whole load of old friends next weekend, I'd like it if you could come with me, I'm sure you'd remember them from years ago!" Chris asked Analeise as she peeled the yellow parking ticket off her windscreen.

"Typical!" she waved the expensive piece of paper in the air.

Chris laughed.

"I owe you 40 quid I suppose!!" he said.

"Its my fault!! Yes, I'd love to go, it would be great to see everyone again after all these years" she replied.

"Great" he kissed her on the cheek "It's a date, I'll give you a call in a couple of days"

He turned round and confidently staggered away, he must have known that Analeise was watching him. He lifted his arm and waved without turning round.

"Cocky bastard!!" she thought, grinning like a Cheshire cat!

She was the cat that got the cream! At least, she felt like it!!

CHAPTER TWELVE

*A*naleise just couldn't wait to phone Pauline with her news when she got home that evening, she didn't even care about the parking ticket.

"He hasn't changed, he is so nice!!" she excitedly said to Pauline, who didn't sound amused.

"They're all nice Ana!!" she said with sarcasm.

"What's wrong with you today! You sound like you've lost the roll-over lottery ticket!!" Analeise said, disappointed that her friend didn't have the same enthusiasm as her.

"Men, that's what is wrong" she replied, "Its Clive, he hasn't called, and wont take my calls!!" she started to cry.

This was a first for Pauline. She was always optimistic, trivial things never normally would bother her.

"Maybe there is something wrong with his phone" Analeise said solemnly.

Pauline was silent.

"I'll call round later, I'll bring you some ice cream," she said, trying to make her feel better.

"Whatever" Pauline replied, and hung up.

Analeise's bubble was burst by now, and all excitement of Chris had drastically faded into the back round.

Later that evening she called round complete with 'Ben and Jerry' to find Pauline still wearing her pyjama's. Her hair was stuck up like a Mohican, and her face was as white as driven snow!

"Oh Jesus! Have you done anything today?" Analeise asked.

"Apart from stalk Clive?" she replied "No"

"Here, try this" Analeise handed her a very large bowl of cookie dough ice cream.

"What am I going to do?" Pauline asked as she started to play with the thick, creamy substance.

"Stop calling would be a start!" Analeise cried. "There's probably a very simple explanation! I didn't realise he had such a hold on you."

"I'm being stupid, I know" Pauline humbly said. "Anyway, I'm pleased about Chris. I really hope he doesn't hurt you"

"Give us a chance!" Analeise replied, "We're only having a drink!!"

"Which will lead to..." Pauline laughed.

"At last, a smile!!" Analeise hugged her dear friend.

They sat and watched 'Pretty Woman' on DVD, ate their ice cream and put the world to right!

As Analeise was leaving, Pauline's landline rang. She made a sprint across the lounge and whacked her foot on the coffee table. Analeise was in fits laughing at her.

"Oh Hi Babe" she said with a smile across her face. Analeise shook her head, waved at Pauline, who had found happiness again!

"Thank God" she thought.

She made a promise to herself never to have those awful feelings of hurt again. Seeing Pauline that evening really brought it back to her. She wondered why she was so obsessed on meeting someone so fast.

The next morning Analeise got a call from the estate agents.

"Hi Analeise, a call just to say that your offer has been accepted" the voice said.

"OH YES!!" she shouted, "That was quick!!"

"The owner wanted a quick sale" she replied.

"What do I do now?" Analeise asked.

"Have you a mortgage sorted out yet?" the anxious voice asked.

"Oh, I have to do that, I didn't realise this was going to happen so soon!" Analeise apologised.

"Then you'll have to get a solicitor to handle the legal end of it." She added.

"Ok" said Analeise "I'm on the case!!"

She came off the phone and jumped with joy. She contacted an independent mortgage advisor and made an appointment for the following day.

Analeise could hardly sleep that night, anxious about a mortgage. She hoped she would qualify for one.

Her appointment was for 11.00am; she was there at 10.45.

"I'm a bit early" she apologised.

Analeise and Martin went to see Tracey about a year ago when he falsely promised her that they would buy a house together. Of course she had no idea at the time that it was a wild goose chase! It was just to stop her from nagging him all the time; he had secretly decided that he was going to leave her eventually.

"Its ok, Tracey can see you now" the receptionist showed her to Tracey Sellers office.

"Hi Analeise" Tracey stood up and shook her hand. Analeise always liked her; she was tall, attractive and had very kind eyes.

"Long time no see," she said with a great smile. Tracey was very professional and great at her job.

"Hi Tracey, I hope you can help me," Analeise said. "My circumstances have changed since the last time I seen you!"

She spent 2 hours with Tracey; half of that time was spent talking about men, pubs, relationships and make-up! They had a lot in common. Being bottom of the class at Maths Analeise hadn't a clue whenever it came to anything to do with numbers and she trusted Tracey to keep her right.

"Don't worry, leave it with me" Tracey assured her.

"Great, thanks very much" Analeise was very grateful for all the help that she had been given.

Repayments, Endowments and ISA'S didn't really register into her pink, fluffy head much to Tracey's amusement!

"Why don't you meet me and the girls for a drink this Friday after work, we'll be in Christies bar on the Lisburn Road." Tracey asked.

"I'll do that" Analeise smiled "I'll see you there"

They both really clicked, they had the same interests, knew the same people, and loved to socialise. Tracey was full of fun.

Analeise was delighted to be asked for a drink with her and her friends.

She yearned for a social life again, as the last lot of months she had been focusing on work. She was over Martin, and all of her disastrous relationships with Englishmen!!

She was ready to wipe the slate clean, and start afresh as a happy single homeowner!!"

CHAPTER THIRTEEN

*T*hat Friday, as Analeise was leaving her last appointment for the day, she got a phone call from Chris Drummond.

"Hi there! Are you still on for tomorrow night? There is a party at Lilly's Club in Belfast."

"Oh, yes of course" She said smiling.

They made arrangements for Chris to pick her up at 7.30 and said their goodbyes.

When Analeise got home from work at 6.00, she got ready for her night out with her new friend Tracey and her friends!

Christies bar was full to the brim of white-collar workers discussing business, getting plastered, and generally talking shit!! Analeise looked around frantically for a face she recognised.

"Hey!!" a voice shouted from the corner of the room. It was Tracey, with about 8 friends and 6 bottles of champagne!

"Hi there!!" Analeise introduced herself to all of the bubbly girls who were full of bubbles literally!!

It was 7.00 in the evening and everyone was hammered!!

"If you cant beat them, then join them!!" Analeise said to herself and got tore in to a bottle of champagne!

She found herself getting entwined in a conversation about Martin with Gemma, an ex-girlfriend of one of his friends. She met her a few times whenever Martin and her ex-boyfriend Joe went socialising together. She had been at their house for a few parties. They were even at their wedding! Gemma was a delight to see again, she had beautiful red hair and pale skin and beautiful green eyes. Analeise was pleased that they had split up as she thought Joe was a bit of a prick (As were all of Martin's friends!) and knew Gemma could do much better. She was smart, intelligent and very sweet.

"Oh, yes. That Martin Moran didn't half love himself!!" She rambled, "You are too good for him!! Look at you!!"

Analeise knew she was being kind, but all this 'scorned woman' talk was becoming tiring. She had moved on to the next level.

"So anyway Gemma how is life with you anyway?" Analeise asked her, hoping never to hear the words Martin Moran ever again.

"Pissed as a fart," she laughed as she poured everyone another glass of champagne.

"Analeise, let me introduce you to your solicitor" Tracey waltzed over to Analeise and escorted her to the bar.

"Ana, meet Daniel Bowers, he will be handling the sale of your new house."

"Oh no!!" she thought, "He's a bit too sexy to be a solicitor"

"Pleased to meet you" she shook his very soft hand.

"And you" he replied. His green eyes twinkled.

"Would you like to go for dinner sometime?" he asked.

"Quick mover Daniel!!" Tracey laughed.

Without flinching once, the cool, calm Daniel just said "Just being friendly".

Analeise couldn't believe what was happening. Here she was with her new friends, being invited to dinner by her new sexy solicitor. Who, by the way was a knockout!! He was the coolest guy she had ever seen; he stood 6 feet 2, not the most handsome guy around, but his eyes were so sexy. Just one look from him and she had goose bumps all over. His lips were so perfect that they looked like an artist had drawn them. He had a little something special about him and she just couldn't put her finger on what it was!

"Well" Analeise blushed. "You have my number"

She was mortified, and didn't know why. Anyway she had her date with Chris the next evening.

"Feast or a famine!!" Analeise whispered to Tracey as Daniel got them both a drink.

"I'm going out with an old flame tomorrow night, can't have too much of a good thing!!"

"Enjoy yourself" Tracey said as she raised her glass.

"Just don't get involved with this one" She nodded over to Daniel as he clumsily carried their drinks back.

"He'll break your heart in two!!" she whispered.

"Looks the type" Answered Analeise.

"What are you two wenches talking about now?" Daniel asked as he handed them their drinks.

"Nothing!!" the girls said at the same time.

Analeise and Daniel spent a good part of the rest of the evening talking about houses, mortgages etc. She didn't really know what she was talking about half the time but did a very good job in bluffing and generally talking shit. As the girls were leaving, Daniel helped Analeise with her jacket.

"I'll give you a good discount if you have dinner with me" he asked again.

"Sounds like good value to me" answered a very drunk Analeise, and said goodbye.

"You so have him wrapped around your finger Ana," said Gemma as they stepped outside. "He never invites girls for dinner, it's usually the other way around. Keep it like that!"

Analeise didn't really care as she was really looking forward to seeing Chris the next night. She had a great evening with her new bunch of friends. They all decided to meet again the following week. She hadn't drunk as much champagne in her life.

She got a taxi, and talked even more shit to the poor innocent driver the whole way home!!

CHAPTER FOURTEEEN

*H*angover from hell!!!
"Why did I drink so much?" Analeise asked herself as she stared at her red eyes in the bathroom mirror.

She crawled back into bed, and brought a bucket with her just in case!

Having thrown up a few times that morning, she thought at around 1.00pm that it was time to get up!

The telephone rang, and she secretly hoped it would be Chris postponing their date until tomorrow night, as she knew it would take a stick of dynamite to make her look remotely human again.

"Hi babe!" cried Pauline in her merriest annoying tone.

"What!" asked Analeise angrily.

"Who ate the jam out of your doughnut? Grumpy!!" she replied.

"I feel like a bag of shit, oh and by the way, I look like one too!!" answered Analeise.

"Not my fault you're an alcoholic!!" Pauline laughed. "What time are you seeing Prince Charming?"

"7.30, I can see it far enough, the fumes of alcohol will kill him. I have already thrown up 4 times, don't know if it's nerves or just a good old fashioned hangover"

"Just make sure you brush your teeth anyway!!" Pauline suggested still sniggering.

"Thanks for the advice!!" replied Analeise. "It's gonna take more than a toothbrush to sort me out!"

Analeise was greyer than grey! She had to do something, so decided to brighten up her skin with a nice re-hydrating facemask, followed by a fake tan.

Then, off to the hairdresser for a blow-dry.

By the time she got home, it was 5.30, she knew she would have to eat at some stage, but dreaded it, as she was afraid of throwing up. The nerves were starting to kick in.

She went into the kitchen and opened the fridge to be greeted by 2 eggs and a pot of Strawberry yoghurt. "Damn", she thought. She put two rounds of bread in the toaster. As she awaited her magnificent feast to cook, she walked into the bathroom and couldn't believe her eyes!

Analeise looked like an 'Oompa Loompa' from Charlie and the Chocolate Factory.

"Oh my God!" She shouted.

She had gone a bit overboard on the old fake tan!

"What am I going to do now?" She thought, and phoned Pauline.

"I swear to you I'm Fucking Orange! Chris won't know whether to peel me or kiss me!" she cried.

Pauline couldn't stop laughing, and kept laughing much to her annoyance.

"It isn't funny, seriously what am I going to do? You know about these things, surely you have had a customer that has had this problem."

"The only advice I can give sweetie is, exfoliate" Pauline tried to contain herself. "I wish I could see you now."

"Well, thanks for the *great* advice, I have to go as I have only got an hour to sandblast my face and get ready." Analeise hung up on her fanatical friend.

Two tubes of exfoliating gel and an hour and a half later, the buzzer went.

"Hi, its me!!" came the voice of Chris.

Analeise felt sick, she quickly checked herself one more time in the mirror.

"Not bad for a write off!!" she thought, and stepped outside.

Chris was standing outside his car with the passenger seat open for her.

"You look great kid!!" he said, and gently kissed her on her very soft exfoliated cheek.

All of a sudden everything was great in Analeise's life again.

They went to Lilly's Bar, a popular, Trendy watering hole. The music was a bit 'hard-core' for her, but she didn't mind. The décor was extremely minimalist, in fact it looked like someone decided to design a nightclub and then couldn't be arsed and lost interest in the whole project. The ladies toilets were upstairs and when they were eventually found they looked like a Builders Yard. She wondered if that was supposed to be modern design!

"Maybe this was the 'new' thing?" Analeise thought to herself as she reapplied her make up in the misty mirror (Which was great – it didn't make her look orange!)

Things had really evolved since she remembered going out to clubs (Or Disco's) as they were called in the good old days. No more lit up dance floors, or guys asking girls to dance, and she really missed the 'slow set' that 80's DJ's used to play half way through the night. (It was great if you pulled someone, but not so good if you were a lonely pint!) This was all new and it was all a learning experience for her.

Analeise and Chris fitted in perfectly.

He was a complete gentleman the whole evening, tending to her every wish. She had a great time; she met with old acquaintances she hadn't seen in years. Barrie McAllister Chris's best friend was there. Analeise had known him years before she even met Chris. They were all good friends before Martin decided that he didn't want his new girlfriend to have heterosexual male friends. Barrie was a womaniser, but all he was to Analeise was a good friend, he was very tall, dark, devilishly handsome and always had a girl on tow!

"Jesus, where have you been for all these years? You have missed some great nights out!!" he said as he twirled her round.

"I know, I'm just glad to be back again in the land of the living." she replied sincerely.

Chris couldn't keep his eyes off her all night. He tended to her every wish. She felt like the Queen of Sheba!

They had a wonderful time, talking, dancing and generally getting pissed.

When it was time to go home, he ordered her a taxi, kissed her passionately, and promised he would call her the next day, it was the end of a perfect night.

And it was the most perfect date.

CHAPTER FIFTEEN

The next day, as promised Chris called Analeise to check she got home in one piece. They arranged another date on the following Sunday, he invited her to his house, where he would cook dinner.

That week also, she got a surprise phone call from Daniel Bowers, her new sexy solicitor.

"Hi Analeise, how are you" he asked.

"Great, thanks for asking" She replied coyly.

"I was wondering if you could call to the office some time this week" he said politely.

"Oh, I've been invited to more exciting venues in my day might I say, but if it floats your boat; then all right" she said flirting the whole time.

"I just need to see you about the sale of your house Analeise, the office *is* the best place." He replied in a serious tone.

Analeise was mortified! She had forgotten for a split second that he *was* her Solicitor!

She was pissed off with herself for acting like this! "Just be yourself!" she thought.

"Y-yes, of course, Mmmmm, lets see" she stuttered, "How is Thursday morning?"

"Good, see you then" he said, and hung up.

"Cool bastard" she thought, her face was blushing the whole time. There was something about him that made her nervous, like a teenager meeting her pop idol for the first time. She hoped she would be more assertive when she seen him on Thursday.

It took Analeise around 2 hours to get ready on Thursday morning. Firstly because she was meeting with a prospecting client and secondly, she was meeting her new, sexy solicitor that morning.

She decided to wear her best trouser suit, and a new pair of open toed 4-inch heel sandals. The sandals were a real indulgence even though she looked ever so slightly deformed whenever she walked in them.

At 11.30, Analeise hobbled into the offices of MacLean and Bowers Solicitors to be greeted by a very busty young secretary.

"Hi, can I help you?" she asked, as she looked under her spectacles very secretary-like.

"I have a meeting with Mr Bowers this morning, my name is Analeise Magowan."

"Just go on through, Daniel is expecting you." The secretary said as she pointed to the door on the right with her pen.

Analeise took big steps into the office, as it would minimise the 'hobble' of her walk to his very untidy desk.

"Hello again!" Daniel stood up and pointed to a chair. "Take a seat" he looked her up and down in one quick glance.

She felt like George Clooney was interviewing her for the starring role for his next movie. 'Why was she so nervous?'

"Thanks" she sat down.

"Sorry about the other night, I was a bit drunk." He put his two hands behind his head confidently. "Now, you're buying for the first time, am I right? Oh, by the way, why are you Analeise Magowan all of a sudden? Isn't your name Moran?"

"Yes, my married name is Moran" answered Analeise nervously "But I want to start as I mean to go on, I'm going back to my maiden name."

"Big move" he said as he leaned forward with a slightly puzzled look.

"I need a fresh start" she replied with a grin.

They got straight down to business. The meeting only lasted for 15 minutes, when it was over, Analeise got off her seat and shook his soft hand *professionally* and proceeded to take big steps to the door.

"Oh, will I see you tomorrow night at Christies?" he asked.

"Don't know" she replied, "Depends on how drunk you are?"

She smiled.

"I'm always drunk," he said, as if dismissing her flirtatious remark.

What was his game? Did he fancy her? Was he trying to lead her on?

Analeise just couldn't get to the bottom of him. One minute he is throwing on the charm, next minute he's completely snubbing her. What Analeise *did* know, was that he was very, very clever.

Analeise met with Tracey, Gemma and the girls the next evening for after work drinks in Christies Bar.

"This is becoming a habit," she shouted across to Gemma, who was at the bar getting in the first round.

"A very good habit" Gemma laughed.

Analeise helped her back with all the drinks.

"Well, tell us all about your date with Chris?" Tracey asked.

"He was a total gentleman to me," she said as her eyes glistened like diamonds. "I really like him, he is cooking me dinner on Sunday night"

"Sounds serious" Gemma replied as she handed her a couple of bottles to carry back to the table.

"It's only wine this week, we can't go mad all of the time," she announced to the table of thirsty women.

Analeise was really enjoying herself. Her new friends were a breath of fresh air for her. They were fun, friendly and most of all; they were there for her. Things were going very well in her life. She didn't see much of Pauline recently as she was spending every weekend with Clive, one week she would go to London, and the next, he would come to Belfast. Analeise needed to be around positive people, and she was in perfect company!

They all stayed for another few drinks, and then they decided to head off to a nightclub.

As expected, unreliable Daniel Bowers didn't show his face.

'Cherry' nightclub was a place Analeise hadn't been before. Martin used to talk about it all of the time, she secretly hoped he wouldn't be there, as she hadn't laid eyes on him for a few months.

It was one of those places, were it was totally full to the brim of pretentious, over styled beautiful people in their mid-twenties. Analeise didn't think that a nightclub of that size could hold such amounts of people so alike. What she *did* know was that the place was perfect for someone like Martin.

She was glad she had had a few jars, as she didn't think she could cope with it completely sober.

They all pushed and shoved to the bar to get more supplies, it was like a cattle market literally! Young pretty boys, eyeing up their next conquest, and young waif like girlies with extended hair drinking their Alco pops through straws and not able to stand up straight.

"What are you having?" Tracey shouted at the top of her voice, as she pointed to the bar (just in case nobody could lip read what she said!!)

"WINE!!!" everyone shouted, pointing back to the bar!

As Tracey was elbowing her way back, Analeise got a tap on her shoulder.

"Excuse Me," said the adolescent boy in her ear "My friend over there would like you to dance with him" he pointed over to his red faced mortified friend. She felt like she was back at school, and started laughing.

"Forget it!!" said the boy, and did the walk of shame back to his anxious friend.

Analeise couldn't stop laughing, "I feel awful," she said to Tracey who handed her a half full glass of wine. "I didn't mean to laugh, it just took me unawares. Is that what you do now? Just get your friend to ask you? Whatever happened to boring old fashioned chat-up lines??"

"This place is very young, that's all, or are we just old? I don't know, come on for a walkabout" Tracey said.

"Its not the sort of place I'd like to spend every weekend!" Analeise said as she pushed through the feisty pre-pubescent bunch. "If this is all that is on the market, I will throw the towel in right now!"

"Show us your tits!" Shouted a blonde 'surf dude' to Analeise as she shuffled her way through the crowd.

She was mortified, shocked and slightly ' turned on' all rolled into one!

"Imagine the cheek of him!" she said to Tracey who was beside herself laughing at the look on Analeise's face.

They didn't stay for very long. It was far too full, they could hardly move.

Tracey and Analeise shared a taxi home, as Tracey got out at her house, she gave Analeise a kind hug and said " Have a great night on Sunday I'll give you a call during the week, you will get the key of your house soon!"

The whole night really made Analeise think hard about her life. She didn't want to be a desperado, but felt that a ship had just sailed and she wasn't on it.

"Jesus, I am turning 34 and single," She also realised that the nightclub wasn't too young.

She was just too old!!

CHAPTER SIXTEEN

On Sunday, thank God, no hangover this time. She had plenty of time to get herself ready. She had a great day, she called round to her mums for her lunch. Then later in the afternoon she met Pauline and Clive for a coffee.

"So, what's the story with this Chris person?" asked Pauline curiously as she shovelled spoon fools of sugar into her tea.

"I like him, in fact I really like him." Then Analeise leaned over to Pauline and said quietly in her ear "I am really horny!"

Pauline started to laugh.

"What did she say?" asked Clive curiously.

"She's looking for a shag!!" Pauline said loudly.

"I didn't say that!!" Analeise was mortified. "It has been a while, if you know what I mean. I'm a woman in her prime!"

"Yes, that James guy was the last hump you have had!" Pauline said bluntly.

"Hump is probably the best description for that one" laughed Analeise.

"You women are unbelievable!!" Clive laughed. "Oh, by the way Trevor has been asking about you!" he looked over at Analeise who was shuffling in her bag.

"Didn't hear that!" she mumbled.

"Only kidding," He said smiling "He thought you were a snob!"

Analeise chose to ignore his comment as Pauline sniggered into her tea.

"Ok, you lovebirds I'm away to beautify myself for my dinner date." Analeise got up and said her goodbyes.

"I'll call you tomorrow babe, be good! Easy on the fake tan!" Pauline shouted as Analeise walked out completely mortified.

Analeise had dilemmas as to what to wear. She wanted to be smart, but to look like she wasn't trying too hard.

"Jeans, and crisp white shirt it is!!" she decided after endlessly staring into her wardrobe for a half an hour.

She also chose nice lacy underwear, just in case.

On the journey to Dungannon, she sang the whole way while constantly chewing on polo mints.

He had a beautiful split-level bungalow surrounded in well kept shrubs with red and yellow roses in the garden.

Chris opened the door with his very usual gorgeous open smile, which showed every perfect tooth. He kissed her on the lips.

"Hi, come on in!!"

Analeise handed him a bottle of Chablis.

"My favourite! Thank you."

His home was the epitome of good taste. It was perfect, classy and charming just like him! Everything was open planned with a huge conservatory overlooking a massive garden with even more beautiful roses.

He had cooked prawns in filo pastry for starter, and insisted he did it all himself! Then it was pan-fried salmon for main course, and he had a tiramisu for dessert. It was perfect, the food, the conversation, everything! He had gone to so much trouble Analeise had secretly hoped she wouldn't have to return the compliment anytime this century as this was completely out of her league!

"Some more wine?" Chris asked as he lifted another bottle from the fridge.

"No, I shouldn't, thanks anyway" Analeise replied as she raised her hand.

"Water, cola, or anything?" he asked.

Analeise could feel this wave of excitement coming from the pit of her stomach. The more she looked at him the more she just wanted to jump his bones there and then!

"You" she laughed nervously.

He didn't say anything, and there was an uncomfortable silence. So Analeise took the reigns and walked over to him and started to kiss him passionately. Her heart was beating like a drum. This was not normal for her and she couldn't believe she was doing this.

She started to unbutton his trousers. He had this, either permanent grin or sheer and utter shock written across his face. Analeise couldn't decide which one. She had come this far; she had to carry on being the dominatrix! She put her hand on his crotch, and then she moved inside his boxers. He was very hard… she was very wet. She started to unbutton her shirt to reveal a very sexy, lacy bra, he cupped her breasts and kissed her neck passionatly. He lifted her up and carried her over to the 2-seater sofa in the conservatory then he pulled off her jeans and knickers and kissed between her legs. Analeise was begging him to enter her. She stood up and told him to lie back. Chris lay on his back on the sofa, then Analeise mounted him; she couldn't stop. She was crying in excitement, she came within 2 minutes he couldn't beleive what was happening to him. Then he turned her round and entered her again. He asked if she was ok…

"Y-Y-Yes, I couldn't be better:" she cried.

"Are you on anything I mean." he seemed impatient.

"NO, oh sorry." she said awkwardly.

"Lie back!" he demanded, the shock-smile thing was still affixed to his face.

He came all over her front, crying in ecstasy. He then got up and walked to the bathroom.

Analeise lay there thinking, "What just happened there?" she felt like shit. It was the quickest quickie she had ever had!

Chris appeared back in the room wearing a dressing gown, holding a box of tissues. He gave them to her, and started to tidy up the dishes.

Analeise cleaned herself up and got dressed immediately; there was a sense of uneasiness in the air.

She walked over to Chris and thanked him for dinner, and instead of helping him with the dishes or offering to make coffee, she asked him for her jacket!

"Y-yes no problem" he sheepishly walked into the hall and handed Analeise her jacket; she was just standing in the hall with her bag round her shoulder.

"There you go" he helped her put it on and opened the front door.

"Thanks for dinner" Analeise said with complete sincerity. She was so embarrassed about the whole ordeal. It was like some porn star had taken over her body for 10 minutes. She didn't expect to act like that.

"Give you a call" Chris said as he waved her goodbye.

Analeise could notice a difference this time from the last two dates with him. He always suggested another date; this time was just 'I will call you'.

He felt she just wanted to shag him and he was disappointed.

It all happened so fast.

Chris liked to seduce women but not like this! He was sorry he went through with it. It just wasn't worth it.

Analeise was mortified and she knew she had made a big, big mistake. But there was not a damn thing she could do to change that.

CHAPTER SEVENTEEN

Days had passed, and Analeise couldn't stop thinking about the evening that she spent with Chris, she was convinced he would never want to see her again. He hadn't called.

"What possessed you to just leave like that?" Gemma asked her, as she blobbed half a jar of ketchup on her chips.

Analeise had met up with Tracey and Gemma for lunch, near Tracey's office, as she had news about the house.

"I don't know, I've been milling it over my mind constantly."

"Well, I think the bloke is gonna think you're just a sex machine, any hope of a relationship is probably out the window at this stage." Tracey said solemnly to Analeise.

"You are a walking disaster when it comes to men!" Gemma laughed.

"If it makes you feel any better, Daniel has been asking about you." Tracey smiled.

"I can't work that guy out!" Analeise said as she shook her head.

"I met a bloke!!" Gemma announced.

"WHO??" Tracey and Analeise said at the same time.

"His name is Mitch!!" she said with pride. "Not very trendy though"

"We can always work on that one!" Tracey answered as she poured more tea.

"I have known him for a while, I met him through work, we just hit it off at the weekend!"

"Result!" Laughed Tracey, who was very happy with her solid relationship with Maurice, a very sensible banker. He adored her.

Tracey was always able to give great advice to her friends, she was very clever, and was completely 'Girl Power'… She took no shit, nor did she expect any of her friends to either!

"That's my problem, I could never meet anyone from my work, unless I was gay" said a very defeated Analeise.

"There is a thought" sniggered a very happy Gemma who hadn't a care in the world. "Maybe Mitch has some friends for you?"

"Oh God no more blind dates for me!" Analeise laughed.

They all finished their lunch and Analeise went back to Tracey's office with her.

"I have news about your house Ana" Tracey said as she logged in to her computer.

"The seller doesn't want to move until August."

As it was only May, Analeise felt a little disappointed.

"It will give you more time to save for a bigger deposit and you would be better off when it comes to furnishing the house!" Tracey said optimistically.

"True" said Analeise. "Ok, it makes sense. I'll just have to stay in that hell hole until then."

"I will inform the mortgage company," Tracey said. "If you want I will also inform Mr Bowers??"

Tracey looked at Analeise curiously.

"What are you getting at at?" Analeise said puzzled.

"Why don't you phone Daniel?" Tracey asked.

"Surely he knows" Analeise replied.

Tracey laughed, "Of course he knows, he was the one that told me!"

"I'm not smart enough for you!!" Laughed Analeise.

"No, he was enquiring about you, I think he likes you"

"He does not, He likes to play games, and I'm not very good at those!!" replied Analeise. "Anyway, I am not very good at relationships in general!!"

"Ok, its up to you" Tracey raised her hands as if dismissing the whole thing.

Analeise needed some time to clear her head before she decided to start jumping head first into the next disastrous relationship!

Later that evening Analeise went to Marks and Spencer to get some essentials for her fridge, as she was walking through the very essential 'ready made meals' section she heard her name being called.

"Is that Analeise Magowan?" asked the tall blonde girl standing at the checkout.

Analeise approached her; she was delighted to see that it was her very old and dear friend Daryl Mc Kinney.

"HI!!" Analeise hugged her, she was delighted to see her, and she was also a little embarrassed as she hadn't been in contact with her for years. Whenever Analeise first met Martin, he was such a control freak; he hated the fact that she had good, true friends. 'I don't approve of your friends' he would always say, until Analeise completely cut them off, because it was more hassle than it was worth having to listen to him complain every time she seen them.

Daryl hadn't changed a bit; she was still very stylish, and very slender. She was a great hairdresser and was really modest and kind. A real genuine person and was always a very good friend to her.

"Look at you" Analeise said. "You look great!!"

"How are you?" Daryl asked.

"Single" Analeise announced. "Listen, I'm really sorry about not being in touch, he just hated me having friends"

"Don't worry" assured Daryl "I had heard through the grapevine, you know what Belfast is like, why didn't you call me?"

"I was too embarrassed, I didn't like to" Analeise said as she blushed. She knew she should have stayed in touch with Daryl and the gang; she had such a great time with them before she met Martin.

"Never worry! We are in touch now." Daryl showed her a photograph of her beautiful daughter Dania.

"WOW! She is lovely, you must be so proud!" Analeise said.

"She is a right handful," Daryl answered as she shuffled the picture back in to her wallet.

"Did you ever find the man of your dreams?" Analeise asked curiously as she only ever remembered Daryl with Josh whom she met at school. It never worked out as Daryl found out whenever they decided to live together shortly after their daughter was born.

"Don't believe in such a thing!" she smiled "What about you? Any children?

Analeise put her head down, she longed for a child whenever she was with Martin, but he just would not tolerate even talking about children. She always remembered him saying "If you ever get pregnant I swear I will hate you forever!"

It was enough to put her off for life.

"No" she said, dismissing the whole subject.

"Why don't you come round to my house Saturday night, a few of the girls are coming round, then we will be going out for a few jars" Daryl suggested.

"I would love to" answered Analeise "No hard feelings?"

"Its me you're talking to, friends will always be friends, just remember that" Daryl said as she clumsily leaned her basket on one of the shelves of very tempting sweets.

"Here's my telephone number and my address" she started to write on a scrappy envelope that she found in her handbag.

"It is really great to see you again" Analeise said, delighted to have bumped into her oldest, dearest friend after all these years. "I will see you on Saturday"

They said their goodbyes, Analeise was a great believer in fate, and she knew someday she would be re-united with all her old pals again. It was only a matter of time. Martin had kept her back all these years, but now it was time to start making up for those years again, and her moment had come.

CHAPTER EIGHTEEN

Saturday had arrived; Analeise was really looking forward to seeing Daryl and the girls again. She had gone out that day and got herself a new fitted skirt and corset style top to match, it looked great it really accentuated her curves to full extent. She got a taxi down to Daryl's house.

"Hi!!" Daryl shouted as Analeise arrived "You look great!" she immediately shoved a large glass of wine into her hand.

In the house Trudy, Debbie, and Abbey were already there; she had met Debbie before, but didn't know the others.

"This is Trudy" Daryl pointed to a very serious looking, quiet girl in the corner, she wore bright red glasses, and about 3 layers of clothes. She looked very artistic Analeise thought. She nodded over curiously at Analeise.

Abbey was beautiful; she was very petite with long blonde hair and a very warm smile.

"I'm Abbey," she said as she shook Analeise's hand.

She instantly felt comfortable with each and every one of them. Trudy was meeting with a bloke later on that evening so she was getting wired into a bottle of wine, meanwhile running back and forward to the loo with a touch of nervy diaorreah!!

"What the hell happened to you all these years!!" asked a very drunk Debbie. Debbie Mallon was one in a million, she was tall, and classically attractive. Long shiny brunette hair, outstanding bone structure and perfect teeth. She was constantly on a diet and would spend days starving herself. She didn't give a damn what she said and to whom! She was always fixing herself and she openly talked about periods, boobs, and anything that came into her head! She totally loved herself in the most endearing way. "Have I got too much make-up on? Are my boobs like spaniels ears? Is this ok on me? Do I look like a Slapper? Were normal questions she would ask on a regular basis while looking in the mirror.

She was a dizzy cow and Analeise adored her. She realised how much she missed all of her old friends and wondered how she coped through the years without them.

"I have missed out on far too much fun, that's what I've been doing!!" laughed Analeise.

"Do you think my boobs look flat in this top?" she asked ignoring her comment as she tried to fix herself while holding a full glass of wine.

They all had a few wines and then ordered a taxi to take them to O'Brien's, an intimate R&B nightclub. Analeise had never been there before.

It was perfect; it was relaxed, not too busy, nice mix of people.

After a few drinks and bit of 'bumping and grinding' Analeise and Daryl left Abbey and Debbie on the dance floor fending off some very randy 'grinders'.

They went outside to take the weight off their feet in the beer garden.

"I'm having a ball!" said Analeise who was completely plastered.

Just as she got off her seat to stagger to the toilet, she spotted a familiar face out of the corner of her eye.

"Chris!" she said slowly.

"Chris who?" Daryl turned round on her chair.

"Analeise, its Chris Drummond. Remember him from years ago??" She nudged her.

Chris walked over to their table.

"Hi girls!!" he smiled with confidence.

Of course, Daryl had known Chris from 12 years ago whenever Analeise dated him. She never approved of him, thought of him as too much of a charmer. She didn't think that he was good enough for Analeise, although they didn't date for long enough before he cleared off to South Africa.

"Ana, look who it is!!" she said surprised'.

She had no idea that Analeise jumped his bones the week previous.

Analeise was mortified; she didn't know what to say.

"Hi there, what are you doing here?" she asked without giving eye contact.

"How the hell are you?" Daryl interrupted.

"I'm here doing the same old thing as you two I'm sure!" he looked at Analeise, who was still stunned. She didn't know how he felt after that night.

"See you later, enjoy yourselves!!" he said, and gave Analeise a knowing wink.

She felt like crying, she hadn't heard from him all week, and here he was on a night out with his friends, she didn't know whether he wanted to see her again or not. She told Daryl the whole story.

"You know what he's like!!" Daryl said, "I'm sure he was delighted to get a shag!"

It didn't make Analeise feel any better.

"Well, whatever happens, I'll not do that in a hurry again!" Analeise said, nearly apologising for her actions.

"Oh yes do!!" laughed Daryl. "He will never hurt you if you just see him whenever it suits you"

Analeise was confused; she just wanted to be normal. Whatever happened to meeting someone and falling in love? It seemed that that era had gone; it was a whole new generation out there. Women use men as men use women.

Everybody plays games.

She didn't really like the new generation of dating. It seemed a lot simpler in the olden days whenever there were no mobile phones. She couldn't keep up with all this texting.

Daryl couldn't be bothered with any of it, Dania's father Josh, plays a big part in Dania's life, but Daryl couldn't be annoyed with the whole relationship thing, so she goes out with him whenever it suits her, goes on holiday the odd time with him. But refuses to be his girlfriend.

In theory it seems easy, but Analeise thought maybe in years to come that it might be a little bit lonely. She definitely wanted to be loved.

Everyone went back to Daryl's house except for Trudy, who hit it lucky with Tim, she had been nervous all night until she downed 2 bottles of wine for a bit of Dutch courage.

"So what happened between you and Chris?" Debbie asked Analeise as Daryl was in the kitchen making potato wedges and shepherds pie.

"I just dogged him and left, and haven't heard from him" Analeise replied.

"What the hell do you expect!!" Debbie said as she vigorously rubbed a baby wipe across her eye, trying to remove her mascara.

"Move on" said Abbey, then attempted to use Daryl's mobile phone to call Trudy.

"Hey slapper!!" she shouted down the phone. "Just making sure you're safe!!"

Then she laughed.

"Daryl's making a gourmet dinner, Deb is rubbing her eyes out of their sockets and Analeise is crying over Chris" she said to a curious Trudy who should have had other things on her mind at that moment in time.

"What's she doing?" asked Debbie as she fought to get the phone out of Abbey's hand. "Should she not be in the throws of passion by now! Tell her to fuck off!"

Everyone laughed

"Is Trudy not having sex with him?" Daryl asked as she handed everyone a large plate full to the brim.

Everyone stuffed their faces, it was the nicest thing ever, Daryl was famous for inviting everyone back to her house and making all kinds of food in the middle of the night, no matter what time they got home at.

At 3.30am Abbey and Debbie got a taxi home.

Analeise stayed in Daryl's house, she slept in Dania's room, not that she got much sleep. She kept on thinking about Chris and the terrible mistake that she had made.

Maybe she would call him.

CHAPTER NINETEEN

The next morning Analeise was awakened by "Who's that in my bed?" she thought she was dreaming of goldilocks until she seen a little dark haired girl before her.

"Oh, hello. I'm Analeise, a friend of your Mum's, I was out last night with your Mum and I stayed" Analeise jumped up.

"I'm Dania, and that's my bed" she looked under her eyes at a very hung over Analeise.

"I know I'm sorry" She couldn't wait to get out of this hostile situation, she felt terrible.

"Stop being cheeky!!" came a voice from downstairs.

"Ignore her Ana, her dad just dropped her off" Daryl apologised.

"I'm up now anyway" Analeise scurried into the bathroom.

She got ready, and walked downstairs where a very mature 8-year-old Dania was practising her dance steps to the sound of Britney Spears.

"I'd better be heading off now," Analeise shouted into the kitchen where Daryl was in the process of making sausages and eggs.

"No, have some breakfast" she persisted.

Analeise hadn't been treated so kindly in a long time, it was great to be around her friend Daryl again, and it was like old times.

Later on that Sunday after a hearty breakfast with Daryl and Dania Analeise headed back home to catch up on some paperwork she was behind on. She thought again about Chris, and decided to just call him.

It rang, "Hello"

"Hi there, have a good time last night?" She asked.

"Y-Yes, is that Analeise?" he asked.

"Oh, sorry yes its me" she replied. "Do you fancy getting together sometime?" she said impatiently.

"Ok, how are you fixed for later on?" he said.

"Alright" she answered, "What do you want to do?"

"Why don't you just come round to mine, we can have a quiet night in" he said.

Before Analeise could think, she had agreed to go to his house at 8.00 with a DVD. It was a far cry from being taken out or have dinner cooked for her, but she just had to see him.

He opened the door wearing his jogging bottoms and a Nike T-shirt; he looked like he had been wearing them all day. Analeise had made a big effort, she had spent the day pampering herself, washed her hair, picked out appropriate clothing, applied her make up to perfection.

Something had changed his feelings for her, and Analeise wanted to change that.

"I decided not to bring wine," She said as if he would 'get' the in-joke, but it was like water off a ducks back.

"I'm dying anyway" he walked over to his infamous 2-seater sofa and lay length ways, so there was no room for her. She sat on the one-seater chair opposite the very large television screen.

He was hostile, and made it very obvious, he didn't offer her a drink, coffee, tea. Nothing.

"Well kid, did you enjoy yourself last night? Any men?" he asked smugly.

Analeise was horrified.

"No men…. What do you think I am?" she replied quickly.

He laughed.

"So, come on over here and keep me company" he swung his legs round the sofa and patted the very lonely seat beside him.

Analeise sat beside him, and they watched the movie.

Whenever it was over she asked for a glass of orange juice or something.

"Sorry, I never thought to ask you earlier." He apologised and got up and walked to the fridge. As he walked back, he took off his t-shirt. He looked incredible. Analeise couldn't keep her eyes off him, and decided whether to sleep with him or not.

"Feeling the heat?" she asked.

He leaned right over and kissed her, this time the kiss seemed more passionate than before.

She couldn't resist, before she knew it she was naked and they were making love on the perfectly polished floor. It was incredible, it was better than before, it seemed more intense, more powerful, and lots and lots more orgasms.

This time after the sex, she took him up on his offer of a shower. When she had finished, he had a coffee waiting on the kitchen table for her.

She kissed him and started to drink her perfect coffee.

"Thanks" she said.

"For the shag or the coffee??" he laughed.

"Both, I suppose" she said into her steaming hot drink.

"You seemed a little, standoffish' earlier" she said.

He started to tidy up all of his belongings, which lay on the floor and put them into a neat pile. He totally ignored what she had said.

"So where are you tomorrow?" he asked.

"Newcastle, County Down, then out to the West of Ireland" she replied, waiting for a proposal of lunch or something.

"I'm in the office all week, its really busy at the moment." He said.

There was an uncomfortable silence.

"Well, I'd better be off I suppose" Analeise said.

"Ok then" Chris said as he escorted her to the door.

"See you..." Analeise waited for an invitation, or a suggestion from him.

"Yes, see you.. Enjoy Newcastle!!" he said, and closed the door. No watching her walk to her car or watch her drive into the night.

Analeise had to be careful, she was really starting to like Chris, her head was telling her to stop, but her body was just giving in.

She didn't care, it felt great.

CHAPTER TWENTY

The next evening Analeise had to pack up her clothes, as this was the week she travelled to Galway and the West coast of Ireland. It was a beautiful drive, but after a while it got very lonely staying away from home.

She had to decide what to wear for the whole week, was it going to rain? Was it going to be sunny and humid? The weatherman never got it right and ten out of ten times Analeise packed the wrong attire!

She was up to her eyes in clothing whenever Pauline rang with some news.

"Hi, just thought I'd tell you that I'm moving to London!!" she screamed down the phone.

Analeise was delighted for her as she ate, slept and breathed Clive from the day and hour she met him.

"When?" Analeise asked in shock.

"Giving a months notice, then I'm off!" she replied excitedly.

Analeise was lost for words, Pauline was her right arm, and she would have crumbled without her whenever Martin left. Maybe she was slightly jealous of her perfect transition. Girl meets boy, they fall in love and live happily ever after.

"Sure, you can come visit us!" she cried, trying to convince a very silent Analeise.

"Yes, of course" she said very slowly.

"Anyway, its your birthday next week babe, we gotta do it in style!" Pauline said.

"That's a nice present from you anyway!" Analeise said angrily.

"Hey, don't be like that, you don't know what is in front of you, the world is your oyster!" she snapped.

"My oyster!!" Analeise sounded close to tears. "What am I going to do now?"

She was really feeling sorry for herself, the year she had since her break-up had been nothing but a string of disasters! Granted her career was going well, but she suddenly realised that she was very, very lonely.

"I'll organise a night out before I go!" Pauline said quietly and said goodbye sheepishly.

Analeise sat down and burst out crying. It was coming up to her 34th birthday and she was very single and didn't like it one little bit.

That week was like a blur for Analeise, she drove to Athlone Co. West Meath on the Monday, worked her way through Galway on the Tuesday, head for County Mayo on that evening, stay in Castlebar that night. Wednesday she would work her way through small towns in the area, and then head for Sligo on the Wednesday night, then finish off the long journey on Thursday through Sligo and Donegal. Meanwhile staying in small country hotels and eating dinner on her own where she desperately tried not to look like the local town hooker! She had plenty of time to think.

She thought about Pauline, and her new found life in London, and also of Gemma, and her new beau Mitch. They seemed so happy.

Why was she so keen to settle? " I was settled for 10 years?" surely she would have come to her senses by now.

"Maybe I just need a little time on my own," she thought. She tried so hard to be positive.

"No men for a while" It was the best thought out plan she had, she decided to focus on the house, maybe go travelling the following year. Yes, she was starting to realise that the world *was* her oyster and not a big smelly sock as she had originally thought.

By the weekend, Analeise had turned over a new leaf. A new train of thought had entered her head. She had loads of time to settle. She had great new friends, was getting a great new house, and her birthday was the following week!

Analeise was starting to like herself again.

Daryl called her that Friday evening to invite her to a kickboxing event that her Boss was organising.

"Come on, it will be a laugh, there will be hot bodied Frenchmen there! Lets call it your birthday night with an added extra of horny Frogs!!"

"Well, its certainly different!" Analeise said. "Alright, you have pulled my leg, anyway I can't sit in on my birthday!"

"Good!" Daryl said, "See you next Saturday!"

Just as Analeise was starting to relax, and get heavily involved in Friday night telly, Pauline called her.

"Hey there baby, what about a nightclub for your big birthday?"

"No can do chicken" Analeise replied. "I'm going to watch horny Kick boxers"

Pauline laughed, "Whatever tickles your fancy darling!"

They agreed to meet for a birthday lunch on the Saturday instead.

Analeise promised herself that she would have the best birthday ever!

CHAPTER TWENTY ONE

*T*he following week flew in, and it was Friday afternoon, Analeise's favourite time of all! She promised herself a big long steep in the bath, facemask, and the works to prepare for the French revolution.

Her phone rang; it was Tracey with a very busy bar in the background.

"HEY BABE, GET YOUR ARSE ROUND HERE!" She shouted, nearly deafening her.

"I was going to have an early one," said Analeise who was very tempted.

"Come on, we'll buy you a birthday drink! Won't take no for an answer!!"

"Only a couple then seeing it's my birthday," said Analeise, who considered herself the luckiest girl in the world with such great friends.

It was only this time last year when she sat all night waiting for Martin to show up to take her out.

He didn't. It was only a matter of weeks whenever he left her-stranded!

What a difference a year makes!!

Within an hour Analeise was ready and on her way to Christies bar.

Whenever she arrived, everyone was there, complete with their usual quantity of champagne bottles on the table.

"There's one here with your name on it birthday girl!" shouted Tracey.

It didn't take Analeise long to catch up with them.

They stayed for a few hours and put the world to right, just as they were leaving Analeise got a tap on her shoulder.

"What's the occasion?" asked Daniel.

"My birthday!" answered a very drunk Analeise.

"Are you the stripogram?" she laughed.

Her inhibitions were completely out the window at this stage, she didn't care about anything.

He whispered in her ear "How's about a kissogram instead?"

"Ok" she answered.

They stared at each other for a split second, and then Daniel leaned over to her and kissed her gently on her lips. Analeise wanted more, it tasted so good.

"Will we leave you guys alone?" asked Gemma.

Analeise and Daniel just stared at each other; the sexual chemistry between them was blatantly obvious.

"I think so," said Tracey.

They all said their goodbyes to Analeise and Daniel who decided to find somewhere a little more quiet upstairs.

"What just happened there?" asked Daniel as he handed Analeise a large Bailies with ice.

"Search me, I had planned on a quiet evening until Tracey tortured me to come here!"

"Sometimes things just happen for a reason" Daniel said philosophical.

Earlier on Analeise was drunk as a skunk, now she was feeling 'yellow mellow' in the company of Daniel. They spent the remainder of the evening just chatting and getting to know each other.

At the end of the evening Daniel ordered two taxis, kissed Analeise passionately as he escorted her into her cab and promised he would call her the next day.

She was floating on air, she had a great night and was glad she made the effort to go out, but promised herself not to get too excited about Daniel.

She had made far too many hasty mistakes in the past.

CHAPTER TWENTY TWO

*A*naleise awoke with the sound of the phone ringing, when she answered

"HAPPY BIRTHDAY TO YOOOOOO, HAPPY BIRTHDAY TO YOOOO, HAPPY BIRTHDAY DEAR SMELLY...HAPPY BIRTHDAY TO YOOO!!!!"

"That was lovely Pauline, how's yoooo?"

Pauline laughed "Babe, can I come up to your place, I have your pressie, cant do lunch. Promised Mary I'd take her to Bingo"

"Of course chicken, you shouldn't have gone to the bother of a pressie!" said Analeise, still very blurry from the night before.

"See you in 10!" Pauline hung up.

Analeise lay for a while and reflected on the night before. The thoughts were nice.

She jumped into the shower, as she finished scrubbing and exfoliating Pauline was banging down the door.

"Easy tiger!" Analeise said as she made way for a very busy Pauline.

"Glad you dressed for the occasion!" said Pauline as she stared at her dripping wet friend.

"Give me a minute, what's the hurry anyway?"

"Fucking Mary! Bloody bastarding Bingo, I promised her before I went to London, I'd take her out, and this was the desired choice! Can you believe out of all the places to go, she wants to go to the fucking 3-2-1 Club!!"

"Each to their own taste!" Analeise laughed.

"I just hope nobody sees me going in there I'll be mortified" Pauline said as she handed a perfectly wrapped gift to Analeise.

"Thank you babe!" Analeise hugged her.

"My only Saturday off, and I'm shouting 'full house' with mum and all the old fogies!!"

"Never mind, maybe you'll win the jackpot!" Analeise said. "Do you want some breakfast?"

"Don't have time sweetie, have a great birthday and I'll call you to-morrow, we'll organise something in the next couple of days" Pauline hurriedly ran down the stairs to be confronted by Brian the alcoholic.

"Hello luv, I locked myself out, can I use your phone?"

He stunk of stale alcohol and burgers.

"ANA!!" Pauline shouted. "Ehhh, just getting you help now"

Analeise looked down laughing at Pauline trying to compose her-self in the company of Brian.

"Get down here!!" Pauline shouted nervously.

"Haven't s-seen you b-f-fore" stuttered Brian who was having problems standing upright.

Analeise asked Brian for his fathers phone number as he stood completely blank faced.

"I'm outta here!" cried Pauline "My life is so damn glamorous!" she said sarcastically "Anyway" she whispered, "How could he be so drunk? It is 10.30 in the morning!"

Analeise just shrugged.

Pauline got a quick getaway..

"Four three, no…four two six six… erm…four three six two nine nine…. I think," said Brian as he pointed his finger to his brain, as if it made a difference.

Analeise dialled the number; thank god it was the right one. She explained that she lived upstairs, and Brian had locked himself out again.. It was only a matter of minutes before his very caring father came round to rescue his destitute son.

Never mind, it was her birthday today and she knew it was going to be a cracker!

Later in the day she called Daryl to ask what the dress code was for these kickboxing things.

"Anything, I'm just wearing jeans"

"Ok, jeans it is!"

Analeise got ready and headed for Daryl's house where they opened up a bottle of wine.

"Good start to a night!" said Daryl as she applied the final touches of her make-up.

As they stepped into the taxi Analeise's phone started to ring. It was Daniel, true enough he promised he would call her, and call her he did!

"Happy birthday old fogie!" he said.

Analeise was delighted that he called.

"Listen, I'm on my way out, but do you fancy going out for a drink tomorrow night?" he asked.

"Well, yes" she said smiling the whole time.

"Ok, I'll call you tomorrow afternoon with arrangements" and just hung up.

"Short and sweet!" she mumbled to herself.

"Who was that?" Daryl asked as she climbed into the front seat of the car.

"My solicitor" Analeise answered "We're going for a drink tomorrow night!"

"He sounds full of chat!" she said sarcastically.

Analeise still couldn't work the guy out; maybe this was just the way he was!

She was still very wary of him, as he seemed like the sort of person who just liked to play mind games.

"I'm going to tread very carefully this time" she said.

When they arrived at the venue, it was full of shaven headed, tattooed, overgrown gorillas. Analeise wondered if this was the type of place she would have chosen to spend her 34th birthday. It didn't matter; she was with Daryl and was sure she would have a good one no matter what.

It started off pretty good; they downed a few wines in the bar next-door while some French men fought some Scottish men.

"Its quite horny in a perverse way!" Analeise laughed as they finished off their 2nd glass of vino.

They went back inside to be greeted by Abigail, Daryl's boss, and organiser of the event. She was flapping in a very irritating manner.

"We need a ring girl for the final fight!" she said in sheer panic.

The two of them looked at Analeise.

Abigail looked like she was about to explode! She remembered her from years ago whenever she would organise Hair Shows. She always was in full control of the situation.

Not Tonight!

"What are you looking at me for?" she asked.

"Go on, you would be a great help!" Abigail pleaded

"I'm not strutting around in skimpy shorts!" she shouted.

"You don't have to wear shorts!" Daryl said.

"This is a wind-up!!" Analeise was horrified.

"I just need you to walk round the ring in between rounds, its no big deal!" Abigail said. "You look great!"

"I've done it before, it's easy!" Daryl said with ease.

"Ok" Analeise gave in, and then wondered what she had let herself be talked in to.

Of course, a few more wines had to be consumed before she humiliated herself in front of everyone in the room!

"Oh by the way" Daryl announced after a couple of drinks "I've never done ring girl before!!" then started laughing.

Analeise was disgusted.

"You twisted bitch!" she said slowly. "Why did you tell me you did?"

Daryl couldn't stop laughing, she had a sick sense of humour and Analeise knew it.

"You'll be great, it's easy!" she said solemnly.

"Easy for you to say!" Analeise decided to stop drinking at this stage, she was feeling slightly pissed.

About half an hour later Abigail came flapping over to the girls.

"Analeise, you have to come with me now and sit at the ringside" she trailed her over to sit beside her.

"The big fight is about to start," she whispered in her ear.

She handed her a plaque card with '1' on it. "Just walk around once holding this above your head, then come out and be ready for the next round and so on, ok?"

Analeise thought it seemed simple enough.

"Easy peasy!" she assured her smiling.

Then the fighters came out. Close up they looked pretty scary, they got into their corners, and it was Analeise's cue.

She got underneath the rope when one of her shoes fell off!

She went back to retrieve it when she heard some sniggers from the front row.

"Never mind" shouted Abigail "Just get on with it!"

Analeise was mortified. All she could see was a very large room of strangers staring at her wearing one shoe! She threw the other one off and proceeded to walk round the ring barefooted, bouncing off the rope on each corner, hoping not to fall on top of one of the fighters. All she could hear were cheers and chanters from everyone, including Daryl. "YO BIG GIRL!" shouted a scottish fan wearing a tartan hat. It was the most humiliating thing ever! She got back under the rope to the safety of darkness where no one could see her red face.

"Not bad, apart from the shoes!" Abigail said with a smile.

"You were a bit quick, walk slower the next time!"

Analeise was about to tell her to stick it.

Then the fight started, and Abigail handed Analeise another card showing '2'.

"How many are there?" asked a worried Analeise.

"Until its over!" she laughed. Just then the fighter wearing the tartan shorts thumped the 'huge' Frenchman, and he fell to the ground with an almighty thump. The crowd were fanatical; the noise erupted all over the hall.

He had knocked him out.

"Looks like you got out of that one easy" said a disappointed Abigail as she took the card off a very relieved Analeise.

"You mean that's it?" she said.

Abigail put her head down; she had planned on this fight being the talk of the town, now it was the talk of the town for the wrong reasons. She had been organising this event for her Kickboxing Boyfriend for months and had hoped that the biggest fight of the evening was going to be spectacular.

She sat in shock for a few moments.

The Scottish fans in the crowd were going crazy, cheering on their champion.

Analeise stared at the scene before her in disbelief, and then the Scottish champion looked over at Analeise and as if to stock his claim, he gave her a big wink.

"Oh shit!" she thought as she scurried back to Daryl.

"Lets go" she said, "You've got nerves of steel, I couldn't have done that!"

Analeise was proud of herself. They said their goodbyes to Abigail who thanked Analeise for her kind efforts.

"I'll book you for the next time!" she said.

"You're ok, I think I've had my moment of fame, but thanks"

The girls laughed and walked down the road to the nearest pizzeria.

The rest of Analeise's big birthday night went a lot more relaxed from then onwards, they had pizza, garlic bread and Italian ice cream to finish off.

They then got a taxi back to Daryl's house. Both of them were stuffed to the gills and they then retired to bed.

Analeise slept like a log all night, she woke up completely refreshed. She heard Daryl in the kitchen singing to herself and wondered what time it was.

"Well sleepy, how does it feel to be half of 68?" she asked.

"Thanks for that thought!" Analeise laughed.

Then she remembered that she had agreed to go for a drink with Daniel tonight.

"Oh Jesus, I forgot about tonight, I'm meeting Mr.Solicitor!" she said as she tried to straighten out her hair.

"Do you want me to do your hair?" Daryl asked kindly.

"Oh could you, you would be a real star!" Analeise answered.

Daryl was a great hairdresser, and always offered her services to all of her friends. Most of them took advantage of her, but Analeise never liked to ask as she felt that she was putting her to too much trouble.

Analeise had very curly hair and hated it, she always tried to straighten it herself, and when she did it would look curiously like candy floss.

Analeise spent the rest of the afternoon in Daryl's house. Her mum had dropped round Dania, and Analeise was fascinated as she watched her perform her gymnastics and her dance routine. She was a great kid, a 'chip off the old block' she would call her.

At 4.00 Analeise took herself and her slinky straight hair back home, and on her way home she got a call from Daniel.

"Be at my house for 8" Was all he said.

"And where would that be?" she asked.

"23 Dungiven Park" he answered.

This was a strange one she thought. "Why couldn't he come for me?"

They agreed that she would collect him in a taxi at 8.00 and they would go to a bar in town.

As she was getting ready Analeise was ever so slightly anxious about this date, Daniel had made her nervous from the day and hour that she met him. Why did she agree to this date? What possessed her to put herself through all of this again? She wondered if she had completely lost her mind.

Anyway, her hair was looking good and she might as well show it off!

Too late now to have doubts.

CHAPTER TWENTY- THREE

*T*he taxi arrived on time.

"Dungiven Park please" she asked the driver.

It was only about 2 miles from the flat, and it was on the way to the centre of Belfast.

When the taxi pulled up at Daniels house he waved from his front room, he then walked down the path towards the taxi without closing the door. He jumped into the car, shortly followed by another young lad, and shortly followed by yet another younger lad!

Analeise looked at him in amazement. What the hell was going on? A gangbang?

"Mercury Bar please" he said to the driver.

"Hi, I'm Ana" she introduced herself to the two young boys still in a state of shock.

"Oh, sorry Analeise this is Chippy my lodger, and his mate Gary" Daniel chirped in.

"Are you two going to the Mercury then?" Analeise asked them.

"We're all going!" Daniel said.

Analeise was speechless the whole journey, even more confused about this strange but interesting Daniel Bowers.

When they arrived, the young lads bounced out of the taxi, and Analeise fumbled in her purse to pay the taxi driver.

Daniel leaned into the front and handed her a pound coin.

"There you go" he said, and got out.

'Did he just take the piss?' She thought.

The taxi man started to snigger.

"That's eight pounds love," he said to Analeise who was completely horrified.

Daniel was standing on the pavement waiting for Analeise hands in pockets.

He did look good though, every time she had seen him he would have been wearing his business attire. Tonight he was wearing blue jeans, and a crisp white casual shirt complete with an ever so sexy smile!

They went into the bar and joined Chippy and Gary to find that they had already started guzzling down beers.

"Wine?" Daniel asked pointing to the bar. For a split second Analeise thought he was *asking her* for a wine!!

Why was she so nervous? So far, he hadn't been the most courteous!!

"Oh, yes please" she replied.

They had a few drinks in the Mercury Bar, Daniel had spent a lot of time talking, and entertaining his two young friends who at this stage had pulled a couple of women! He was full of chat, a great personality, and a great entertainer. Totally adorable Analeise thought. He had made her laugh all night.

They then headed to Thornton's Wine Bar, where it played very loud 'house' music. It wasn't really Analeise's taste, the crowd seemed a bit young.

She couldn't really get talking to Daniel very well for two reasons, firstly the music was pounding from the speakers, and secondly her lovable date seemed to know everyone in the place!

"Are you with Daniel?" asked this skinny blond haired girl.

"Yes" Analeise replied into her ear.

"He's a laugh!" she said and walked away.

It was a very bizarre night; it was not really going the way Analeise had expected it to. Daniel, adorable and entertaining as he was, was not really spending a whole load of time with his date!

Just as Analeise was contemplating going home, Daniel walked over to her and said, "We're going to a party." And took her by the hand outside to an awaiting taxi.

Analeise decided to sit in the back seat this time in case she got fleeced again!

"Could you stop off at Casey's on the Ormeau Road," he asked the driver.

"Getting a carry out!" he said to Analeise who felt she had consumed enough alcohol for one evening.

"Nothing for me" she said and raised her hands in defeat.

In fact she was ready to go home, if she had of known it was going to be a complete bender, she would have stayed at home. Three nights on the trot was starting to wear her down. Maybe 12 years ago, it would have been normal, but not now! How did Daniel stick the pace so well? Analeise had hoped for a quiet drink, and not some mad pub-crawl. She had hardly said a sentence to Daniel all night.

When they arrived at the party, it was full to the door with noisy, excitable people. There were bodies of all kinds everywhere guzzling on bottles of Budweiser. A guy who looked like a car thief was standing in the hall dancing on his own. A young couple were having a game of tonsil tennis on the stairs. It was a bit like student digs and she wondered why a 32 year old Solicitor like Daniel would have any desire to be there. It was mayhem and she asked him nicely if she could go home.

"Home?" He was astounded. "What do you want to go home for, we're not long here!"

She felt obliged to stay in the complete madness for another while. Then at 3.30am she had had enough! She walked over to Daniel who was sitting talking shit in some poor sod's ear.

"Daniel, can we go now? I have work in the morning" she said apologetically.

"I'm staying, go you on pet" he said as if dismissing her.

Analeise was furious; she couldn't believe that he was prepared to let her go home on her own. What was his problem?

"Fine, I will go!" she said and stormed out, climbing over bodies to get to the front door.

"What a freak!" she thought.

It only took 5 minutes before a taxi arrived at the front door of the house of insanity.

It was 4.00am whenever she got home, completely exhausted and completely confused. She was even more baffled about this Daniel Bowers guy than ever. He was a professional person, why did he feel the need to stay up so late and party with people so young? One thing she knew was that she would never go on a date with him ever again. If this was his idea of a 'drink' then maybe the guy had some kind of problem.

Analeise looked in the mirror at herself whilst she was removing her make-up, she felt a bit let down and very disappointed in this mysterious man that intrigued her for weeks.

She checked her forehead to see if there was a sign on her head saying

'I love dysfunctional men'!!

Strangely enough, there wasn't!

CHAPTER TWENTY- FOUR

*F*irst thing the next morning, Analeise felt the need to call Tracey with a post mortem on the night before.

"I went on a date last night!" she announced.

"Who?" Tracey asked Impatiently.

"Daniel" Analeise said slowly.

"Lets meet for lunch, you can tell me everything!" Tracey said excitedly.

Analeise agreed to meet her for lunch, but knew that Tracey would be as disappointed as she was.

Analeise agreed to meet Tracey at her office on High Street, and then they would call Gemma who worked only a few doors away.

"Ok, we'll go to Papa Capaldis across the road, they do great Creole chicken!" said an anxious Tracey and put the phone down. She lit up a cigarette and gave Analeise an almighty smile.

"Well!" she said as she nudged her ' not so' excited friend.

"Well nothing" Analeise said with a blank face. "Thanks for telling me he's a complete party animal!"

Tracey laughed.

"Tell Me," she said still laughing.

At this stage Analeise was beginning to feel that she had been set up.

They walked to the restaurant, which wasn't too far away to be greeted by another 'anxious for gossip' friend.

Gemma was already there, and was clutched to a menu.

"I heard!" she cried, "Tell me!"

Analeise was bedazzled at their excitement, and wished she had the same enthusiasm!

"Girls, I gotta tell you!" She started to explain. "He arrived for the date with his fucking lodger and his mate!"

Tracey and Gemma's faces went blank.

"No way" said Gemma, and slammed her menu on the table. "He didn't bring the juniors with him" she said it as if she knew he had done this kind of thing before.

"Juniors?" Analeise asked puzzled.

"Its just what we call them, they are like his little groupies!" Tracey tried to explain.

"What the fuck is all that about?" Analeise couldn't believe what she was hearing.

The two girls looked at Analeise with complete pity on their faces while she tried to work out why the hell he ran around with guys young enough to be his sons!!

"Is he a gay boy?" Analeise asked puzzled to the rapturous sounds of laughter.

"No Ana" Gemma explained "We have known him a long time, he likes to go out, party, live the life of a 21 year old. Don't know why, I just think he must be going through that 'thing' that men go through whenever they get into their 30's.

"I told you to take him with a pinch of salt Ana" Tracey said with compassion.

"It doesn't matter anyway," Analeise said to them. "I never want to see him again, he's a disaster!"

Tracey nodded in agreement. "Yes, he is a disaster, but a good laugh"

"Yes" Agreed Gemma "You can't help but like him!"

"If I had of known he was going to treat me like that, I would have given the whole evening a bye-ball! You know he gave me a pound to pay for the cab on the way to the bar!!" Analeise said as she lifted a menu as if dismissing the whole subject.

Tracey and Gemma were in shock. They couldn't believe what he had done. They knew he was a bit mad but didn't realise that he would involve someone like Analeise into his crazy, bizarre world. Tracey was sorry now she tried to get them together.

They all enjoyed their lunch of Creole chicken with chunky chips and a side order of sour cream. They didn't discuss Daniel one more time until they were all saying their goodbyes.

"So how was it left?" Tracey asked curiously.

"It wasn't!" Analeise answered with a stern look.

Tracey knew not to speak any more of Daniel Bowers.

On the journey to her next call of the day, which was a Department store in the centre of Belfast, she couldn't help but think about what Gemma had said about men whenever they reach a certain age.

She was right! Martin visited Wankerville whenever he turned thirty; he started dressing like a surf freak on speed!! It was as if he was trying to prove something. Maybe she should avoid men who were early thirties. Then she remembered Chris Drummond, he had just turned thirty. Maybe she should just avoid men full stop!!

As she was walking into the Department store she saw a familiar face standing at one of the make-up counters.

It was Penny Brightman, a brilliant make-up artist that used to work with Martin on photo shoots, she even had done Analeise's make up the odd time for photo shoots years ago. Analeise instantly liked her from the moment she met her, she had been Martins friend for years before she really got to know Analeise properly. They used to go for coffee on a regular basis, and talk about their next fashion shoot. Analeise never felt threatened by her. She was sound. Martin had lost contact with her for some time and this would be Analeise's first meeting with her since the break-up over a year ago. She was tall, elegant, slim and (as always) perfectly made up much to Analeise's annoyance.

"Hi there!" she gave Analeise a big hug.

"Great to see you!!" Analeise was genuinely delighted to see her.

"How have you been?" she asked sincerely.

Analeise wondered if she had known about the break up, and wondered how she would react remembering that Martin was her original friend.

"Have you heard?" Analeise asked as if apologising.

"Yes, I'm devastated" she replied.

Analeise just looked at her and wondered if she should call Martin a shithead or not!

"I'm ok!" Analeise raised her hands in the air and took a deep breath to swallow the lump, which was starting to form in her throat.

"He's such a wee shit!" Penny said.

Analeise started to laugh, and felt relieved.

They went for a coffee to catch up on old times.

"I wasn't sure whether to call you or not Ana" Penny explained as she poured a brown sugar into her very foamy cappuccino. "I didn't know how you would be with me, you know being Martins friend and all that"

"Its ok, I understand" Analeise said, "Do you ever see him?

"No, never" Penny shook her head. "Where is he living?"

"With some chick somewhere, that's all I know" Analeise said, staring into the whirlpool she had created in her coffee cup!

"And you?" Penny asked.

"Still in that flea-bitten pit, although I have bought a house in Lisburn but don't move until August." Analeise answered.

"Where in Lisburn?" she asked excitedly.

"Birch Avenue" Analeise said.

"No way!!" Penny laughed, "We live in Birch Park! Just round the corner"

Then Analeise vaguely remembered visiting Penny and her devoted husband Jamie years ago just after her daughter Samantha was born, just before she made the unenviable mistake of marrying Martin.

"That's right!" Analeise said. "I never thought, I went to view the house and just got a great vibe!"

"Its really nice round there, I'm so pleased. It means we can keep in touch!" Penny said with enthusiasm.

Analeise and Penny talked for another half an hour.

"I'd better go, I haven't done a hands turn today!" Analeise said as she looked at her watch.

She was genuinely pleased to see Penny again and was happy to know she would be living around the corner from her.

They swapped telephone numbers.

"You can come to our Halloween Party!" Penny said to Analeise as they were leaving their seats.

"I know its only June!" she put her hands up apologetically. "But we have it every year, and its great!"

"Would love to!" Analeise answered.

They said their goodbyes and Analeise went into the Department Store with a confident smile.

It was incredible how the last year had tuned around for her, all of a sudden all her old friends have turned up out of the blue.

"One door closes, and another one opens!" Her Mum would always say.

Mums are always right!!

CHAPTER TWENTY-FIVE

*B*usiness for Analeise was starting to slow down a bit as the summer was drawing in more and more. Salons were busy with waxing, tinting, and false tan etc... Everyone was on holiday, and no one was spending any money on facials or anti-aging creams.

Analeise was running around chasing her tail at the moment,

She was on her way to Dublin for their monthly Sales meeting. Analeise was dreading it.

"Hi there!" She was greeted by a big smile from her boss Kevin the minute she walked through the door.

"Hello there" She said reluctantly and wondered what the big smile was all about.

"My office in 10 minutes" he said, and hurried away.

Analeise walked into the small, and dingy tearoom where Tanya and Patti, her colleagues were deep in conversation.

Analeise was the only employee who came from the North of Ireland, so she only needed to be in head office for sales meetings or in times of crisis.

Tanya and Patti represented the same skincare brand as she did only in the Southern Counties of Ireland although they would communicate on the telephone at times, they only seen each other once a month.

Tanya, a well built strong, business type stopped talking immediately.

"Analeise!" she said with a big smile "How's you?"

"Good thanks" Analeise said slowly "What's going on today?"

Tanya was like the company's daily newspaper, she knew everything long before anyone else did.

"Nothing" she answered. "How's business? Did you have a good month?"

"Shit, thanks" Analeise answered and started to make a coffee for herself.

"Coffee anyone?" she asked. There was silence. "How was yours?"

"Don't know, I think it was ok." Tanya said vaguely.

Analeise knew she was lying. She always had brilliant months! She had to hand it to her she was a brilliant rep; she adored the company and gave 100% of her time to it.

"I've had a shit one too," Patti piped in.

Patti was more on Analeise's wavelength whenever it came to work. She normally got up at 8.00am and finished around 5pm like most people. Tanya was different; she got up at 5.00am and finished at 8.00pm!

"That's ok" Analeise stirred her instant coffee "We won't look as bad if two of us have done shit!" She smiled at the two of them and walked upstairs to the invoice office to hand Betty in her cheques she had collected from her clients over the last few days.

Betty, a 56-year-old human bulldog.

She would call all of the clients and remind them of how much money they owe, and not come off the phone until they agreed to send a cheque to her. She would bark, and bark and not care who heard her. She was rude, and she knew it.

She drove Analeise insane.

Clients would complain to Analeise every day about her manners, and she would have to apologise on behalf of her.

"Have you got money for me?" she asked as she peered over her overcrowded desk.

"I am fine Betty, and how are you on this fine day?" Analeise said sarcastically.

The joke as usual went right over Betty's overworked head.

"I need your cheques now because I've to go to the bank and lodge them before lunchtime" she said as she held out her bony hand.

SAINTS, SINNERS AND TV DINNERS

"Calm your head Betty, I have them here." Analeise answered impatiently. "Do you think I came up here just to bid you good day?"

Betty laughed, and tried to be light hearted.

Analeise didn't laugh, handed the cheques and walked back downstairs to find Kevin standing talking to a tall, attractive blonde.

"Oh Analeise this is Tara, she has just started with us, and will be your new colleague up North!" he said with glee.

"Pleased to meet you" Analeise shook her very well cared for hand.

"She'll be travelling with you for a while!" Kevin announced, and then walked off.

"I'm from Newtownabbey" Tara said.

Analeise was delighted to have someone in the company with the same accent as her!

"Great, have you met the others?" Analeise asked.

"No, I'm just in the door!"

Analeise waltzed Tara into the tearoom to find that Tanya and Patti had been joined by laugh-a-minute Jennifer; the receptionist who had the personality of a garden snail, her hair resembled grated carrots and was as much fun as a wet weekend in Donegal. A smile would completely finish her off. Analeise tried constantly to get some kind of reaction from her to no avail!!

"Girls, this is Tara. She's from the North!" she said proudly showing off her new colleague.

"Hi" said Tanya "I heard you were starting"

"Surprise, surprise" said Analeise under her breath.

"I've met you before" Patti said, "Did you work in Cleavers Department Store?"

"Yes" Tara said with a big smile "I worked for Dermarome there"

Tanya walked out of the room unhappy at the fact of someone knowing something she didn't!

"Hi" came the words of a very insignificant Jennifer who raised her hand and blew her nose at the same time.

"Ok gang!" Kevin peeked his chunky face into the tearoom. "My office"

They all gathered into the small office and sat around Kevin's cluttered desk where he had the shortest sales meeting known to mankind.

It lasted approximately 9 minutes! He gave everyone their figures for June, gave them their targets for July and told everyone to get out and start selling.

Everyone, especially Analeise was ever so slightly pissed off!

"I have just driven 2 hours for that!!" She was disgusted.

"Who does he think he is!"? Tanya said. "I could have been in Cork today with a new client!"

"He's a tosser!" Patti said.

Meanwhile Tara couldn't make head or tail of what she had let herself in for.

They all hung around, much to Kevin's annoyance for a few hours, doing errands and odd jobs they couldn't do whilst driving a car!

Analeise set sail for her journey home at 1.30pm.

She organised some time with Tara so she could travel with her for a few days just to get her into the swing of things.

Analeise was home at 4.30, a bit tired and a bit deflated.

Was business that bad that Kevin had the need to start someone else?

Analeise started to doubt her abilities, and thought that maybe Tara would be her replacement after she was sacked!

Maybe she was just a little paranoid after such a crappy day and a terrible sales month.

Analeise was determined not to be beaten; July was going to be a great month!

CHAPTER TWENTY-SIX

*F*or a few weeks, Analeise had put everything into her job. She didn't slow down for anything or any one!

She had been out travelling with the new talent known as Tara Potter who was completely adorable!

They were very much on the same wavelength whenever it came to relationships. Tara had just turned thirty and found the whole single thing completely boring. She had lived in Dublin for a few years where she worked in the Department store for Kevin. Then she moved to London, where she found a job as an interpreter for a large company. She stayed for another few years but knew it was time to come home. So she called Kevin asking for a job within the company working closer to her hometown.

She had the same interests as Analeise, she was a really genuine person, and Analeise was starting to consider her as a very good friend.

Whenever it was time for Tara to start calling to salons on her own, they agreed to stay in touch a lot and maybe go to the movies once in a while.

For Analeise it felt great to have a work colleague who came from the same area as she did, she would feel more like part of a team rather than an outsider who seen everyone just once a month. It also motivated her.

She had a great July as she had hoped.

She also had a few messages from Daniel Bowers over the last few weeks, which she decided to ignore much to his annoyance. The more she ignored, the more he was determined to get an answer.

He never called; he just kept sending weird text messages at all hours of the day (and night!). Text messages were a new and very irritating thing to Analeise. They always seemed to be mis-interpreted. She just preferred to call someone, just like the good old days! were people just too damn lazy and couldn't be arsed talking? Texting was something she was going to have to get used to and go with the times!

She finally sent one back to him agreeing to have lunch sometime. He didn't make her nervous anymore, he just freaked her out.

She hadn't heard from Chris in quite sometime and decided that maybe she would just give him another call. Or maybe not, she really wanted to see him again and this would be the only way!

Pauline had settled in London with Clive to start their new life together. They never got their night out before she left; she had far too many things to do. She had made a few phone calls to Analeise in the last few weeks reporting on the Department Store in Oxford Street and how bitchy the other girls were. Pauline would boast on how she gave 'that Kathy Lincoln from Estee Lauder' a piece of her mind! What a complete cow she was and how jealous she was of her Etc, etc!!

Analeise had been gathering up bits and pieces for her new house. She had bought two new cream sofas, a fridge, a washing machine and a magnificent glass coffee table. She had spent the last remaining weeks in 'Grotsville' packing odds and ends into cardboard boxes. It was exciting for her to do this as she knew it wouldn't be long before she would be moving to her own place at last.

A few weeks later Analeise decided it was time to start going into cupboards and start sorting out all the junk that lay dormant there for years. She knew it was going to be tough as a lot of the crap belonged to Martin.

As she was sifting through things swimmingly; there they were...

The wedding photographs; every single one of them in a brown envelope!

She had forgotten about them, and also forgot the fact that Martin never bothered to ever get an album for them.

She sat on the floor and cried, and cried. It was the hardest thing she ever had to do. It was as if something very special had died and was never buried.

She phoned Martin, it only rang for a few moments.

"Hello" he said quickly and out of breath.

"Hi" Analeise said solemnly "Its me, I am doing a bit of sorting here. Do you want any wedding pictures?"

Martin was silent for a moment. "Wedding pictures? What for? To hang on my wall?" he joked.

Analeise was trying to be serious and was not amused at his negative response and started crying again.

"Are you sorting out stuff now?" he asked, realising that Analeise was in no mood to joke.

"Yes, We need to get things closed off once and for all" she said.

He agreed to be there within the hour.

Whenever he arrived 30 minutes later Analeise was still sitting on the floor surrounded by Family photographs, holiday pictures, Martins first professional photos of her. So many memories had flooded out and Analeise's heart was breaking in two.

"Hey, are you ok?" he asked a very exhausted estranged wife.

It was the first civil thing he had said to her since their break-up.

"Not really" Analeise answered not even looking at him. "I don't want to take everything here, I'm sure you would want some reminders" she said as she stared at a photo of the two of them on a holiday in Greece six years ago.

The two of them spent the guts of two hours sorting out photos, birth certificates, insurance documents, and all other kinds of bullshit that married couples share. They looked back and laughed at a few things and talked about funny times they had together.

"So, when do you move?" Martin asked her.

"Next month, thank God" she replied with a smile.

"Good for you" He said, "I have bought a house too"

"You're a dark horse aren't you?" Analeise said angrily.

"Didn't feel the need to tell you, we have split up remember?" he said as he stood up.

Analeise raised herself to her feet and looked him in the eyes and said "I'm going to see a solicitor, I want divorced!"

She couldn't believe what she had said, but Martins comment to her just pushed her over the edge.

"You can do what you want with your money," he said with a smile. "I don't care to be divorced because I never want to marry again. Why do you want divorced?" he asked.

"I want to move on with my life, and I feel it will help" Analeise said.

"Have you met someone else? Is he the one pushing you to do this?"

Analeise was horrified!

"Believe it or not Martin, I have my own life, and I am more than capable of making my own decisions now," she yelled.

"All grown up aren't we!" he laughed.

"Fuck you Martin! You were nothing but a control freak, you had to make all my decisions for me before and now you don't like it. Well.. Newsflash Big Shot I have my own life now, and I'm sure as hell glad you won't be a part of it anymore."

Martin was silent.

"I'm away!" he said and walked out the front door.

As she watched him leave, clutched to the only remnants of 10 years together her stomach churned with a feeling of sadness, anger and hatred all rolled into one. All those mixed emotions of good times shared had yet again been smashed into tiny little pieces of hurt.

She had made her decision, and it really was time to move on.

A new house awaited and a whole new single life. Her life. Her decisions.

CHAPTER TWENTY-SEVEN

*A*t last, it was moving day. Kevin had given her a few days off to move into her new house.

It was a hard few weeks for her, as she had to organise everything herself as well as work for a very demanding Company.

She had made a few phone calls to Daniel Bowers about the dates, times and conditions of the move. The conversations were purely professional. On the last phone call they agreed to meet for lunch whenever she got settled in.

Analeise had seen Tracey a few times regarding 'signing her life away' on a few documents. She doesn't know what she had of done without her. She insisted on buying her dinner sometime.

But at the moment it was all systems go!

Analeise was so excited; she had everything she owned packed into cardboard boxes. Her sofas, and the rest of the furniture that she had bought was at her brother Ben's house. He and his wife Pamela helped her a lot in the last couple of weeks. They hired a van and helped her load, and unload all of her things. Her Mum was great too, in fact everyone in her family were a great help to her. It was then she realised that she was so lucky to have the best people in the world on her side.

They were all very proud of her and what she had been through in the last year and a half. Here she was moving into her new house.

Ben and her Dad assembled her Bed for her, at this stage it was 10.30pm and everyone was exhausted.

"Come and stay with us tonight" Pamela kindly suggested "It will be more homely for you"

As Analeise looked around the cold, unfurnished house, she agreed with her.

Pamela was a great sister-in-law. Analeise considered her more like a sister than anything else. She was also very supportive whenever Martin had left her. There was always a place for her at their house. Analeise didn't want to abuse her kindness, but she was always grateful for her support. She had been married to Ben for 4 years and their relationship grew stronger year upon year. It would inspire Analeise and make her realise that not every man was a complete shithead. She aspired to have a man in her life that was as good to her as her brother was to his wife.

She was up very early the next morning, and couldn't wait to get back home to start organising all of her things.

She had a phone call on that Friday afternoon from Penny Brightman asking her to have tea with her and the family that evening as she was probably sick of eating takeaway!

She was right; Analeise had been living on pizza for days as cooking was not her speciality at the best of times!

At 6.30 she walked round to Penny's house, it was literally a one-minute walk from her house. She couldn't believe it was so close!

"Hi there" smiled a very glamorous Penny at the front door.

Analeise looked like a tramp in comparison, she didn't mind as she had been up to her eyes in dust and grime all afternoon. Her Mum was there all day with her scrubbing the oven until it looked like new!

Her Mum offered her tea also, but she had given enough help for one day and went home tired and weary. She was such a star.

"You remember Analeise," she said to her tall, blonde and attractive American husband Jamie.

"Of course I do!" he said as he rose from his very comfortable armchair.

"How are you?" he asked as he walked into the kitchen.

"I'm great thanks," she answered.

"I remember being in this house before." she said to Penny who was mashing potatoes in a large pot.

"I just had the baby, remember you and Martin called round?" she said.

Analeise could barely remember, as all her times with Martin at the end of their relationship seemed very vague.

"You were very quiet, I sensed there was something wrong even then!" Penny said.

"Yes, you're right." Analeise said as she remembered a very dark night a few years ago. Martin and she had been at his mother's house, then Martin announced that he was calling round to see Penny and Jamie. Analeise wasn't keen on going, as she hadn't bought a present for their new baby daughter Samantha. She was ashamed and felt terrible.

They stayed only an hour and argued the whole way home.

"I'm sorry about all that. I have really changed you know!" Analeise said.

"What are you apologising for?" Penny said.

"About how odd I was then," Analeise said humbly.

"Wise-up!" Jamie said. "You weren't odd, Martin was the oddball! Imagine leaving you in a crowded bar! I still can't believe he did that!"

Jamie had met Martin a few times, but Martin couldn't be bothered with him. The reason being was that Jamie always beat him at whatever they were playing. Whether it would be golf, snooker or darts. "Typical Yank!" he would say irritated at the thought of being beaten.

Analeise really enjoyed her home cooked dinner, it was great to see, and spend quality time with Penny and her family. Samantha, their daughter was three, gorgeous and was the image of her mother!

At 9.30 after catching up on all the gossip and talking about old times Analeise decided to go home.

"Now call round anytime, there is always someone here!" Penny said with sincerity.

"I will" Analeise answered, "You'll probably be sick looking at me, it won't be long before you're hiding behind the sofa whenever you see me"

Penny and Jamie laughed.

She went home to her new house and slept in it for the first time ever. It was the best sleep she had had in quite some time.

A few weeks had passed and Analeise was getting into the swing of things in her new domain. She took Tracey for dinner one evening as a thank you for all her help in mortgage matters. Tracey tried desperately to link Analeise up to one of Maurice's banking friends. She totally refused point blank to go on another blind date ever again! Gemma also insisted that she meet with Colin who was a dear friend of Mitch. "He's a bit chunky, but a really nice guy!" She told her one evening on the phone. Analeise just had visions of 'Chunky Tortoise Man' in bad brown trousers and shuddered at the thought! She wasn't having it from any of them. She hated the fact that all of her friends felt the need to link her up with someone. It was as though she wasn't 'complete' without a man in her life! She did like the idea of someone to love again though.

"There is a formal coming up, you'll have to come!" Tracey said as they said their goodbyes.

"I've never been to a formal before!" Analeise answered excitedly.

"Just thought I'd warn you that Daniel wants to invite you," Tracey said smiling.

Analeise started laughing.

"You *are* joking!" she said.

"Don't tell him when he calls that I told you, just sound surprised."

"Ok, ok!" Analeise put her hands in the air. "I'd like to go, it'd be a laugh!"

"Good!" Tracey clapped her hands together.

Analeise was desperate for a good night out and anxiously awaited the call.

The next day, Daniel called her mobile as she was dashing into a salon in Belfast City Centre.

"Hi there, how was the move?" He asked.

"Great" she answered impatiently.

"Can you talk?" he asked.

"Not really, I'm just about to walk into a salon" she said.

"Would you like to go to a formal next Saturday night!" he asked quickly.

Analeise tried really hard to sound surprised "Oh, very nice!"

"Yes, ok then!" she said smiling.

"Pick me up at 6.30 in a taxi," he said much to her displeasure.

"Not if you are bringing your fan club!" she snapped.

"Tracey is going," he said.

"Oh, very nice" she said again, also trying really hard to sound surprised.

"See you at her house then!" she said assertively.

"Ok" he said. "See you then" and put the phone down.

Analeise smiled to herself, and hoped that this date would be a lot better than the last one!

CHAPTER TWENTY-EIGHT

"What are you wearing?" Tracey asked Analeise anxiously on the Saturday afternoon.

Her phone call got her out of the long hot bath she had been steeping in for 20 minutes.

"Red dress" Analeise said, trying to dry herself and hold the phone at the same time.

"I'm having a bit of a disaster here!!" She sounded stressed. "Fucking dress wont fit!"

"Have you not got another one?" Analeise asked concerned.

"They're all the same size!" she said.

"I've got a black one that might fit you?" Analeise suggested.

"Don't worry, I'll find something" she said "Just wanted to call to see how you were!"

"I'm fine," She answered, "Just getting organised."

"See you at mine later! Come a bit earlier and we'll have some champagne"

"Ok, I'll bring a bottle!" Analeise said.

Analeise arrived at Tracey's house at 6.15. Maurice answered the door whilst dancing to the sounds of the Bee Gees.

"Looking good!" She said and kissed him on the cheek.

He looked great, his jet-black hair was shining, and perfectly styled and his black dinner jacket did him justice. He was a complete sweetheart and a great, patient boyfriend to Tracey. Analeise only met him once very briefly whenever he picked her up from Christies bar one

Friday night. He treated Analeise like he had known her all of his life. She felt very at ease in his company.

"I'm upstairs!" Shouted Tracey from the bathroom.

Analeise handed Maurice a bottle of bubbly.

"We have some here" He handed her a glass and poured some golden, sparkly liquid into it.

"Are you ok up there?" Analeise shouted up the stairs at Tracey.

"Coming down now!" she sounded hassled.

"Is she ok?" Analeise asked Maurice who was sifting through his CD collection.

"She does this every time we go out!" he seemed uninterested.

"Does what!" asked Tracey who was standing in the hall at the bottom of the stairs.

She looked stunning. Her black off one shoulder dress was gorgeous; her purple georgette shawl really finished it off.

"Always a pantomime before we go out!" Maurice handed her a glass of champagne.

"Let us see your dress Analeise!" Tracey asked as she gulped her champagne down very quickly.

Analeise was still wearing her full-length grey coat, which wasn't the most glamorous.

She reluctantly slipped the coat off to reveal an amazing full-length scarlet red dress, which fitted every inch of her curves.

"WOW" said Maurice, much to her embarrassment.

"Is it too much?" asked Analeise

"You've a great pair of knockers!" he said.

Tracey gave him a thump "It is amazing, you'll knock Daniel for six! I can't wait to see his face when he sees you!!"

Analeise pulled her grey coat back over her shoulders again.

The doorbell rang and Analeise got an adrenalin rush.

She heard Tracey greeting him in the hall.

Analeise wasn't sure if her eyes were getting the better of her or not but what the hell was he wearing?

She blushed.

Were pink bow ties back in fashion again?

Maybe paisley patterned pink waistcoats were the new thing?

No. It was the shiny tap dancer shoes that just finished it off.

Was it the 80's revival formal?

Analeise was stunned; he was like a reject from Miami Vice!

"Hello" she smiled at him. "You look well"

She wondered if he knew she was lying.

"Sorry I can't say the same about you!" he said and swallowed a glass of champagne in one quick swoop!!

"Cheeky bastard!" she thought. How dare he!

Why did she let herself be talked into this again? She stared at Tracey and shook her head in amazement.

Tracey sniggered and motioned her to take off her coat. Daniel caught her by the side of his beady eye.

"What are you doing?" he asked Tracey with a smirk.

Analeise was really starting to hate him now. He was always one step ahead of anyone's thoughts. She found it very irritating; the guy was too clever for his own good.

Analeise walked into the hall and removed her coat. Tracey anxiously awaited the 'big entrance'.

When Analeise waltzed into the room again with the greatest of ease Daniel had his back to her.

"More champagne Ana?" Tracey suggested.

"Oh yes please" She said, trying really hard to compose herself like a true sexpot!

"What did you take your coat off for? We're going in a minute!" Was not the response she would have wished for from Daniel after he stared at her up and down like a piece of meat hanging in a butchers shop!

Analeise was past caring at this stage. She had great experience in this type of behaviour from Martin, and was not prepared to let this cheeky, arrogant, '1985 styled' prick bother her.

They finished their drinks and had a taxi take them to the Ewart Hotel in Belfast.

When they arrived Analeise was amazed at the lack of manners that Daniel Bowers actually had.

He took himself off to the bar, which meant that she had to walk into the Grand Hall like a complete gooseberry. She stood close to Tracey and felt every eye in the place staring at her.

She was so conscious of this; she took herself off to the cloakroom just to have something to do.

When she arrived back she couldn't find Tracey and Maurice anywhere.

"Over here!" shouted Tracey from the corner of the room.

Analeise still felt all eyes of pity on her.

"Go and get him!" Analeise said to Maurice as she gave him a mighty shove in the direction of the bar.

"Why are you so worried? You look incredible. Everyone just wants to know who you are, that's all." Tracey tried to compose Analeise who was beside herself with embarrassment. Everyone was looking at her, but they were genuinely staring with admiration. She had absolutely no idea that she looked so stunning.

Analeise needed a drink for Dutch courage.

As they all were assigned to their seats, there was still no sign of Daniel, and the seat beside Analeise was empty.

All of a sudden as she was staring around the room for a familiar face.

She found one and it was Chris Drummond.

He was there with some gorgeous brunette girl; he had not seen her.

Analeise's heart missed a beat. Who was she?

She hoped he would not see her sitting with an empty chair beside her.

She quickly looked away.

Just as Analeise looked up again she saw him walking towards her. She could feel herself blushing from head to toe! Perfect! Now her skin matched the colour of her dress!

"Hi there" he said and kissed her on the cheek.

"Hello, how are you?" Analeise said eyes sparkling.

Chris kneeled down beside her, he looked amazing, he smelt amazing and she just wished she were with him.

"Good, who are you with?" he asked, looking around the table.

"Oh, this is Tracey" she pointed to a curious Tracey who was giving him a good examination with her eyes.

"Hi" she said smiling.

"And Maurice her boyfriend" she pointed to Maurice who was in deep conversation with a Studious looking sod wearing horn rimmed glasses.

"AND ME!" The Scarlet Pimpernel finally showed his face!

Daniel sat in his seat and leaned over Analeise to introduce himself to Chris.

"Pleased to meet you" Chris said and stood up "See you later" he winked at Analeise.

He walked back to his seat where his anxious date awaited him.

"Who's that poof?" Daniel asked a furious Analeise.

"Where were you?" she asked him back.

"Making a few connections," he said as he stared Chris's direction.

"Connections with Jack Daniels I presume?" Analeise said angrily.

Daniel chose to ignore her comment. Instead he started talking to the girl next to him who looked as bored as Analeise.

She took a deep breath and silently wished for this entire nightmare to be finally over.

They all enjoyed their meal of watermelon sorbet to start, then beef Wellington on a bed of green vegetables, followed by chocolate mousse and raspberry coulis.

Analeise was starting to get into the swing of things once the band started playing, she was also so conscious to the fact that Chris was only a matter of yards away from her.

The expensive wine was slowly starting to go to her head.

"Do you want to dance?" slurred Daniel who at this stage had removed his dinner jacket and was pinker than pink!

"Ok" Laughed Analeise.

Whenever she got to the dance floor, she just couldn't believe her eyes.

Daniel was dancing like Barney the Dinosaur in a fit!

He looked like someone had just wound him up! Analeise looked over at Tracey, who at this stage was lying over the table in convulsions!

Analeise couldn't keep her face straight; Daniel was in a world of his own. His dance moves matched his clothes.

The night was just getting funnier and funnier. She had to hand it to Daniel; he just didn't give a shit!

She admired that quality to him and wished she were more like that.

When they sat down, Analeise glanced around the room for Chris and couldn't find him.

She then took a walk to the toilets whenever she bumped into him standing outside the Ladies Loo's waiting.

"Sort of a funny place to meet new people!" Analeise joked.

"I'm waiting for Christine," he said as he pointed to the door.

Analeise smiled.

"So, is this serious?" she asked curiously.

"I don't know" he paused "Maybe" and shrugged.

Her heart sank.

"Good Luck" she tried to say with enthusiasm.

"What about you and... that guy" he asked.

"He's my solicitor" Analeise answered "Nothing heavy"

"Good catch!" he said smiling. "Apart from the Spandau Ballet outfit!"

"He's a nice Guy!" She said in Defence.

"Don't mind me!" Chris laughed.

His face lit up whenever his close to perfect girlfriend waltzed out of the toilets smelling like the ground floor of Boots the Chemists.

"This is Christine!" He said to Analeise as he proudly showed off his catch of the day.

"Hi.... Nice to meet you" she shook her hand gently.

"Good to see you Ana" Chris said and ushered his lady to the door.

Analeise was close to tears at this stage.

Chris was all she wanted, he was a gentleman, kind, considerate, gorgeous; and she threw it all away on a stupid one-night stand.

When she went back into the room Daniel had done another runner.

Tracey was engrossed in conversation with a lady dressed as a 'lemon meringue'. And Maurice was still talking to 'Horn Rimmed Glasses Man'.

Analeise sat on her seat and listened as the band played 'True' by Spandau Ballet and wondered if she would ever have another chance with Chris again.

"Want to Dance?" asked Daniel who gave her the fright of her life.

"Why the hell not!" Analeise smiled.

At 2.00 Daniel ordered a taxi for himself and Analeise. Tracey and Maurice headed home earlier.

When they arrived back at Daniels house it was heaving with people.

Chippy his kindergarten lodger was having a party.

Analeise just wanted the night to end.

"I want to go to bed?" She pleaded.

"First on your left" Daniel replied and got tore into a bottle of vodka.

As much as Analeise liked Daniel, his lifestyle was just not to her liking. Where did he get all this energy?

She lay in Daniels bed and felt very guilty about thinking of Chris. She thought of him until she fell asleep.

CHAPTER TWENTY-NINE

*A*naleise woke quite early the next morning to the sounds of a half naked snoring solicitor.

Her head was pounding, she was still wearing her now very wrinkled dress from the previous night.

She sniggered to herself as she looked at Daniel, wearing only his boxers and his hideous pink waistcoat!

She had to hand it to him. He was quite funny. He entertained her the whole night with his dancing and his stupid jokes. He had a great outlook on life. He just didn't give a fiddler's fuck what anyone thought of him.

Analeise envied that.

She went downstairs to fetch a pail of water to be greeted by a couple of people sleeping half way up the stairs. They looked like they were on their way to bed and just passed out on the way there!

She climbed over them to find two more bodies lying on the sofa and one on the kitchen floor. It was total madness.

She drunk the water from the only clean cup she could find in the whole kitchen. The sink was piled up to the ceiling with dishes.

Whenever she got back to the bedroom Daniel (who's head looked like an onion!) had wakened up.

"Thanks for the water!" he said sarcastically.

"I didn't know you were wakened, it's like a war zone down there!" Analeise pointed to the door.

She tried to calm down his Mohican as he looked into space uncaringly. Then he leaned over to one side and let rip the loudest fart she had ever heard!

She jumped up disgusted.

"Suppose you never fart?" he said smiling and wafting the covers.

"You are a stinker!" she laughed. "I'm going now!"

"What about a fuck?" Daniel said laughing.

"Very tempting!" she said, as she brushed down her wrinkly dress "But no!"

"I'm a legend!" he smiled.

In her eyes he wasn't a legend, he was a clown with an obvious drink problem.

At 10.00 that morning Analeise got a taxi home still laughing about the night before. Daniel was an absolute character. One in a million. But she wasn't really attracted to him any more. She adored him as a friend, but that was all. He wasn't the cool, sexy guy she had originally thought. He was just as mad as a brush and didn't care about anything. He would never treat her the way she wanted and knew she deserved better.

She thought of Chris again. Why could she not get him out of her head?

She had a shower when she got home. As she was drying her hair Tracey phoned.

"How did it go last night?"

"Great" Analeise answered, "Daniel is funny"

"He likes you," she said.

"My arse!" Analeise cried, "He was full of compliments! Anyway what did you think of Chris?"

"Didn't really get a chance to check him out very well, but very good looking!"

"He's got a new chick," Analeise said slowly. "I can't see it going anywhere. Her name is Christine"

"Chris and Chris!" Tracey laughed, "Give it two weeks, Chris and Chris just doesn't sound right!"

Analeise and Chris sounded much better to her. What the hell was his problem? They got along very well, had great sexual chemistry and they clicked. Easy Peasy!

Analeise just wanted to get her life back on track again.

It was time to start pursuing a divorce.

That was the next thing on her agenda.

Later that evening Analeise went to her Mums house for her tea and discussed the procedures of finding a divorce solicitor.

"It's going to cost you Pet!" Her Mum said worriedly. "You have only moved into that house!"

"And that's why I want to move on with my life!" Analeise argued.

"Have you got a boyfriend?" Her Mum asked curiously.

"Chance would be a fine thing!" she said, then gulped her cup of Luke warm tea down in one go.

Analeise had enough probing for one day, so she kissed her dear Mother goodbye and set sail for home.

She phoned Tracey to ask if she knew anyone that could handle a divorce for her.

"You going ahead with it?" Tracey asked whilst munching on a pack of crisps.

"Definitely" Analeise was determined.

"I can give you the number of this girl Eleanor, she's cheap if it's a quick and easy job" she replied.

"Sounds good" Analeise said anxiously.

She wrote down the number and made a promise to herself to call her the next day.

That Monday morning Analeise called Evans and Company Solicitors and made an appointment for the following week.

She also called her newfound friend Penny Brightman to see if maybe they could meet for dinner sometime.

"I really fancy a night of drinking and dancing, I'm really in a party mood!" she asked excitedly.

"That'll do too!"

She was pleased to get another night out. She needed them at the moment, she felt that she was slowly getting older and older and was missing all the fun and possible opportunities to meet people.

Analeise's life was really starting to fall nicely into place, but she didn't realise that. She was running around like a headless chicken.

She knew there was something missing.

CHAPTER THIRTY

*A*naleise finished work a little early on the Friday afternoon, and went into the City Centre to find a new outfit for her night out.

She couldn't find anything. Everything she tried on made her look like a lump of tripe so gave it all up as a bad job.

She went through all of her clothes and decided just to wear an old pair of Levi's and a white sleeveless vest.

At 7.30 Analeise walked round to Penny's to find her dancing to Abba and drinking tequila shots.

This was a very rare occurrence as Penny was business like to the very core.

She always had her professional head on whatever the occasion.

"Hey Ana!" she wrapped her arms around her. "You've got a lot of catching up to do" Penny said and stuffed a shot glass into her hand and ushered her into the kitchen.

"How many have you had?" Analeise laughed. She was totally shocked at Penny.

"About four!" Penny put three fingers up then poured herself another shot of 'mad woman's potion!'

"Its half seven!" Analeise cried "Its not a race. The bars are open until one!"

"Never mind! Lets get pissed!" Penny said.

"Yes, lets get pissed!" Analeise said reluctantly and raised her glass in the air.

They eventually got a taxi to take them to Wendy's Nightclub.

It was a great place to go, as the music was really good. Unfortunately the place was famous for being a bit of a pick-up joint full of desperate over 30's!

Analeise wanted to go somewhere else, as she didn't like to be associated to such a place.

"It'll be a laugh!" Penny said. "The music is good, and there is loads of room to dance. Any way we haven't been out for ages!"

"Ok I just hope no-one sees me going in. I don't want to be associated with the 'groovers' that go here!" Analeise laughed.

Penny was really drunk after drinking 4 tequila shots in the house. It didn't take much to get her plastered.

Whenever they arrived. The place was empty!

It was very big and was surrounded in intimate booths. There were two very long bars, which were mirrored the whole way down (Which made them look even bigger). Even the DJ Box was empty!

Penny was a bit shocked.

As was Analeise!

They walked up to the bar to get some drinks.

"Will it get busier than this?" she asked a vacant faced 17-year-old glass washer who either didn't hear her or just couldn't be arsed answering her stupid question.

Analeise started to laugh.

"Did he have his crystal ball under the bar?" Analeise tried to say with a straight face.

They had their choice of seats so decided to sit on the nice comfortable booth just facing the entrance.

"I'm mortified!" Penny said.

"Early birds catch the worms!" Analeise said looking round the big empty room.

She found the whole thing very amusing.

As the night progressed it was starting to get busier and busier. About an hour later the place was heaving with people. The girls were glad to get their great seats with a great view of the dance floor.

The music was great; they were dancing to every song.

Analeise decided to take a breather and sat down.

As she looked around to find her dancing queen friend a young, blonde haired, green-eyed pretty-faced guy was standing opposite her.

"Hello" he said. "Are you single?"

"Yes" she replied.

"Are you over 25?" He asked again.

"Yes" said a very flattered Analeise

"Can I sit down?" He asked politely.

"Of course" She said. She couldn't believe how mannerly he was, and how gorgeous he was!

By this stage Penny had made her way back to the seat to re-hydrate her system with ...more wine!!

She pointed over to him and gave a big wink and a 'thumbs up' much to Analeise's embarrassment!

Analeise thought he was great; his name was Adam Kearney, He was 29 years old and was a musician.

He had an unbelievable smile, and his eyes just glistened. His blonde locks were shoulder length, which made him quite rugged as well as very pretty. He looked like a Calvin Klein model.

Alongside being drop dead gorgeous Adam was very funny. He entertained all of them with his very winning personality.

He sat with them until 12.15.

They had decided to get a taxi home early in order to avoid the big taxi rush, which was so apparent in Belfast. All bars and nightclubs finished at 1.00 and everyone would be turfed out on the streets at the same time!

Adam and his friend Mark walked the girls to their awaiting taxi.

Analeise had given her telephone number to Adam earlier, so they arranged to meet on the Monday night for a drink.

He tried to kiss her but Analeise was too embarrassed in front of Penny who at this stage was trying her best to stand up straight!

"Call you tomorrow!" he said as she stepped into the taxi.

"What a catch!" Penny shouted as she clambered in on top of her.

"You both look great together!" she said proudly.

Analeise was high as a kite.

This would be one night when Analeise would have very sweet dreams.

CHAPTER THIRTY —ONE

The next day after a very long shower Analeise decided to walk round to Penny's house.

Jamie opened the door.

"I gotta warn you" he said "Its not a pretty sight!"

Analeise started laughing whenever she seen Penny lying on the sofas still wearing her pyjama's.

"Have a good time last night?" Analeise asked.

"If you want tea, you'll have to make it yourself!" Penny said slowly and quietly.

"Every picture tells a story!" Analeise said as she shook her head.

"Look at you all loved up!" Jamie said with a smile. "I heard all about it!"

Analeise was radiant considering she had a full night of drinking and dancing.

"I know, look at you!!" Penny said, "How come you don't feel like shit?"

"I had a shower and a good breakfast!" Analeise said proudly.

"Has he phoned?" Penny asked raising her eyebrow.

"Jesus Christ, Its 11.30am!" Analeise snapped, "Give us a break!"

Jamie was laughing as he walked out of the room.

"She just wants another wedding to go to, that's all!" he pointed to Penny who was holding her head in fear that if might fall off.

Analeise stayed for a coffee and they all talked about the night before. Penny didn't move from her seat and promised herself she would never drink again.

At 1.25pm Analeise headed back home, to find that in her absence her phone had rang twice.

Adam had called her and left a very nice message to thank her for a nice evening and that he would call her later.

"What a nice guy" she thought.

Later that afternoon while she was on her hands and knees miserably cleaning her bathroom the phone rang. It was Adam.

"Hello, how are you?" he asked.

"Great" Analeise said as her face beamed. "And you?"

"I'm even better now," he charmingly said.

Analeise *was* charmed.

"I'm sorry I couldn't take your call earlier" she said, "I was round at Penny's"

"Its ok, how is she feeling today?" he asked with humour.

"Not the best" she laughed.

"So, are we still on for Monday?" Adam asked.

"Oh yes!" replied Analeise with glee "What time?"

They arranged to go for a drink at The Pheasant Pub, and he would collect her at 8.00.

Analeise was beside herself with excitement. She danced around the house for the rest of the afternoon.

Doing the housework seemed like a very easy task now!

Over the last couple of days Analeise had been walking on air. She had met the most gorgeous, witty, incredible guy ever!

She phoned every one of her friends to spread the good word about this wonderful creature.

"Don't get too keen" Daryl warned.

"Don't jump in too fast!" Pauline said.

"Be careful with your feelings!" Tracey explained, "Just don't get hurt"

Everyone was being very sincere with their advice.

"What's everyone's problem!"? Analeise complained to Penny on the Monday lunchtime as they dined in Hungry Hugh's.

"I've met Mr. Wonderful and everyone is so negative!"

"They just want to protect you, that's all" Penny tried to reason to Analeise.

She wasn't having it.

"I'm a big girl!" Analeise proudly said ignoring the signs.

"You have a lot of love to give, just don't give it to the wrong person" Penny tried to explain.

"He's perfect!" Analeise argued.

"How do you know that Ana?" Penny tried to stay calm because Analeise was starting to get into a flap! "You will just know it whenever someone right comes along. Please believe me."

Analeise put her head down. She knew she was always trying to run before she could walk; always jumping into things headfirst and making big mistakes.

"Just go tonight and have a nice time." Penny said and smiled at her desperate friend.

"Ok, will do" Analeise was resigned to the fact that everyone meant well in their warning comments.

She couldn't wait for 8.00.

He was 10 minutes late.

Analeise was sitting waiting for him ready for action. Shoes, handbag, coat..

Eventually she heard the horn pumping outside.

She then took a deep breath. "Thank god" she thought to herself. She was very close to taking a palpitation!

"Hi" she said as she jumped into his shiny blue sports car.

The R&B music was pumping from his stereo. He turned the sound down.

"Hello gorgeous" he said smiling.

Analeise just melted inside.

They went to The Pheasant Bar just outside Belfast. There was a nice mix of people; not too busy. They found a seat at the very back close to the large open fire.

Analeise chose to drink orange juice, as she wanted to keep her wits about her for the whole duration of his company.

They got along the best the whole night. They laughed, they told jokes, and they found so much in common.

Analeise knew that Adam liked her, which made her feel more at ease.

He left her back home at around 11.00.

They said their goodbyes and Adam kissed her on the cheek.

He said he would call her the following day.

Analeise was in heaven. 'At last; the perfect guy!' she thought to herself as she was getting ready for bed. "No more games!"

The following day as Analeise was dashing back to her car after spending 2 hours with a client in Omagh. Her phone rang.

Without looking to see who it was she answered with her business tone of voice.

"Hello, Ana speaking!"

"Hello Adam speaking" was the reply.

Business tone out the window Analeise smiled from ear to ear.

"How are you?" she asked.

"Good" he replied. "I'm just in the house writing some songs"

She was more than impressed.

"Nice!" she said, "I'm getting rained on in Omagh!"

"I win!" he laughed.

"You definitely win," she said. Her heart was beating faster than ever.

"Do you fancy lunch sometime this week?" he asked.

"Yes!" she quickly replied. "What about Friday? I'm always in Belfast on Fridays"

"Friday it is then!" he said. "I'll talk to you during the week to make arrangements"

Again, her day was made.

It just took that small phone call to make Analeise the happiest girl in the world. It was all she wanted. Someone incredible just like Adam to take a genuine interest in her.

CHAPTER THIRTY-TWO

*A*naleise worked really hard for the rest of the week. She opened a few new accounts and got great orders. She had a great outlook on life. She also met with her new divorce solicitor Eleanor on the Wednesday afternoon who told her that she would get the ball rolling very quickly as there were no children and no house to deal with.

"It will be very clean cut as long as he consents," she told her as she fiddled with her pen.

"As simple as that? Just sign a paper?" Analeise asked curiously.

"The courts have been closed over the summer months, so there will be a bit of a wait. I'll do my best to get a date as soon as possible." Eleanor said smiling. She had a very pleasant smile. She was very petite and very well dressed. She seemed to relate to Analeise and her stupid questions. She then shuffled all of her paperwork around her desk in a lazy attempt to tidy it.

"I'll be in touch if I need you" she said.

"What do I need to do?" Analeise clumsily asked.

"Nothing, that's what you pay me for," She said patiently, smiling.

Analeise had agreed with her that she would be paying for the whole divorce herself, as she knew that it would just prolong the agony of trying to get money out of Martin.

She would be in full control of the situation and was happy about that.

Daryl was very proud of her at the moment.

Analeise was round at her house on the Wednesday night.

"You seem very contented?" Daryl said as she made her tea and doughnuts. "Must be this new man!"

"I think I've found the man of my dreams" Analeise announced. "And being a divorcee is on the cards!!"

"Just be careful," she warned as she handed her a very warm cup of tea filled to the brim.

"I KNOW!" Analeise yelled. "Just give me a break!"

Daryl started laughing.

"Do you think you could have filled that cup up any fuller?" Analeise asked as she struggled to sip her boiling hot tea.

Daryl uncaringly kept laughing.

Analeise sipped her boiling hot tea and nearly jumped a mile!

"Jesus! I nearly lost my fucking lips there!!"

Daryl laughed even more.

"You are hectic!! I wish you would calm your head sometimes!"

Analeise saw the funny side. Daryl had a twisted sense of humour and she knew it well.

"Did you make that super boiling on purpose you sick cow?" Analeise said smirking.

"How did you guess?" Daryl laughed.

Analeise saw the funny side. Daryl was a practical joker and was always playing tricks on Analeise. She remembered years ago going on a ski holiday with her and a big crowd of friends. One evening she got back to the hotel room early and removed all the bulbs from the lights and hid behind one of the beds until Analeise came back. Whenever she eventually got back, she spent 5 minutes trying to switch on the lights. She crept into the room to phone reception.

Daryl jumped out and scared the living daylights out of her! Analeise thought she was going to take a heart attack there and then. Daryl was a joker, but was a very dear friend.

She coloured Analeise's hair that night so it would look shiny and healthy.

It looked great.

She was delighted.

Analeise and her shiny hair met Adam on the Friday afternoon outside Aero Bistro at 1.30. It was very busy and there was lots of buzz about the place.

Adam and his gorgeous smile arrived bang on time.

He kissed her gently on the cheek.

"Hope we get a table" Analeise said as she tried to hide her very obvious nerves.

"Its ok, I have it booked" Adam smiled.

Analeise was on cloud nine, she felt that this wonderful man was just whisking her off her feet and she was on another planet.

A very attractive waitress escorted them to their seats.

"I have a CD for you" Adam said as he shuffled into his denim jacket pocket.

"Who is it?" She asked excitedly.

"Me" He handed her the shiny silver disc.

She stared at it nearly expecting it to do something miraculous!

"Have a listen when you get a chance" Adam said, "Give me your honest verdict!"

"I will!" Analeise said with glee.

She was so happy. She couldn't believe that this amazing person was actually with her. Even the very attractive waitress was giving Adam the eye. He had the ability to charm the birds down from the trees.

Analeise was freefalling right in the direction of Adam Kearney and she loved every moment she spent with him.

At 3.00 they said their goodbyes and agreed to see each other on the Sunday night.

Analeise and Daryl were going to Massey's bar and nightclub and Analeise said she would meet him there.

"You are going to love him!" She excitedly said to Daryl on the phone on the way home from Lunch. "We're still going out on Sunday night?"

"Yes" said an uninterested Daryl who was patiently waiting for her next client to walk through the door. "Mrs Kelly is late again and it's going to keep me behind all day. I hate this fucking job!"

"I'm sorry babe!" Analeise said.

"Ok, see you on Sunday. I'll do your hair if you want" Daryl said, trying to sound enthusiastic.

"I'll come round to yours early" she said.

Analeise played the CD in the car that Adam had given to her.

The lyrics were so romantic

'I'm blinded by the love in your eyes'
'I know I'm someone special you don't realise'

He had the most angelic voice.

Analeise couldn't believe that he wrote this song. It was beautiful in a cheesy sort of way.

'Why was he never famous?' She thought.

She couldn't wait to see him again.

Analeise was on cloud Cuckoo Land on the Saturday and Sunday.

She went to her Mums house on Sunday for her Lunch and hardly ate a thing.

"What's wrong with you?" Her Mum asked concerned.

"I think I might be falling for someone," Analeise answered.

"Who is it!" Mum asked curiously.

"He's a musician, and he is incredible!" She said swooning.

"You're a bit of a dark horse! When did you meet him?" she asked again.

"Last week" Analeise answered.

Her Mum was none too amused!!

"Last week! Sure you hardly know him for Gods sake!"
Analeise was sorry she told her now!
"It doesn't matter!" Analeise said angrily. "I have to go!"
She stood up and put on her jacket.
Her Mum gave her a big hug and said no more about it.

Analeise wanted to look incredible for her meeting with Adam again. So she put on a pencil skirt, which skimmed every curve and a white halter neck top.

She drove to Daryl's house singing the whole way to Adam Kearney's new CD.

Daryl as usual was sitting in her towelling dressing gown smoking her 30th cigarette of the day.

"Is your hair washed?" She asked as Analeise waltzed through the door.

"Yes" She replied. "I'm fine thank you and how are you grumpy drawers!"

"Fucked off!" Daryl replied and took a long draw from her cigarette. "Its
Josh. He's a bastard. Wouldn't take Dania tonight!"

"Where is she?" Analeise asked concerned.

"With my Mum!" Daryl drew again from her cigarette.

"What's the big deal? So long as someone is minding her" Analeise looked at Daryl bemused.

"You're like Puff the magic dragon sitting there!"

"Men are all a shower of wankers you know. Just watch yourself with this Adam guy!"
Daryl warned her.

"I know, I know!" Analeise moaned.

Daryl took her time getting ready. Analeise didn't want to rush her as she had very kindly done her hair straight and shiny.

"Will I book a taxi now?" Analeise shouted up the stairs patiently to Daryl who was knee high in clothing.

"Yes, give me 10 minutes" Daryl shouted down the stairs hassled.

When they arrived at Massey's it was totally hiving. Finding anyone there would be like finding a needle in a haystack.

"Lets go to the loo!" Analeise suggested.

"We've only fucking got here!" Daryl complained, "You got the runs or something?"

"No!" Analeise shouted "Its so we can see who is here!"

"Wine?" asked Daryl as she pointed to the direction of the bar.

Analeise stood in the crowd and didn't recognise a soul.

Whenever Daryl came back from the bar she pointed to the direction of seats at the other end of the bar.

"The boys are here!" she shouted into Analeise's ear.

"What boys?" She asked as she was being ushered through the feisty crowd.

Whenever they arrived at the seats they found a whole load of old familiar faces;

Bob Robertson and Barry McAllister who were Chris Drummond's friends.

They were very old friends from the crowd that Analeise and Daryl ran around with whenever they were in their early twenties. They were real charmers and complete slags! Very good looking, successful guys who broke the hearts of many women. It took them years to eventually settle down. Daryl and Analeise were just glad to be their friends.

Daryl had kept in touch with them all of these years. Barrie McAllister hadn't seen Analeise since her last date with Chris.

"How the hell are you big girl!!" he jumped up and gave her a bear hug.

Daryl was delighted to see him too as it had been a while.

"Where are the rest of them?" Daryl asked curiously.

"They all faded!" Bob answered.

They had been at a stag weekend in Scotland for him with about 6 others. He was getting married the following week. They decided to end their mad weekend in Massey's.

Analeise felt a tingle on the back of her neck and turned around expecting to see Adam.

"Hello Chris!" she said shocked.

There he was looking every bit as Analeise had dreamed about since the night of the formal.

"How are you Analeise?" He stared into her eyes.

"Good" Was all she could say.

He sat down beside his buddy and patted the seat beside him.

"Have a seat!" he smiled.

"Its ok, I'm supposed to be meeting someone here" She said very uneasily and continued to scope around the room.

"New man!" Chris said cheekily.

"Suppose you could say that" Analeise answered quickly.

Then out of the blue appeared a very sexy Adam dressed in his usual denim attire.

He kissed her on the cheek.

"Everyone" she announced "This is Adam"

Adam shyly raised his hand.

Bob and Barrie raised their drinks and Chris stood up like a complete gentleman and shook Adams hand.

Analeise felt a little bit awkward.

"I'll let you get back to your friends and I'll see you later" Adam said to Analeise and kissed her on the cheek again.

It was obvious he was a little bit intimidated.

"Who is James Dean?" Chris asked.

Everyone laughed.

"His name is Adam!" Analeise said angrily.

"He 'is the one and only'" Daryl said sniggering.

"You're all a shower of wankers!" Analeise said and stormed off to the toilets.

When she returned Chris was chatting up an attractive blonde with big jugs, Daryl was deep in conversation with Bob about the joys of parenthood and Barrie McAllister was on the phone to his girlfriend in London.

"Great!" she thought.

"Is anyone going downstairs to the Disco Frisco?" Analeise asked.

"Me!" Daryl stood up.

The two of them eagerly bounced down the stairs to the sounds of the 'Nolan Sisters'.

The bar of the nightclub was wall-to-wall desperado Sugar Daddies!

"Talent's good" smirked Daryl.

Analeise was in fits of laughter.

"I think we'll have a good night" she said, "Music is good!"

They got their drinks and found a spot close to the dance floor.

Around 10 minutes later Bob, Barrie and Chris arrived and walked in the direction of Daryl and Analeise who were being chatted up by 'Del Boy and Rodney'.

Analeise felt uncomfortable in the company of Chris as a single girl. She knew she would just have to get used to it as she had realised that Chris just wanted her friendship and a few friendly 'shags' from time to time. She pretended to him it was all she wanted too. She couldn't possibly let him know her true feelings for him. Anyway she was with the new leading man in her life now. Where was he anyway?

Del boy and Rodney eventually got the hint that they were getting nowhere with Daryl and Analeise whenever the lads arrived. In fact they thought the girls were ever so slightly taking the piss!

"Not click then?" Chris whispered into Analeise's ear.

"Leave me alone" She was agitated "Where is Pamela Anderson then?"

Chris laughed.

"What about your girlfriend Christine?" Analeise asked curiously.

"What girlfriend?" He smiled. "Where is your boyfriend?"

Analeise shrugged.

She walked around the room pretending to look for someone, but really she needed desperately to get away from Chris for lots of reasons. She then stumbled upon Adam who was with his two friends David and Mark.

"There you are my sweet!" he said as he kissed her on the cheek.

"This is Analeise, but better known as Ana," he announced proudly to his curious friends who couldn't keep their eyes off her tits. "This is David and Peter."

"Hello" Analeise said shyly, trying desperately hard to cover her breasts with both of her arms making her look distinctively like the Hunchback of Notre Dam.

"Where are your buddies?" He asked looking nosily around the room.

"Over there" She pointed in the direction of the little dark nook they had chosen earlier on.

"Drink?" He asked politely.

"No, I've got one over there thanks!" Analeise pointed again to the dark cave at the back of the room.

"Not staying then," Adam said quietly.

"What?" Analeise couldn't hear him.

"Nothing" Adam replied awkwardly. "See you later on I hope"

"Y-Yes" Analeise replied quickly and walked back to Daryl and the lads.

"Blown out?" Bob asked Analeise as Chris grinned like a Cheshire cat.

"No!" She replied defensively. "I'm with Daryl tonight"

"Can we watch then?" He laughed.

Analeise didn't get the 'in house' lesbian joke and fired all of them a dirty look.

"We'll pay 500 quid to watch you two get down to some steamy action."

Chris said as he pointed to Analeise who was horrified and Daryl who was laughing her ass off.

"Five hundred each!" Daryl said. "Or a ski holiday"

Analeise genuinely wasn't sure if the boys were serious or not. She truly secretly hoped they were only joking.

Daryl held Analeise's hand and stroked it for a joke.

"I'll pay £3.50 for that!" Chris said laughing.

Then Analeise saw the funny side to it. They were only joking, of course they were. They were all friends at the end of the day.

Analeise felt very uneasy being in the company of Chris, especially knowing there was someone else in the room that she had a genuine interest in.

She felt a little confused.

Bob and Daryl were tripping the light fantastic on the dance floor, giving it heaps!

Analeise felt it was time to pay a little more attention to Adam. At least he wasn't making disrespectful remarks towards her.

This time when she walked over he was deep in conversation with a pretty girl wearing a very short skirt.

"Hello again!" He smiled cheekily. "How long are you going to give me this time?"

Analeise laughed. "I'm sorry, but I'm back for good now"

"Good!" He said, "This is Denise, a very good friend of mine"

"Pleased to meet you" Analeise said as she raised her glass.

"And you!" she replied with a kind smile.

She kissed Adam on the cheek and said her goodbyes.

"I used to be in a band with her," Adam explained to a slightly jealous Analeise.

"Is that all?" She asked curiously, smiling.

Adam grinned from ear to ear. Analeise didn't probe any more.

They decided to go to a quieter part of the room where they could talk more.

Analeise fancied Adam so much now; she couldn't resist his humour, his smile, his very winning personality and his ability to keep her amused without her even wondering about Chris, or in fact if Daryl had died and was in Dance floor heaven!

The night was coming to an end now and Analeise wanted to carry on talking to Adam. She dreaded the lights coming on. So she excused herself and went to the toilets to check just in case she had swallowed the ugly bug pill in the duration of the evening.

She was fine, but re-touched her make up just to be on the safe side!

When she walked out of the loo's Adam was standing waiting for her. She couldn't believe it. What a gentleman. She then lost complete self-control and walked over to him and started to kiss him very passionately. He tasted amazing, his lips were so soft, so pure, and she couldn't get enough of him. Meanwhile the lights had come on. When he eventually came up for air all of Analeise's friends were standing right behind her!

He smiled shyly at them.

Analeise turned around to find the two boys and Chris standing staring at her.

She felt like a schoolgirl caught kissing the boys behind the bicycle sheds!

"What do you want?" She asked cheekily, trying to hide her humiliation.

"We're going, what are you doing?" Bob asked.

Analeise looked like an alien with no lips, all of her make up that she had previously applied to perfection 5 minutes ago was smeared all over Adams face.

"Going!" Analeise answered slightly embarrassed. "There is no need for these white-bright lights!"

"See you upstairs" Chris said, "We're going for a burger!"

This felt bizarre for Analeise.

"Better let you go then" Adam wasn't giving her eye contact. Analeise was very self-conscious about her smeared off make-up.

"I hate this part of the night, don't you?" Analeise said as they walked up the stairs.

"Yes, I'd better find my friends" Adam replied. "Can I call you tomorrow?"

These were the words she longed to hear.

"Yes that would be great" she replied with a smile.

He kissed her softly on the lips and they said their goodbyes.

As Analeise floated outside Daryl and the boys were waiting patiently for her.

"Where were you sneak?" Daryl asked laughing.

"Where were you Ginger Rogers?" Analeise asked as she fumbled into her bag in a desperate attempt to find lip-gloss.

"Well" asked Chris "How's lover boy?"

Analeise was really embarrassed about the whole thing happening right in front of Chris Drummond.

"He's not my lover!" She snapped in defence and walked on.

"Didn't look like that to me!" He caught up with her. "You had him pinned against the wall! You're a wild animal Magowan!"

"What do you want Chris!" Analeise looked at him.

"A burger!" he laughed.

"You're drunk!!" Analeise realised she was exhausted and walked away from Chris and joined the others who were in deep conversation about their favourite foods.

"You ok?" Daryl asked, concerned how her confused friend might feel.

"Sort of" she shrugged. "I'm not hungry."

"We'll just get a taxi home now," Daryl announced and suggested she might make one of her midnight delights back home.

She directed Analeise towards a taxi rank.

As they were all saying goodbye Chris approached Analeise and gave her a kiss on the cheek. "Call you tomorrow" he whispered in her ear.

Analeise was horrified. Why now did he decide to call her after all these months? Was it because it might be a challenge for him to win her from another man? Or was he just trying to fuck her off completely?

"Whatever!" She replied and stormed into the taxi rank.

"Its gonna be about 20 minutes!" Daryl announced.

The words were falling on deaf ears, as Analeise's mind was somewhere else completely.

"What's wrong glamour puss?" Daryl looked at her very flat friend.

"You know something Analeise said dreamily "I'm in Limbo Central right now waiting for the 'Prince Charming Express' to come sweep me off my feet!"

"No you're not!" Daryl said "You're in a fucking taxi rank waiting for a sweaty taxi man to take you home."

"Chris just said that he would call me!" Analeise said staring into outer space.

"Aren't you happy with Adam?" She asked.

"Yes, I really like Adam, but I really like Chris!" She said slowly, hoping to find the answer at the end of her sentence.

"Chris is a waste of time" Daryl warned "Forget him!"

Analeise really tried, but couldn't.

Why did he have such a strong hold on her?

Adam was wonderful.

She must try and put Chris Drummond out of her head once and for all!

CHAPTER THIRTY-THREE

*A*naleise had to get up early the next morning as she had and appointment in Dundalk, about 65 miles away from Belfast.

She stayed as usual in Daryl's spare room. She left a note for her to thank her for her hospitality and left her to snore and make the most of her day off.

Analeise's head felt like someone had been drilling into it all night. She stopped at a garage for a takeaway coffee and doughnut.

"Healthy" she thought to herself as she stuffed the soft doughnut down her fat neck in 2 mouthfuls!

When she arrived at the salon, the dizzy receptionist informed her "Sorry Analeise, Barbara called and said she couldn't see you today" and shrugged.

Analeise was speechless.

She stared at the poor girl for a minute or so. Her mind went completely blank, then in a moment of rage said "Do you know I drove down here specially?"

The receptionist shrugged again.

"Sorry" was all she could say.

"Barbara will be a long time waiting for me to come back here!" Analeise snapped and stormed out the door tripping up on the carpet on the way out!

"This place is a death-trap!!" she shouted pointing at the frayed piece of carpet trying to hide her embarrassment.

Two blank faced women with moustaches (in obvious need of a

good waxing!!) sat in the reception area watched in amazement at Analeise.

She got back into her car and couldn't stop the tears from pumping out of her eyes.

It wasn't the fact that she had driven for nearly two hours to get there. She felt so worthless. She called her dear colleague Tara Potter to offload her woes.

"What a bitch!" she screamed "I was going to call you anyway to cheer you up!" Tara sounded excited.

"Please don't tell me you have a new job!" Analeise pleaded.

"Better" Tara teased. "How do you fancy going to New York?"

Analeise screamed in her most high-pitched glass breaking voice.

"I'll take that is a yes?" Tara laughed.

"When?" She asked.

"My friend Ricky from London works for a company that gives tickets for Virgin Airlines to very good clients and he had a couple spare" she explained to a very ecstatic Analeise.

"Free?" Analeise shouted.

"All we have to pay for is accommodation!" Tara said.

"I'm there!!" She said with glee. "Just need to clear the time off with Kevin! Shouldn't be a problem anyway!"

"Good, can I leave that one with you then?" Tara asked.

"Leave it to me!" Analeise said. "When are they for?"

"Two weeks time" Tara replied.

The journey back home didn't seem as bad now until she got a phone call from Eleanor the solicitor.

"Hi Analeise, just to let you know that we still haven't had any word back from your husband, so it will be the end of November before we can get a court date."

"Bastard!" Analeise thought.

"Ok, I'll give him a ring just to remind him, thanks for calling" She said politely.

She tried really hard not to let it bother her. She wondered why Martin hadn't bothered his arse to sign the papers.

"He always was a lazy bastard," she thought.

She phoned Kevin just to confirm the time off with Tara.

"Hello there Analeise" He said in a chirpy tone.

She was delighted to hear he was in a good mood. It would make life a little bit easier.

It was a doddle! No problem, Kevin was a sweetheart.

Now Analeise had a great adventure to look forward to in a couple of weeks.

While she was in a good mood, she decided to call Martin and gently remind him of his great task of signing a piece of paper!

"I must 'hoke' it out, I have it lying around somewhere!" He answered dryly.

"Find it," she said firmly. "It's not much to ask of you, is it? I'm not exactly taking your last penny or anything Martin. Its very reasonable. It's a signature for gods sake!"

"Keep your wig on. I said I'd find it!" Martin slammed down the phone.

Analeise was pissed off with him. Why did everything concerning Martin have to be a major drama?

Analeise arrived back home that afternoon and got wired into some paperwork in the house whenever her landline rang.

"Hey Kid, how are you?"

Analeise recognised the voice. It was Chris Drummond.

"Hello, how are you?" she replied nervously.

"Good thanks, was just thinking about you there." He said slowly.

Her heart was racing.

"What are you doing?" she asked.

"I'm in Lisburn, can I call round?" He announced. "Would love to see your new house!"

Analeise felt the blood draining from her face.

"I'm just doing some paperwork, I suppose you can," she said casually.

She was crapping herself. She came off the phone and ran to the mirror to check her face for any flaws.

She touched up her lipstick, but didn't want to do any more to herself in case it looked like she was trying too hard.

Then she ran into the bathroom to see what state it was in. Didn't want any pant liners, fake tans or hair removal products to be lying around. She was naturally beautiful of course!!

At least she wanted Chris to think that!

She needed to use the toilet but refrained just in case he arrived while she was mid-flow!

She walked around the house not knowing what to do. She wanted to look ever so casual.

15 minutes later she was wondering if he had gotten lost or something.

She didn't want to call him. She didn't want him to know that she was awaiting his arrival.

Another 30 minutes passed.

Where the hell was he?

She continued working on her weekly expenses but not concentrating. She couldn't stop wondering if he was at the wrong address.

"Fuck it!" she said to herself and dialled his number.

"Sorry Kid, meant to call you. I had to go on home. Maybe we'll meet up sometime?"

Secretly Analeise was disappointed and pissed off at getting herself into an almighty flap. The bastard was probably just playing a game to see if she would be available for him. Analeise just couldn't see the wood for the trees!

"Ok, give me a call sometime" she said.

She didn't really know what she was saying because she was so embarrassed

Anyway she had Adam. What did she want from Chris anyway?

She dialled his number but got no reply.

She left a chirpy, but not too 'desperate to see him' message.

4 hours, 17 minutes and 35 seconds later (Hey, who's counting!) she was driving round to Daryl's house. She suddenly remembered that she hadn't heard from Adam.

"Maybe he's dead!" Daryl said with a smirk.

Ignoring her twisted sense of humour Analeise wondered if she should call again.

"He's a wanker anyway!" Daryl announced.

"Where the hell did that come from!!"? Analeise shouted.

"Probably got the hump because of Chris," she answered shovelling a chocolate éclair into her mouth!

"Why?" Analeise was puzzled.

"He felt a bit intimidated in our company" she replied with a mouth full of fresh cream.

"Anyway I'm going to New York in two weeks!!" Analeise proudly announced.

"I don't know what you're worried about anyway. It has been a few hours, he's probably busy!" Daryl said uniterested "New York sounds much more exciting!"

Analeise knew she was right but still wondered why Adam hadn't returned her call.

CHAPTER THIRTY-FOUR

The two weeks running up to Analeise's trip to New York, she couldn't stop wondering about Adam. She had called him a few days after the first call with still no reply. Everyone told her to just forget him. Which she tried desperately to do. She was so confused. The last few months were like a human whirlwind. She flew head first from one disaster to another! Chris. Adam. Daniel. Assholes!

"What's his problem?" she asked Tara when they were in the airport. "Is he just lazy? Did I do something wrong?"

"No answer is your answer!" She replied coolly. "I'm reading this great book on how to 'get in' to a mans mind!"

"I think I might need to borrow that book!" She replied.

He was so nice. He seemed so keen. What happened?

She was so looking forward to this short break. Her head was pickled.

Tara and Analeise flew first of all to London that evening and stayed with Tara's dear friend Ricky who supplied the tickets for them.

They called in for some take-away pizza on the way back to his house and got wired into a bottle of white wine when they got there.

Ricky- all 18 stone of him was totally adorable. He looked like Humpty Dumpty and reminded Analeise of a very bad blind date she had a few months ago! He was single and Analeise knew he had the 'hots' for Tara. What guy would just give away two free tickets to New York?

Analeise was exhausted and retired to the spare room around 11 o'clock shortly followed by Tara.

"He so fancies you!" Analeise whispered to Tara when she got into the big spare bed.

"No, he's just a friend" she said innocently.

"I've got one eye on the door." Analeise sniggered "That big boy will be in here before this night is over you mark my words babydoll!" She sung. "My first my Last, My everything!"

Tara wasn't having it. She completely ignored her pulling the entire duvet off Analeise.

First thing the next morning (No appearance in the middle of the night from Humpty!)

He left them off at Heathrow Airport where they would get their Virgin Atlantic flight.

"Take care you!" He said as he kissed Tara on the cheek. Analeise didn't get one.

"Nice to meet you" he said as he shook her hand half-heartedly.

Very Exciting!! 3 hours later they boarded the big Jumbo Jet!

7 hours later they arrived at JFK Airport.

They were beside themselves with excitement.

They got a taxi to their hotel on Eighth Avenue.

"Yellow cabs, can you believe it!!" Tara said with sheer and utter excitement as they stepped into an 'Indian Take-away Flavoured Cab'.

The unimpressed Taxi driver pretended not to speak English as Analeise had asked, "Where is a good place to eat?"

Silence

Not to be put off in any way, she continued "Any nice restaurants?" Silence.

"No worries, I'm sure we'll find somewhere!" Tara said, trying not to laugh.

Neither of them had ever been to New York before so the whole thing was such an experience.

Their hotel room was huge. It had two double beds on one side of the room and a living room area on the other side with a couple of two-seater sofa's facing each other, coffee table in between and a very large television up against the wall.

They were a bit wrecked when they arrived, but decided to take full advantage of the 'Big Apple' and all it had to offer.

"No point in sleeping!" Analeise said trying to shrug off the jet lag.

It was 10.00pm in London time, but only 5.00pm New York time, so they decided to go out and grab some action.

"Lets go for an adventure!" Tara said as she looked out the window of the 23rd floor.

They went outside and took a walk up West 34th Street admiring all the shops along the way.

"Macy's!" Tara shouted at the top of her voice like she had just found the Holy Grail!

The two girls ran towards the entrance like they had never seen a department store before. They were like a couple of children in a toyshop as they walked around the cosmetics, which took over the whole of the ground floor.

By 7.00 they were absolutely shattered, so decided to head back to their Hotel and have an early one. They planned their whole day ahead on the long walk back.

They were up with the birds the next morning.

At 7am Tara decided to go out for coffees while Analeise had a shower.

When Tara arrived back they both laughed at the fact of them being up so early. Tara was never the best of risers in the morning. There was no doubt that they hadn't given themselves time to adjust to the five hours time difference.

The two of them were ready for action at 8.00am.

They headed out for some breakfast. They found a little diner in the corner of the block. Tara had pancakes while Analeise decided to have bagels and cream cheese, which went to her stomach like a lump of lead!!

It was still a bit early for the shops so they headed for the Empire State Building and did the tour. They waited in the queue for an hour but when they finally got to the top they really knew that it was worth the wait. The views were exquisite.

Then afterwards after a Hot Dog from a street vendor (Analeise insisted they have a New York Hot Dog!) they got an open top Bus to take them on a tour of the city. They got off at Battery Park and decided to go over to Staten Island and then take a ferry to see the Statue of Liberty.

By now it was 3.30 and they were shattered, but nothing was going to take them back. They wanted to keep on going.

Analeise was feeling a little bit light headed. She wasn't sure if it was the fact that she was on the top of the Empire State Building or on a very choppy ferry journey out to the Statue. She was a bit over-whelmed and hoped she wouldn't take a panic attack. They went bargain shopping at Century 21, which took another 2 hours.

"Lets have something to eat!" Analeise suggested hoping it might make her feel better.

"We just have to go to Victoria's secret! I know there is one on Broadway somewhere!" Tara said as she fussed with all her bags.

"Have you any idea how many miles Broadway actually is!" Analeise said as they stopped walking. "I can't walk anymore Tara I am going to die!"

"Ok Granny lets get you some food!" Tara said.

They got a bus to take them back up town and they got off at Central Park.

"Isn't it so romantic!" Analeise said as she gazed around her in admiration. She dreamily walked over to the horses and buggy's to get a better view and at that moment stepped into a big pile of Horseshit!

"Shit!" she shouted as she tried to scrape it on the footpath.

The guy in the front of the cart just looked at her and shrugged.

"Good luck coming your way my friend!" Tara said as she laughed. "Oh the romance indeed!" she continued to mock.

"I stink now!" Analeise moaned as she slid her foot up and down the pavement " Are they not supposed to clean up after them?"

"I think that is a fresh one!" Tara continued to laugh.

They decided to call it a day, so went back to the hotel to change for dinner.

Glad rags on, they headed for Times Square for something to eat.

They decided to try the restaurant on the 82nd floor at the Marriot Hotel appropriately named 'The View'.

Going up in the elevator was like being on a rocket ship!

Analeise's head was spinning around like a top by now.

When they eventually arrived it was very elegant. The restaurant was circular with windows the whole way around showing off the stunning views of the city.

They were ushered to their seats at a window.

By now Analeise felt like she was in space. It was a surreal experience.

They got their menus and nearly choked.

"Twenty dollars for a cocktail!!" Tara said as her eyes sat out on stalks.

"Fuck it" Analeise said, "We're on our holidays!"

They ordered two Cosmopolitans.

When they arrived, they were in small, elegant cocktail glasses.

"Jesus!" Tara said, "One swoop and that'll be gone!"

Analeise laughed. "Just sip and make it last!"

They had a look at the food menu and were very disappointed. They were starving and wanted a big 'all American' burger.

"No burgers or chips not even club sandwiches!" Tara stared at the menu in hope of something relatively tasty.

"Twenty five fucking dollars for a spring roll starter!!"

At this stage Tara's arm was starting to look pretty tasty for Analeise. She was ravenous.

"I could eat the beard off Moses!" Analeise moaned.

She was developing a pretty bad headache now and her dizziness was getting worse.

"C'mon then" Analeise said, "Lets drink up and go!"

They put 50 dollars on the table and walked out.

A table of elegant Italians who invited them for drinks stopped them.

Tempting as it was, they were on a mission for food. So they refrained.

They searched for a pizzeria.

"There we go" Analeise said with joy as they walked into Greene's Pizzeria on the corner of West 43rd Street.

It was the tastiest thing ever. They were silent the whole way through their meal munching and gnawing their way through 2 very large pizzas

It had been a long day so they decided to head back. Even though it was only 9 o'clock in the evening, it was really 2am for them!

The next morning bright and breezy they decided that they had seen enough sites and that it was time for shopping.

They went to Macy's, walked along 5th Avenue, and went to Saks. They desperately searched for Bloomingdale's. By the time they found it; Analeise's tiredness and dizziness had started to kick in again. She was fighting it and refused to let it spoil her short trip to this wonderful city.

Arms full of bags of goodies they found themselves back on 5th Avenue and decided to find Tiffany's.

They were having a ball.

Blocks, and blocks of shops later there it was!

"Isn't it beautiful!" Tara said with excitement as she fumbled to find her camera.

"Take my picture outside it!!" she asked Analeise.

Analeise felt completely nauseous but again ignored it.

When they went inside they looked for the silver jewellery.

Tara saw the most amazing silver cross on a chain.

"How much is it?" She asked the uppity assistant.

"Twenty" she replied.

Analeise and Tara looked at each other in great relief.

"Thousand dollars" the assistant finished her sentence smugly and with a false smile.

"Where is the silver section?" asked Tara who sounded like a complete cheap skate!

"Fifth floor" the assistant said without looking at them.

"Snotty bitch" Analeise muttered under her breath.

"More elevators!" Tara moaned.

Whenever they got to the 'cheap' floor Analeise felt so bad that she had to go and sit down on a very comfortable sofa. Tara was running around trying this and that. She was completely wrecking the head of a very helpful assistant who was hoping to get great commission from her big spend!

Analeise wasn't really sure how she could cope with the rest of the day.

After Tara purchased 2 pairs of earrings and a necklace they stepped outside.

"Why didn't you buy anything?" she asked as she waved her infamous blue bags in the air.

Analeise couldn't see a thing in front of her. She just said "I think I'm going to faint".

Luckily Tara was there to break her fall.

Analeise collapsed into Tara's weary arms.

Tara panicked, as she was now responsible for her friend and all of their shopping.

A kind gentleman stopped and asked Tara if he could be of any assistance. "No!" Tara snapped as she thought that he might mug her.

Onlookers stared at the couple and probably thought that Analeise was drunk.

"Versace, Prada, Gucci" Whispered the dodgy looking bloke holding what looked like a pram with a blanket over the top.

"What?" shouted a horrified Tara who at this stage was clutching to her Tiffany bag like her life depended on it.

He pointed down at the soggy blanket.

"That's not Gucci!" she said dismissively hoping the man would disappear.

Analeise didn't know where she was whenever she came round.

At this stage Tara was telling the 'fake handbag seller' to sling his hook.

"No!" shouted Analeise who was totally disorientated.

"Its bags!" Analeise (Who was sitting on the pavement by now) tried to explain to Tara.

"Show them!" she demanded to the man.

"Come round the corner" he beckoned and pointed to a small alleyway.

"Later!" Analeise said as she struggled to get up.

The man and his cart scurried away quickly like a rat up a drainpipe.

"It's a different world here!" Tara said, her cheeks looking very flushed.

Analeise didn't know whether to laugh or cry.

"I need tea!" she said to her dear protective friend.

"I need a cart like his for all this shit!!" Tara said exhausted looking down at all of their purchases.

They went to the nearest diner possible for some tea, rest and relaxation.

"You are a walking, living disaster!" Tara said as she watched her friend shovel mouthfuls of burger down her neck.

"I'm not used to this amount of excitement in a couple of days babe!" she replied slowly.

They both realised that they tried to cram one week into the very short time they had in New York but enjoyed every minute! They promised they would do it again some day without it being in Fast Forward!

That evening they had dinner in the hotel and had a very early night.

The next morning they headed back to the airport with all of their purchases crammed into their suitcases.

CHAPTER THIRTY-FIVE

*A*naleise needed a few days to get her system back to normal after their 'whirlwind' trip to New York.

After she had arrived home she had received a phone call from Adam apologising for his behaviour.

Of course she forgave him and they went out for a drink the following evening. He was even more charming than before. He gave her a cock and bull story that he was so incredibly busy that he lost touch with everyone and he would never do it again.

She had suggested to him that maybe she would cook him dinner that weekend.

He agreed.

"You can't cook to save your life!!" Daryl said whenever Analeise broke the news of 'the seduction' to her on the phone.

"I'm not that bad!" Analeise snapped.

"Just make sure you know the number of a good Chinese!!" Daryl laughed much to her disgust.

Analeise decided to call Tracey for some culinary advice, as she was always entertaining for Maurice's friends.

"Are you gonna make him a toastie!!" she laughed.

"Good one!!" Analeise said trying to be up beat.

"When is he coming round?" She asked.

"Friday night" She replied half-heartedly. "I don't know why I asked. It just slipped out!"

"Make something easy like Chicken" Tracey said.

"Chicken Kiev?" she asked.

Tracey burst out laughing.

Analeise was humiliated. 'Am I that bad?' she thought to herself.

"What about a tin of Spaghetti Hoops!!" Tracey said still laughing.

"Cheeky Fucker!!" Analeise mumbled. "I'm sure I'll sort something out!"

"We'll have to meet for lunch soon!" Tracey said.

"What about next week sometime" Analeise suggested.

"Next week it is!" Tracey said "Good luck with La seduction!!"

Analeise decided that Friday night would be 'The Night'.

She hadn't shagged him yet and thought that this would be the perfect opportunity.

She wasn't the most experienced whenever it came to buying 'real' food. So she gave herself plenty of time in the supermarket to plan something wonderful.

She bought 'pre-made' crab cakes for starter, fresh chicken breasts, stock cubes and spices, some vegetables and a clove of garlic and decided to conjure up some home made chicken delight for main course. A strawberry cheesecake for dessert and then he would be hers! (This was the plan anyway!)

On the Friday afternoon Analeise finished her work a little early in order to prepare for her big night in!

She changed her sheets, cleaned her house from top to bottom, and had a big long bubble bath with her favourite Chanel fragrance.

She had laid out a Basque, stockings and suspenders to wear under her slinky dress. The night was planned from start to finish.

When Analeise stepped out of the bath, she put on her dressing gown and threw a towel around her hair. She went into the kitchen and stared at the two raw chicken breasts in anticipation.

She phoned her Mum.

"What should I do with these things?" she asked sounding ever so slightly frustrated.

"Pan fry them in stock then add some flavourings" Her Mum said casually.

"What else should I make?" Analeise asked as she was rummaging through her cupboards.

"Vegetables and some potato wedges or maybe roasties?" Analeise's Mum was the most patient person in the world.

Analeise rolled her eyes and wished she had a magic wand.

"Just do your chicken slowly!" Her Mum added as she was putting the phone down.

Analeise decided to 'slowly' cook the chicken in a pan as she was getting herself prepared.

She went up the stairs to dry her hair, do her make-up and put on her underwear.

20 minutes later as Analeise was trying to 'clip' up her Basque the doorbell went.

She panicked and rushed to look out of the window.

"Oh Shit!" she said to herself.

Adam was 15 minutes early.

She threw her bathrobe on again and ran down the stairs like a woman possessed.

"Nice!" Adam said cheekily as Analeise opened the door.

"You're early!" she said curtly.

He handed her a bottle of wine and walked into the lounge.

Analeise ran up the stairs again to finish putting on her underwear.

She was really struggling to clip the top of her stockings to the Basque whenever Adam shouted up the stairs "Something is burning!"

Analeise was having major problems by now so decided to abandon the whole 'stockings' thing.

Then Adam walked up the stairs into her bedroom to find Analeise with Basque on removing her stockings.

She was mortified!

"GET OUT!" She shouted in complete humiliation and ran to shut the door behind him.

Adam was a little bit embarrassed and wondered what the hell she was doing.

He stood outside the room and said, "I'm sorry, but there is a burning smell coming from the kitchen, will I just check it?"

"YES!" she yelled.

"Oh fucking hell!!" she said to herself and removed her sexy Basque.

She put on plain, ordinary bra and knickers and stepped into her dress.

She tried really hard to hide her embarrassment as she walked down the stairs to find Adam trying to surgically remove the crab cakes from the baking tray. The kitchen was a haze of blue smoke.

"Holy Fuck!" she said. Her face was beaming now.

"What were they before they burned to death?" Adam said trying to hide embarrassment all around.

"This is your fault" Analeise said, "You were too early!"

"I'm glad I was or it would have been the fire brigade meeting me at the door!"

He said with a smile.

Analeise vision of the night of seduction had flown out the window now.

"Will we be able to salvage what is in the pan?" Adam asked.

"Just go next door and I will bring you in a beer!" She said as she shuffled Adam into the next room.

Analeise went back into the carnage in the kitchen to find that the pan-fried chicken was now starting to become the pan!

It was stuck like glue!

She tried to 'chip' it away and scrape off the burnt bits.

The potatoes and the vegetables were done earlier on so Analeise blasted them in the microwave to heat them up.

She put the 'best looking' piece of chicken on Adam's plate followed by soggy, overdone vegetables and potatoes.

Not wanting to spoil a good night Analeise called Adam into the kitchen where she had the table set.

Her cheeks were flushed and she had a very 'stressed' look on her face.

"I had problems with the chicken" she apologised before Adam took his seat.

"I can see" Adam was finding the whole thing quite amusing much to her displeasure.

Analeise sat down to eat her dinner. She couldn't enjoy it at all.

"So when did you become a professional chef?" Adam asked with a straight face.

The two of them just laughed.

Analeise just had to write the whole thing off, as she couldn't hide her embarrassment for much longer. She explained to him that cooking was not her best point and she was sorry she suggested cooking.

"Mmmmm, delicious!" Adam said and kissed her on the cheek whenever he finished his cremated meal.

"I would have been better just ordering a pizza. I'm never going to be able to cook!"

She apologised again.

"It was the effort that I appreciate" Adam said charmingly.

They went into the next room with their drinks. Analeise couldn't keep her eyes off him.

He kissed her gently on the mouth, then one thing led to another.

Before long he was starting to undo her sensible underwear.

She had consumed a considerable amount of wine and the touch of Adam was highly intoxicating.

They made love on her sofa and it was incredible.

They lay in each other's arms for about a half an hour later, just talking and laughing about the earlier events of the evening.

Then Adam started to dress.

"Would you like to stay, or have another drink?" Analeise asked, hoping he could not resist her electric charm.

"No, I'll have to get on I have an early start." He lied.

She threw her dress on quickly.

Adam walked to the front door and kissed her again.

"Thanks for dinner" he said.

"It was hardly dinner!" Analeise smiled.

"Thanks for the burnt offerings!" He said again.

Then without suggesting another date he left.

Again Analeise had weird, mixed feelings.

She then went into the kitchen to tidy up. It was only 9.30 and wondered why Adam had to go so early.

The next morning Penny called her to remind her of her famous Halloween Party.

"Guess who I cooked for last night?" Analeise asked her.

"Let me guess. Adam perhaps?" She replied.

"I gave him burnt food, I can't believe it." Analeise said. Her face blushing at the very thought of it.

"Martin always told me that a woman couldn't be good at everything!" Penny said laughing. "Lets say that you are better at other things."

"I should never have offered to cook. I knew it would be a disaster!" Analeise said reflecting on the night previous.

"We consummated our relationship though!" Analeise announced.

"Didn't need to know." Penny said. "Was it not a bit early?"

"You are getting more and more like my Mum!" Analeise snapped.

"I just want you to be happy my sweet!" Penny said light heartedly. "Anyway, what are you dressing up as?"

"A chef!" She laughed.

She took a drive into Belfast centre for a spot of shopping.

As she was crossing the road at the city hall she saw a familiar face walking out of Marks and Spencer.

Analeise tried to compose herself.

"We'll have to stop meeting like this!" Chris said with a huge smile. He looked stunning.

"You are just going to have to stop stalking me!" Analeise replied her face beaming.

"What are you doing?" He asked.

"Just doing some shopping." She said casually.

"What about James Dean?" he asked smiling.

"His name is Adam!" She replied shaking her head. She was also shaking inside.

Chris just laughed.

"I'd better go" He said "Meeting a friend for lunch"

"Female or Male?" Analeise asked curiously.

"My mate Barrie!" He said much to her relief.

"Next time you're in Dungannon give me a call. We could do something." He said suggestively as he raised his eyebrows.

She knew exactly what he meant. Tempting as it was, she really wanted to make it work with Adam.

At least he didn't want her just for sex!

That was what she thought anyway.

They said their goodbyes and yet again Chris was implanted in Analeise's very confused head.

CHAPTER THIRTY-SIX

A few days had passed and Analeise was looking forward to Penny's Halloween Party. She decided that she would dress up as a red devil as she had a red dress, shoes and lipstick. She just had to borrow red horns from Dania!

It was easy and hassle free.

She wondered if she should invite Adam or not. He was in her bad books again as he hadn't phoned her. She decided to just leave it. She couldn't cope with another drama if he would answer his phone or not!

"Well, how did the 'big' night of seduction go?" asked Daryl when Analeise called up to her house for the horns.

"Don't ask!" Analeise rolled her eyes. "Lets just say I won't be doing that in a hurry soon!"

"How are things?" Daryl asked curiously.

"Haven't heard a word since!" Analeise said as she twiddled with the plastic red horns.

"Maybe you have poisoned him once and for all and he is dead!" Daryl laughed.

"I can't for the love of God wonder why I get to meet all these disastrous men?" Analeise said. "What did I do so wrong?"

"There are a lot of fish in the sea. Its just finding the right one for you that's all!" Daryl said light heartedly.

"Fish! I have only met frogs!" Analeise said smiling. "I don't think I could be bothered anymore. It's too much hassle. Maybe I'm just trying too hard!"

"I don't know how you are bothered. I'd prefer a good book!" Daryl said.

Analeise envied that. She wished that she would be satisfied with just a book. Something inside of her strived for something more than that. It was like a machine that kept bouncing back for more. Maybe she was just addicted to the pain.

On the Friday night Analeise dressed as a very sexy devil walked round to Penny and Jamie's house.

They had it decorated to perfection. There were cobwebs everywhere, pumpkins, witches and skeletons took over the whole house. All the interior lighting was Orange coloured bulbs. A lot of effort was made.

As Analeise was the last to arrive the place was absolutely heaving.

"Take a tequila!" Jamie (Count Dracula) said as a bedazzled Analeise searched for another familiar face.

"Look at you!!" Shouted Witchy Penny from the other side of the room. She still looked stunning even though she was dressed as a witch.

She gave her a big hug and started to introduce her to a very colourful crowd.

"EVERYONE, THIS IS ANALEISE!!" She shouted into the crowd.

Everyone carried on drinking without lifting their heads.

"Everybody is pissed! What kept you?" She asked staring right into her pale face.

"Including you!" Analeise said laughing. "You're drunk!"

"Where is Adam?" Penny asked as she shoved a glass of tequila into her hand.

"Don't know and don't want to go there tonight!" Analeise said and raised her glass in the air before downing it in one go!

Everyone at the party was a family and business associate of Penny and Jamie's. There was Jamie's business partner and his wife. They were dressed as Robin Hood and Maid Marion (How cosy). Penny's brother and his wife, dressed up as Anthony and Cleopatra (How romantic). Her sister and her husband, dressed as Fred and Wilma Flintstone (How Cute). Their daughter and her boyfriend, Dressed as Nazi's (How inappropriate!) and of course Smug Couple of the Century, David and Emma, Penny's photographer friend and his wife. They dressed up as Posh and Becks (How totally cringe worthy!)

Analeise didn't really want to be in their company as he was a work colleague of Martin Moran. She had met them a few times in the past as David worked quite closely to Martin. They would have gone to each other's houses the odd weekend and socialised. Analeise remembered one year spending New Years Eve with them. It was the most boring night known to mankind. There were 7 people there including Herself and Martin; everyone there had flu. Then one minute after the 12 o'clock chimes, Emma decided to get the vacuum cleaner out and start doing housework.

Analeise didn't really have an awful lot of time for her. David was really nice, she felt quite sorry for him and wondered why he ever had the desire to marry such a wench.

Unfortunately they were the only people that Analeise actually knew quite well.

"Hi Analeise!" Emma said with a big false smile. "Who are you with?"

"Nobody!" Analeise said and poured another drink for herself. She wondered how she would get through this night without punching a 'smug, cosy couple'."

"I am sorry about you and Martin" she said and walked away without giving Analeise a chance to reply.

"Well, have you been mingling?" Penny said as she stuffed her witch's hat onto her head.

"Hardly!" Analeise snapped. "Its like Noah's Fucking Ark in here! I didn't know it was 'bring your own date and dress accordingly!'"

"It doesn't matter!" Penny said trying to keep her face straight and scurried away.

Analeise was in a room full of people and felt like the loneliest person on the planet.

She should have known that this party would be full of couples.

It was the fact that most of the people there knew that She used to be married to Martin and they looked at her with that pitied look on their painted faces.

She had two ideas.

1.   Go home and cry her beans out.
2.   Stay and get pissed!

"Fuck it!" she said softly to herself.

"Penny, where are all the Abba CD's??" she shouted.

She danced, drunk and answered awkward questions about her broken marriage and then at 12.30 she felt it was time to go.

She excused herself and thanked Penny and Jamie for inviting her.

"Are you sure you're ok to walk round on your own?" Penny asked concerned (And pissed!)

"I'm fine!" Analeise said and kissed her on the cheek. "Goodnight"

She cried her eyes out the whole walk back to her house.

The next morning, Analeise woke up with a completely different attitude. She wrapped herself up warmly and drove to the nearest beach where she would go for a big, long walk. When she needed to reflect on things, the first place she went to was the seaside.

She decided that she was being foolish just moping around feeling sorry for herself and that she had lots to be happy about. A new house, a supportive family and great friends. What did she need a man for? And why give herself all of this unwanted grief?

It was a cold day and there were very little people around which suited her very much.

She thought about Adam and wondered what the guy's problem was. It certainly wasn't her! Then she thought about Chris and the games that he played.

She sniggered to herself whenever she thought about Daniel. He was a complete gem!

There was no bullshit, she knew exactly where she stood.

In the last year and a half her life was an emotional roller coaster. She had nobody to blame for it except herself. Everyone in her life tried to warn her about jumping into things headfirst. But it was her nature to do that. She was impulsive and adventurous and always wanted a new challenge.

She also longed to be loved and cared for. But this time she knew that she would have to start loving, and liking herself again before she could possibly love someone else.

Just at that moment as she was watching the waves crash onto the pier a little black and white pup came clambering in her direction.

"Look at you!" she said as she bent down to cuddle it.

"Sam!!" A voice came from behind her.

A man in a green wax jacket came dashing over to Analeise in a flap.

"He must be yours." She said as she tried to pick the skinny little pup in her arms.

"Has a habit of doing runners!" He said looking slightly embarrassed.

"He's adorable!" Analeise said.

"Thanks." He said. His eyes looked kind.

"I'd love to own a dog, but my job just wouldn't allow it!" Analeise said as she petted his head. "It's quite a big commitment and I travel a lot with work."

"Being happy is the most important thing I say!" he said as he took the puppy from Analeise. "Trivial things don't matter!"

"My name is Analeise!" she said as she held out her hand.

He struggled to find a free hand to shake.

"John!" he said.

"You make a lot of sense John!" She said sincerely.

"I try to. But most of the time I don't practise what I preach!" He laughed.

Analeise stared into his kind eyes again. She was not attracted to him, but he had a quality that she liked. He looked like he would love someone deep down and make her so happy.

"Nice to meet you Analeise. Look after yourself!" He said and ushered the puppy away.

"And you!" Analeise couldn't stop staring at him as he walked away.

She smiled to herself as she watched him chasing after the little dog.

Analeise went home that day in a much better frame of mind.

CHAPTER THIRTY-SEVEN

On that Monday Analeise got a phone call from Tara.
"Fucking bastards" She said quickly "There was a sales meeting today and nobody told us!"

"That was nice!" Analeise said calmly.

"Aren't you pissed off?" She asked surprised.

"Couldn't give one!" Analeise sounded un naturally calm.

"Well, I can't believe that we were not asked. Must be something going on!" Tara sounded hassled.

"I'm just going to phone Kevin and ask him for my figures for October and my target for November. That's all we need to know Tara. Don't take it personally." Analeise tried to console her.

"Suppose they didn't want us down if they didn't really need us!" Tara started coming around again.

"I've worked for this company for too long to start getting paranoid!" Analeise said.

"You're right!" Tara apologised for her irrational behaviour.

As Analeise was feeling very strong willed she decided it was time to call Eleanor the solicitor to find out if Martin had signed on the dotted line?

"Haven't heard from him I'm afraid. I was going to give you a call this week."

She replied in a business tone.

"I can not believe him!" She screamed.

"We will send him another letter Analeise. Try not to worry." She assured and put the phone down.

Analeise wasn't having it. She dialled his number.

"What do I have to fucking do to get you to sign a piece of paper!!"? She yelled down the phone.

"Nice to hear from you!" He said casually.

"Fuck you!" She was aware of her bad manners but didn't care.

"You sound as calm as ever Ana. Life must be good to you?" He replied in a patronising tone.

"Just sign the bloody paper Martin." She slammed down the phone.

The day started off quite well. Very positive. It just took one phone call to her ex husband to send her over the edge again.

Analeise couldn't wait to get the day over her.

She called round to Daryl's house that evening.

"Why the fuck can't he just sign the paper?" Daryl asked as she was lighting up a cigarette.

"Because he is a bully and a complete control freak!" Analeise said as she played with Daryl's luminous pink lighter.

"Any word from Adam?" Daryl asked as she looked under her glasses.

"Nothing" Analeise said uncaringly. "I don't really care any more. I am fed up meeting losers. There has to be more to life than this!"

"There is" Daryl said, "Its just finding it is the problem! Anyway it is Abbey's birthday next week and we are taking her out next Sunday night are you in?"

"Aren't I always in?" Analeise smiled. She was secretly looking forward to a girly night, which didn't involve 'Lovey Dovey' couples.

This was a very busy time of the year for Analeise as it was the big pre Christmas sell in!

All of her salons needed to see her to find out about the exclusive Christmas Sets that Dermarome had to offer. They were desperate to see her. Even salons that couldn't be arsed with Reps calling round insisted on seeing her in November. Normally whenever she would arrive they would moan and groan about the prices. Analeise was well used to this, year in, and year out.

Her diary was choc a block!!

On the Thursday morning on her drive to Cookstown in County Tyrone she thought about John and his very kind eyes. There was something special about him she couldn't quite work out.

She arrived at Eternal Youth Beauty Salon.

"Let us see those Christmas sets!!" shouted Cassie Hamilton as she hurriedly shuffled Analeise into the small reception area of her modest salon.

She poked into her briefcase for the presentation folder.

"They're getting dearer and dearer!!" She shook her head as Analeise rolled her eyes.

"Like everything!" Analeise said impatiently. "Which ones do you like?"

Cassie thumbed through the folder like a child would flick through a 'Toys R Us' catalogue. "Oh yes, want that one! Give me ten of those ones! Oh, look at those!" she shouted as her eyes sparkled.

She placed a very large Christmas order much to Analeise's delight.

The next stop for Analeise was Dungannon and thought about calling Chris Drummond.

She kept on driving and never bothered. She was tight for time.

She stopped for a sandwich in a garage on the main road and ate it while she was driving. She was a professional at doing this. She had it down to a fine art!

It was pretty hard to get parked close to 'Bella' Beauty salon so she put the car in a car park at the other side of the town. She was really pushed for time.

As she was crossing the road a black car passed and pulled in at the side.

"ANA" Chris Drummond shouted, "You're blind as a bat!"

She smiled and walked over to the passenger side and looked in. He was laughing.

"I should wear my glasses more!" she said as she blushed.

"You'd look sexy in glasses!" He said. "Why didn't you call me?"

"I'm pushed for time. I have an appointment in 10 minutes." She said as she looked at her watch.

"There is a lot you can do in 10 minutes!" he said as he raised his eyebrows.

Analeise chose to ignore it.

"So what are you doing today?" She asked.

"This and that you know" he said vaguely "I'm going home for a spot of lunch"

"Good to see you Chris." She said and smiled. "I'm late."

Chris just stared at her.

"Do you want to come back after your appointment?" He asked.

"What for?" Analeise asked.

He grinned like a chesire cat.

"Ok, this is some kind of a game to you isn't it?" She said angrily.

"You're the biggest player I know Ana!" Chris answered. "You know rightly what you want from me and I know exactly what I want from you and it works well!"

"Not any more Chris" She said solemnly and walked away.

"Call you!" he shouted from the car.

Analeise kept walking. She was furious.

She knew she only had herself to blame.

Analeise headed to Daryl's house on the Sunday afternoon where they had few afternoon drinkies and beautified themselves for the night ahead.

They met everyone at Roland's restaurant in the City Centre where a meal was booked for 20 people.

As usual Daryl took forever to get ready so they were last to arrive.

There was Champagne lined from the top to the bottom of the table.

"You've a lot of catching up to do!" Abbey shouted up the table.

Analeise was so happy being in the company of such real true friends.

After the meal they went to Massies Nightclub, which was always great on a Sunday night.

They were quite early so found great seats at the back, which were raised. They could see everything from there.

Everyone was full of champagne. The music was great.

As the place slowly got busier and busier the view was not so good anymore so Analeise and a few girls went down for a dance.

They danced for around 5 songs whenever Analeise felt it was time for another drink.

As she walked off the dance floor Adam tapped her on the shoulder.

"Hello!" he said smiling his usual gorgeous smile.

She gave him a look under her eyes. "Where have you been?"

"I'm really sorry. I just got a bit scared." He said.

"Scared of what?" Analeise asked curiously.

At this stage Abbey and Trudy walked passed and nudged her. They had heard about him but didn't know who he was. They stood behind him sticking their thumbs up for approval. Analeise was doing her best to ignore them.

"I was starting to get strong feelings for you." He said as he stared into her eyes.

Analeise was thrilled and excited. Her heart was beating so fast she hoped she wouldn't take a palpitation. It didn't take much to persuade her, but yet again his charm won her over.

"Wow, my cooking didn't put you off?" she asked light heartedly.

"It was the nicest thing any girl had ever done for me." He said.

Analeise was on cloud nine.

She stood with him for the remainder of the evening where he told her she was the most beautiful woman he had met and his world had turned upside down since meeting her.

It was all complete bullshit of course and Analeise had yet again been wrapped up in his charm!

At this stage Daryl and a few of the others had gone on home and Trudy stayed with Analeise.

"My friend is on her own. I'd better go now." Analeise said as Adam stared lovingly into her eyes.

"Let me give you a lift home." He suggested.

She got Trudy organised and followed him back to his car. He gave Trudy a lift to her house and then Analeise announced that she was staying with Daryl.

"I'm staying in Dania's bed. You can't come with me but you can come in for some coffee." She said.

She wrapped the door and felt like a teenager bringing her boyfriend home.

Daryl answered the door in a big saggy pair of pyjamas.

"Daryl, this is Adam." She said forgetting that Daryl had already met him before,

"I know you," she said.

Analeise was glaring at Daryl hoping she wouldn't give him a hard time for not calling her dear friend.

"I'm away to bed. No noise!" She joked. "I wouldn't let you in if my daughter had of been here!" she pointed to Adam.

Analeise made coffee for them and they went into the lounge. Adam was being very affectionate. He couldn't stop kissing her and she loved it.

"So, will you see me again?" He asked.

"Of course." Analeise stupidly said.

Then one thing led to another. Slowly he began to unzip her top. She couldn't resist him. She didn't care that she was in Daryl's front room and the floor was wooden. They brought the pillows from the couch on to the floor and slowly made love.

It was incredible.

At 3.30 he went home.

Analeise then sneaked upstairs and crept into Dania's empty bed. She couldn't sleep a wink.

The next morning She was up before Daryl. She tried to be as quiet as possible as she sneaked down the stairs and out the door.

She had an appointment in Belfast City Centre at 11.00 that morning. She went home, had a shower and got dressed into her black trouser suit. She was very happy and couldn't stop thinking about Adam.

She was running late and she parked her car in the nearest multi storey car park and made a quick dash to the salon.

When she arrived she was greeted by the receptionist who informed her that the salon owner couldn't see her and to make another appointment.

"Was there something wrong with phoning to tell me?" Analeise said angrily to her.

She made another appointment and stormed out. She couldn't believe that this kept happening to her.

As she left the salon she felt her heart beating really quickly and knew that she was going to take another palpitation. Whenever Analeise got stressed or uptight in any way she would take a panic attack. These things would spring up from time to time with absolutely no warning. The more stressed she got was the more chance she would get these attacks.

She stopped at the side of the street, scrambled into her handbag in search of an emergency paper bag to breathe into. She looked around her to see if there was a quiet place to go, as it was very embarrassing. Most people who witnessed this normally thought she was glue sniffing and it made her more uptight!

As she turned the corner she felt a real tightness across her chest and walked into a man who was dressed in business attire. He knocked her to the ground. His hair was dark and she recalled him being very handsome. He smelt like cinnamon, lemons and home baking all rolled into one. A smell that was mind numbing. As he bent down to pick her off the street he had a real familiar look in his eyes. They looked gentle and kind.

"Are you ok?" He asked kindly.

"Y-yes" She stuttered. She was embarrassed. "I'm so sorry" She stared into his ice blue eyes.

"Don't be sorry. Just be careful. Look after your heart and take care of yourself." He said and just disappeared.

She was bewildered. Who was he? Where had she seen him before?

He was warm and gentle and she longed to be in his company. She stood and looked around her to find where he was.

He was gone.

CHAPTER THIRTY-EIGHT

That evening Adam called Analeise and suggested calling round. She couldn't wait to see him again after him pouring his heart out to her. She felt so lucky.

He came round around 9.00, they watched a DVD and drunk some beers. Analeise was enjoying his company and decided to seduce him on the sofa. It felt as good as the first time. Then at 11.30 he excused himself and headed home.

She went to bed that evening and thought about him. She enjoyed the security of having someone to love. But did he want to love her back? Why would he never stay? She was tumbling very fast like a freight train and she knew it. She also wondered who the stranger in the street was.

He was fascinating.

The next few days were pretty busy in the life of Analeise Magowan. She had received word from the solicitor that Martin Moran had signed his divorce papers and a court date was set for December.

Abbey had also called her to tell her that she had tickets for a concert in the Omni Arena in Belfast in two weeks time.

Analeise's November was becoming quite successful. Adam had called a few times and suggested calling up to see her again.

"Why doesn't he invite you anywhere?" Penny asked Analeise when she had called round one evening.

"We've been out for drinks!" Analeise snapped.

"What is his house like?" Penny asked again.

"It's in the process of being built!" She answered quickly.

"Built?" Penny said as she looked under her eyes at Analeise. "Where is he living?"

"With his Mum." she said. "Why all the questions?"

"Not too sure what I think of him." Penny said suspiciously. "He lost interest after you slept with him didn't he?"

"No!" Analeise snapped "He started messing before I went to New York."

"You're even admitting that he has been messing!" she shook her head.

Penny was very clever and meant a lot to Analeise but she wondered why she had doubts about him. He had poured out his heart to her. Wasn't that enough?

"Just be careful." Penny said with compassion.

"Funny you should say that!" Analeise sat forward. "I had a panic attack the other day and a man picked me up and said the very same thing."

"You should listen Analeise!" Penny said unsurprised. "I would hate to see your heart broken again. You don't deserve it. Your feelings are getting too strong for these boys, just ease up!"

"He said that too!" Analeise was amazed. "Look after your heart!"

"Just listen to them." Penny said calmly. "Your angels are guiding you."

Analeise started to cry. She felt so emotional.

Yet again Analeise hadn't heard from Adam for a good few days so called him.

He didn't answer.

She was looking forward to the concert on the Monday evening.

Abbey met her in the Hard Rock Café close to the Arena where they had a few drinks.

After a couple of beers they thought it was time to head in and find their seats. The place was full to the brim! It was a full house.

They had great seats very close to the stage and whenever the group eventually came on they felt in need of another beer to keep them in the high spirits. The atmosphere was electric and it was a great show.

Abbey went to the bar and Analeise stayed. She was dancing and having the time of her life! Abbey had proved to be great friend to her in the last lot of months. She worked for a radio station and always called her offering tickets for different events. She never forgot Analeise. They gelled from the moment they met.

"Fucking mad queue out there!" She moaned as she handed Analeise her plastic glass full of frothy beer.

After her drinks Analeise went to the loo. On her way out as she was entering the Arena again she bumped right into Adam. She couldn't believe it. There were 80,000 people in the Arena and she had to bump into him!

She blushed from top to toe.

"Hello!" She said as she was looking to see whom he was with. He seemed to be alone.

"Funny meeting you here" he said calmly.

"Where are you sitting?" She asked.

"Down there." He pointed to seats very close to where Abbey patiently waited for her. "Seen you coming in."

"Well, I'd better go." Analeise said awkwardly. "Enjoy the rest of the show"

She scurried away as quickly as she could.

Abbey was singing her heart out when Analeise got back to her seat.

"Queue?" Abbey looked at a very stern faced friend. "What's wrong? You look like you have seen a ghost!"

"I think I might have" Analeise answered. "Just bumped into Adam."

"Where is he sitting?" She said as her head was spinning around.

"Stop looking! He's behind us somewhere!" She snapped.

"What a complete bastard!" Abbey said straight-faced. "You deserve better than that!"

"What is it?" Analeise asked curiously.

"He's with a fucking girl!" Abbey said.

Analeise heart sunk. She felt like she had been hit by a double Decker bus.

She tried, but she couldn't enjoy the rest of the show.

Abbey wanted to go to a nightclub after the concert and Analeise grudgingly went along.

On the way there Abbey tried to talk sense to Analeise, she told her about the time she met a guy and how he swept her off her feet. He treated her like a princess, took her to all the best restaurants and bars, introduced her to all of his wonderful friends and made plans for the future. She was tumbling head over heels. He invited her to his best friends wedding in England and they sat at the top table with the parents of the bride. Everyone was wondering who she was and she adored that he showed her off so proudly. He bought drinks all-day and charged them all to the room. She retired to bed at around one o'clock, but he insisted on staying up late. He arrived back at the room around 3.30 completely plastered. She had already fallen asleep. The next morning (very hung over and no apology for his behaviour) he told her that he had mislaid his credit card and if she wouldn't mind sorting out the bill until they got home. It came to £250 and she was a little shocked. When they got home they arranged dinner at her house the following Sunday. She didn't hear from him all week. When she called to confirm, he seemed a little standoffish! Sunday came and she still hadn't heard anything. So she sent him a message telling him what time to come at. Two hours later she got a message from him saying he was having a family crisis and he couldn't make it.

"What's wrong with that?" Analeise asked intrigued.

"I never heard from him again!" she said as if spitting the words.

"Ever?" Analeise asked.

"Weird text messages saying that he was going through a rough time, and how he didn't want to tell me about it!"

"Had you shagged him?" Analeise was curious.

"Yes!" Abbey said as she stared into space. "He was crap, lasted 5 minutes and he was hung like a field mouse!"

They both laughed.

"Moral of the story is..?" Analeise asked.

"Always have your guard up and always be wary of a charmer!"
Abbey said as she put her arm around her good friend. "I never got my money back. What a wanker!" she shook her head.

"Ever see him around?" Analeise asked.

"It turned out that I heard through the grapevine he was advertising in the personals in the Telegraph. God love the next girl that has the misfortune of walking in his direction!" Abbey said as they walked into Massies Bar.

By the time they got there they had sobered up somewhat.

"Lets go on the wine?" Abbey said as they queued at the bar.

Analeise felt a sensation on her shoulder and looked around only to find Adam standing right behind her.

"Following me?" She said jokingly.

He just smiled. It was pretty obvious that his woman was standing with him.

Abbey at this stage was pre-occupied ordering the wine. Analeise stood directly behind her like a child with its mother at the checkouts in the Supermarket!

Abbey turned around with the drinks and handed Analeise a delicious cold glass of wine.

She looked at Adam like he was a dog that just pissed on her best rug!

He smiled charmingly.

She shook her head and ushered her broken hearted friend to the other side of the room.

"Don't ever call him again!" She said to Analeise who was trying her best to keep her chin up. "I mean it, don't ever listen to his bullshit lines ever ever!"

"It's obvious now why he never took me any place lately." Analeise said thoughtfully.

"Imagine being his poor girlfriend?" Abbey said trying her hardest to reassure her. "Just remember my story and learn from your mistakes!"

Analeise just had to think positively now. Adam was no good. He was a charmer and had her stringing along for nothing. She was so vulnerable! She fell far too quickly and hardly even knew him. She was a bit disappointed in herself.

Why was she so desperate?

She would just have to be more careful in future.

CHAPTER THIRTY-NINE

She tried her best to forget about Adam. She was taken for a fool and had to deal with it. Everyone was right about him.

Why couldn't she just listen to people?

She decided to give Chris a call. Maybe he wasn't so bad after all.

"Hello there. Was wondering what you were doing?" She asked relieved that he answered!

"Nothing much. Do you want to come round?" He said casually.

"Yes, I'll see you in an hour." Analeise knew what the night entailed and didn't expect anything else.

She had a quick shower and threw on a pair of jeans and a big chunky jumper.

As she was driving down the motorway she heard a strange sound from her car. She turned down the radio and drove slower.

It was pitch black outside and quite cold and she knew that she would have to stop.

She stopped and walked round the car.

"Fuck it!" She shouted and kicked the wheel.

She had a puncture. She got back into the car to call Chris to tell him to come out to help her.

In the rush of getting ready in a hurry she had left the house without her mobile phone!

She sat there in the dark for a few minutes and wondered what to do. She knew there were telephones at the side of the road but didn't know how far away they were from her.

She decided to drive the car slowly to the nearest phone. It was the only option!

The wind was very strong and it was starting to rain.

Analeise was starting to feel a little bit scared.

As she started up the car again a black car stopped in front of her and a man got out to help.

"Having problems?" He asked as he walked over to the driver's side of her car.

"I've a puncture and can't change a wheel." Analeise said as she opened her door.

"Have you got a spare?" He asked.

"Y-yes" She ushered him round to the boot of the car. "Its full of stuff!" she apologised as she started to empty all of the Dermarome Sample products and Paperwork crap from the boot very quickly.

The man was silent. He changed the wheel for her within minutes.

"You don't know what is round the corner." He said kindly and stared into her eyes. "Be careful"

Again his eyes were so familiar to her. Piercing blue. His cologne smelt of cinnamon and lemons. It was so dark she didn't really see his face.

"Do I know you?" She asked him as he walked back to his car.

He didn't answer and drove away.

Analeise sat frozen to her seat for 10 minutes. She couldn't get this man out of her head.

Who was he?

Why was he always there when she needed him? She wasn't frightened of him. She felt warm and loved whenever he was around. It was as if he was watching over her or something.

Just like an Angel.

She arrived at Chris's house 45 minutes late.

"I thought you had an accident or something!" He said as he took her coat off. " I phoned but there was no answer."

"I forgot my phone!" She said. Her cheeks were burning. "I had a puncture on the motorway."

"Did you fix it yourself?" He smiled.

"I wouldn't know where to start!" Analeise laughed. "Someone stopped to help me."

"A man no doubt!" Chris grinned.

"Yes" She said quietly and thoughtfully. "A very kind man."

Analeise decided not to tell Chris about her encounters with this incredible person, as he could never understand.

Chris offered her a coffee. "It will warm you up!"

She sat down and couldn't stop thinking about the stranger.

"You look a million miles away kid!" Chris said as he shoved a very hot mug into her hand.

Analeise tried for Chris's sake to forget the man for now and concentrate on her night with the gorgeous and sexy creature she had before her!

He sat down beside her and played with her hair. She stared into his eyes. They were so blue like big deep swimming pools.

If only she could look at them every day.

He wrapped his arms around her and kissed her passionately. She couldn't resist him. It felt so good, so right. For a moment she felt like she belonged to him. It was a nice moment.

He took her hand and walked her up the stairs into one of the bedrooms and threw her on the bed. She giggled. Chris lay on top of her kissing her lips, then her neck. He then pushed her jumper off and Analeise felt like something had taken over her body. His lips moved down on to her breasts. Then he started to un button her jeans. She wanted him inside of her at that moment and hurriedly removed his clothes. Within seconds they were both un dressed and were making incredible love on Chris's carefully made bed.

When they had finished Chris held her tightly. He made her feel like the only woman on the planet. He kissed her again. It was so romantic until Chris said

"You're a great fuck!"

Why did he have to go and spoil something so beautiful?

"You're so romantic!" Analeise said sarcastically as she started to put her clothes on.

"What do you mean?" He said defensively.

"You didn't have to say that!" She said fumbling with her jeans.

"I cant do anything right!" he raised his arms. "Anyway I'm not telling you lies!"

She thought about what he said and knew he was right. At least he wasn't playing games with her. She should know the score by now. She knew that all she was to him was sex. She so desperately wanted him all of the time but knew they weren't right for each other. Why couldn't she accept that? He was like a drug she needed all of the time.

Or was it just someone?

Analeise went home that night and realised she was on a road to self-destruction if she carried on the way she was going.

The next few weeks were very busy as it was drawing close to Christmas. Analeise was far from organised as she had thrown herself into her work.

She decided to go to the Supermarket as her fridge was like Mars.

Very empty with a few fuzzy things lying around!

She filled her trolley with ready-made delights, which made her life oh so easy. No cooking involved!

Great.

As she was deciding which cheese to experiment with she heard a woman calling her name "Analeise?"

She turned round to find David and Emma the 'Perfect Couple' from the Halloween party. They were dressed like they had just been to Church.

"Hello." Analeise said as she blushed. She was now sorry she didn't make a bit more of an effort dressing.

Tracksuit bottoms with the arse hanging round her knees didn't exactly spell 'Classy Chick doing my shopping!'

"Just getting our Turkey!" Emma said gleefully like Mother Earth.

Analeise gazed into their trolley to find what resembled a dead ostrich!

"Who are you feeding? A small country?" Analeise said smiling.

"We're having a traditional family Christmas." She said proudly as she looked into Analeise's 'Meals for One' in her trolley much to her annoyance.

"I just can t be arsed cooking." Analeise said defensively as she fumbled with a small block of Mature Cheddar.

"Are you going to your Mum's for Christmas?" David asked.

"Yes" Analeise answered quickly trying really hard to not look at all bothered.

"Have a nice one anyway!" They both said smugly and went on their way.

Analeise pulled a face at them as they turned their backs. She went directly to the checkout just in case she had the sheer humiliation of meeting them later on.

The next day Analeise had her court date and for some weird reason was dreading it.

Eleanor had informed her that it would only take 10 minutes as Martin had already signed the consent papers and would not be required to attend.

She put on her best business suit and drove to Craigavon Court where Eleanor was already waiting for her. Analeise looked hassled.

"Are you ok?" Eleanor asked coldly.

"I'm nervous!" She said as she fiddled with her car keys.

"No need." She assured "Lets go upstairs"

They sat at the back of the empty, cold courtroom and Analeise looked all around her.

"Where is everyone?" She asked Eleanor as she imagined a John Grisham novel.

"We are going into the judge's quarters. It is very informal, you will just have to say an oath and I will do the rest of the talking." She said shuffling her papers.

"ANALEISE MORAN" a man shouted from the top of the courtroom.

"That's our cue!" Eleanor said as she led Analeise into the small room at the corner of the courtroom. She had never been in a real courtroom before and felt that she was being sentenced for death!

In the small, stuffy room sat a very stern female judge and another Lady taking notes. They sat down around the table and the Lady handed Analeise a bible and asked her to repeat after her.

Eleanor then said a load of formal bullshit to the judge and the judge asked Analeise if she had been living apart from Martin for over a year. She was so nervous, and really hoped she wouldn't take another panic attack. It would be the worst-case scenario! Imagine being wheeled out of court breathing into a paper bag!! Oh the sheer humiliation!

"Yes." She replied very shakily.

The Judge then handed Eleanor a legal sheet of paper announcing that it was a six-week wait before Analeise could marry again.

'Chance would be a fine thing!' She thought to herself.

They were excused and left the room.

"That's it?" Analeise asked.

"It will be six weeks before you get your decree absolute which means you are officially divorced and can legally change your name back." Eleanor said as she handed her the official letter. She was so matter-of –fact about the whole thing. This was her marriage and it had now been 'dissolved' as the judge's terminology described it! Analeise should have been jumping with joy but she wasn't.

Analeise got back into her car and burst out crying. She didn't know why but felt the need to call Martin. "You are divorced now." She announced.

"Isn't that what you want?" he asked her.

"Yes, but it feels weird!" she said knowing it was finally over. "I just needed closure Martin."

"I know." He said comfortingly. "Are you ok?" he seemed genuinely concerned.

"Yes." Analeise sniffled. "I'm ok."

"I'm here if you need me," Martin said.

"Thanks." Analeise said humbly and put the phone down.

For the next five minutes Analeise just cried. It was another chapter of her life that had been closed. She was relieved in a lonely sort of way. She could only look forward now.

CHAPTER FORTY

*T*he following week Daryl called Analeise to tell her about the official Christmas night out to be held that weekend.

"I could be doing with one!" Analeise said sounding hassled. "I'm not going to my work Christmas party. Its in a crappy Hotel in County West Meath!"

"You're just right" Daryl agreed. "This could be a double celebration! Divorce Party!!"

Analeise laughed. "Any excuse for a night out, but I don't want a Divorce Party if that's ok!"

Analeise had been spending the last week calling to her clients with bottles of wine much to their displeasure.

"Same old bottle of Vinegar!" They would moan.

She took note of all the clients that *did* moan, as they would get sweet fuck-all the following year!

Everyone went to Abbey's house in Belfast on the Friday night; Analeise brought her overnight bag, as she knew a heavy night of drinking was in store.

As they were all getting ready Abbey called Analeise into the hall.

"I heard a few stories about you!" she said innocently.

Analeise was horrified. "What stories?"

"Apparently Chris Drummond is spreading a few tales around the place!" she said trying really hard not to offend her.

"About me?" Analeise asked.

"Yes, he has been bumming and blowing about your relationship with him!" she said, sorry she had brought the subject up. "He's say-ing about your wild nights of passion and that you are mad for it and apparently you have had threesomes?"

"BASTARD!" She screamed. "He is a liar! Who told you?"

"I'm sorry Analeise but you are my friend and I just had to let you know. He is friendly with one of the guys that I work with. We do some business with his PR Company. He's just a wanker and every-one knows it!" Abbey shook her head. She knew Analeise had been through enough wankers to last her a couple of centuries and knew it was only kind to tell her.

"Ana knows he is a wanker!" Daryl was standing directly behind Analeise who turned round in surprise.

"I didn't think he'd be telling half of Belfast about what we get up to. And as for threesomes; it is total bullshit!" Analeise said to her. She was so disappointed in him. She knew he was a bit of a playboy. But not this, it was disrespectful.

Analeise poured herself a very large glass of white wine and downed it in one go.

"Easy tiger, we have all night!!" Abbey said to her.

"I know" She said, "I can't believe him!"

"Forget him!" Daryl snapped "How many times have I told you that he is bad news and not to get involved. Guys can get casual but Girls can't!"

"I'm not involved!" Analeise said, "I'm just angry and he's not get-ting away with this just so easy!"

"GOOD!" both of the girls said at the same time.

By the time the taxi arrived Analeise had already drunk a bottle of wine.

They went to Café Bongo where they had something to eat and then went upstairs. It was hiving with very young people. Wall to wall juveniles! 'Bongo' was a very appropriate name for the club!

"Is it just me or are we the oldest people in here?" Daryl asked with a very straight face.

"Fuck it!" Analeise shrugged and drunk another glass of wine.

The average age in the nightclub was around 19! Daryl was very aware of that but Analeise and Abbey decided to ignore the fact that they were old enough to be mothers of the feisty boys who were dancing in the direction of them. The music was great. Daryl hated every minute of it.

Analeise danced all night and when she wasn't dancing she was drinking white wine.

She had a ball. Daryl and Abbey decided to sneak off to the pub next door where the clientele were more around the legal drinking age! In fact it was the complete opposite of Café Bongo. It was an 'old mans pub' full of pervy men who wore tweed jackets and corduroy trousers. The pub smelled of sweat, tobacco and damp wool. The girls didn't care.

Analeise had no idea they were gone, she found a dancing partner for the rest of the night. His name was Marcus. He loved her to bits. He was young, pretty and he was all that Analeise required at that moment in time.

Whenever the lights came on at the end of the night she looked for the girls. Marcus decided to help her. They stepped outside to find Abbey and Daryl waiting for her.

"Where were you?" She asked, her make-up was smeared all over her face from such serious snogging!

"The Jester!" they both said pointing in the direction of said bar!

"Fuckers!" She said laughing. "Good job I have a friend!" Analeise showed off her prize catch.

"Pretty!" Daryl said staring at the young, drunken boy "Lets go you!"

"I'm bringing Marcus!" Analeise announced.

"No you're not!" Daryl snapped. "You are staying in Abbey's house. Its disrespectful!"

"Ok then I'm going back to his house!" she said angrily and trailed a very excited Marcus away.

"C'mon" Marcus said "Lets go to my Mum's house for a bit of Rumpy Pumpy!"

Analeise couldn't believe what he said, "What did you say?"

"Rumpy Pumpy!" He said proudly.

She gazed at him through her 'wine goggles' and had a reality check. He was taking her back to his Mum's house (Who was probably only a few years older than her!)

"Its ok, I think I'll just go home with my friends now!" She walked back to her friends who were watching her from across the street.

"Analeise!" He shouted, "Can I have your number?"

She kept walking.

"What happened to the boy?" Daryl asked.

"I'm not shagging anyone who says 'fancy a bit of rumpy pumpy'! Especially not with his Mum in the same house, its obscene!"

Everybody laughed and all got a taxi back to Abbey's house where on the way home she invited a few people back for a party

Analeise had enough and went straight to bed.

They all slept in pretty late the next day. Their heads were banging. None more than Analeise's.

They had some tea and toast and Analeise had a brain wave.

"I'm going to call Chris!" She announced.

"What for?" Abbey said. "Don't say I said anything!"

"Not going to mention a thing!" Analeise said.

She dialled his number.

"Hello Kid!" he said "Can't get enough of me?"

"Just thought about you and wondered if I could take you out for dinner. Sort of like a Christmas Present?" She asked trying not to laugh.

The two girls stared at her in horror.

"Would love to." Chris answered quickly. "Where had you in mind?"

"I was thinking of 'Dine' in town." Analeise said.

Abbey and Daryl's mouths dropped. It was the most expensive restaurant in Belfast.

"What about Monday night?" Chris suggested.

"You can stay in my house if you like?" She said suggestively. "I'll pick you up from your house!"

"See you then!" Chris sounded chuffed and put the phone down.

"What are you up to?" Daryl asked.

Abbey was pretty streetwise and had an idea of Analeise's cunning plan.

They all laughed.

CHAPTER FORTY-ONE

On the Monday night Analeise got off work a little bit early to beautify herself. She wore a very sexy black dress. She smothered herself in her favourite body cream. Her make up was applied to perfection. She had arranged to see Chris at 7.00, as the meal was booked for 8.00. She booked the meal under Chris's name just to make him feel special.

She pulled up to his house to find that he wasn't ready.

"Hurry up!" she said as she looked at her watch.

"What about a kiss?" He asked with a cheeky grin.

"Later!" She promised. "Now just get on with it!"

He looked stunning. He wore a crisp white shirt and a pair of very expensive jeans. He smelt divine.

Analeise drove straight to the restaurant.

"What did I do to deserve this?" Chris asked very pleased with himself as she parked the car.

"For just being you!" She said smiling.

They arrived at the very elegant restaurant. It had a great reputation and was always winning awards.

"Table for Drummond" Analeise said to the receptionist and handed him her coat. It was very full that evening being so close to Christmas and their table was romantically in the corner of the room near the back. It had a crisp white tablecloth with 2 large candles in the centre with an exotic red flower with green foliage.

This would be Analeise's first (and last) meal with Chris and thought it was such a shame as they made such a handsome couple.

"You look amazing tonight Babe!" Chris said as he sat down. He couldn't stop smiling.

"Thanks!" She said confidently.

The staff were very attentive. They ordered a bottle of Chablis while they decided on what they would eat.

"Why are you doing this?" Chris asked her as he thumbed his way through the menu.

"Well, we never really went anywhere together and I just thought I would treat you to something nice. That's all!" Analeise said as she fluttered her eyelashes.

He ordered smoked salmon for Starter and a very 'well done' steak for main course.

Analeise decided to have the Camembert for starter and would have the Seafood Pasta for main course.

They enjoyed their starters and Chris talked about work and how he was up for promotion etc. etc. Afterwards Analeise decided to excuse herself and go to the Ladies Room. It was at the front of the restaurant.

She sneaked up to the receptionist around the corner from the main restaurant and asked, "Can I have my coat please?"

"Certainly!" He said slightly surprised.

"Don't say to my friend that I have gone please!" she pleaded, "He is being quite offensive"

"Y-yes of course Madam!" he said as she slithered out the front door.

20 minutes had passed and Analeise had arrived at Daryl's house.

"What did you do?" she laughed. "Did you leave him high and dry?"

"Yes." She said soberly. She had mixed feelings. She had never done anything like that before. She also knew he deserved it.

Meanwhile Chris is sitting in the most expensive restaurant in Belfast awaiting Analeise return from the bathroom. Fifteen minutes had passed and he called over a waitress. "Could you just check the bathroom for my friend? She has been away for nearly half an hour"

"Yes indeed" she said and walked in the direction of the Ladies room.

Chris was starting to get a few looks by now and was feeling a little bit embarrassed.

The waitress walked back as the two Main Courses arrived.

"Seafood Linguine?" The waiter asked Chris.

"Mmmmm, over there" he pointed to the empty seat in front of him. The waiter carefully put the exquisite dishes on the table. His steak looked amazing! He was starving.

"I'm sorry sir, but there is nobody in the bathroom." The concerned waitress announced to Chris who was starting to get a fair idea of what was happening to him.

He dialled Analeise's number into his phone but he only got her voice mail.

"Nice one Ana!!" he said and hung up.

He called the waiter back and told him to return the main courses as he would not need them anymore and that he was leaving.

"I'll just get your bill sir!" he said.

Chris was horrified, humiliated and pissed off all rolled into one. He couldn't believe that nice, sweet Analeise could do that to him.

After paying £60.50 for nothing he then realised that he had no way of getting back home. Analeise was driving and he would have to either have the humiliation of calling one of his friends for a lift or pay 40 quid for a taxi! Whenever he got outside he decided to call Barrie because Chris was never a happy bunny whenever he had to spend any kind of money.

"That bitch left me in a restaurant and I need a lift home!" He said solemnly.

"She got you a cracker!" Barrie laughed.

Chris was not amused.

He arrived half an hour later where Chris was standing at the corner of the street waiting for him.

"Stop by her house on the way. I want to give her a piece of my mind!" Chris said angrily to his friend who found the whole thing very amusing.

"I'm not getting involved mate. I'm giving you a lift home. End of story!!" Barrie said.

"Could you have chosen a more expensive restaurant?" Barrie said with a smile.

"She picked it!" Chris snapped.

He just couldn't understand why Analeise would do such a thing on him.

Whenever he arrived home he called her number again. Phone was switched off!

"Analeise you bitch!" He said, "I can't believe you did that you sad cow. Whatever did I do so bad to make you do such a thing?" then he hung up.

Analeise had spent the remainder of the evening at Daryl's house and felt at 10.00 it was time to go home. "I hope he isn't camped outside my house with a sledge hammer!!" she laughed.

"That will teach him to slander my name around town!" She said to Daryl as she said goodbye.

"You did well Babe!" Daryl said to her. "You so deserve to be treated with respect."

Chris wasn't camped outside her house when she got home. She was relieved.

She thought it was a waste of a good night but at least it showed Chris not to go round telling everyone lies! She also knew it was the end of him and her and wondered if he was even a little bit pissed off! She listened to her voice message and sniggered to herself. She wondered how he got himself home. She knew he was bound to call one of his friends, as parting with money was not one of his favourite pastimes.

On the Friday Analeise finished work for a couple of weeks. She was in desperate need of a break and it couldn't have come quickly enough.

She spent Christmas Eve running around like a headless chicken as she still had a fair bit of shopping to do. She called round to Penny and

Jamie's that evening with presents and they made her dinner for her.

The following day Analeise called up to her Mums as usual and the Whole family went to her Dad's Golf Club for a few pre-Christmas Dinner drinkies.

She had a great, gin-fuelled Christmas Day.

She phoned all of her friends to wish them Merry Christmas.

Whenever she called Tracey Sellers and told her the whole Chris Drummond story she couldn't contain herself any longer. "I love it!! Well done!!" was all she could say. She invited Analeise to a party on New Years Eve and Analeise accepted with pleasure

CHAPTER FORTY-TWO

*A*naleise had a nice quiet Christmas week. She invited Daryl and a few of the girls round to her house on Boxing Day. She spent some time with her brother and his family as well and spent some quality time just doing nothing!

Tracey had tickets for Ruby's Nightclub in the centre of Belfast. It was brand-new and the place to be seen. Analeise bought herself a new silver fitted dress and a pair of knee high boots, which looked totally stunning.

She met Tracey in the bar below the nightclub. It was packed to full capacity with everyone in great spirits! Everyone was dressed for the occasion. Females were 'glitter clad'; Males wore their best shirts and sported their new cologne that they most probably got for Christmas. Tracey went all out for the occasion also. She had bought a designer red dress and looked like she had spent the day being pampered.

"I have!" She said laughing.

"Just right!" Analeise said as she kissed her on the cheek. "Are you up for a wild one?"

"Of course!" Analeise said excitedly

"Happy new Year Gorgeous and I hope the New Year brings you all you deserve!" Maurice said to her and kissed her on the cheek. He looked stunning in his 'new shirt'.

"Thanks" Analeise said. She intended to have a great time!

They stayed for a couple of glasses of Champagne and headed up-stairs to the nightclub where they chose very elegant chairs close to the bar. "We'll get a good view here!" Analeise said.

The décor was red velvet and was stunning. Analeise hadn't been there before but was totally besotted by it. There were nooks and cranny's everywhere all separated by red fur curtains. It looked slightly like some old hookers boudoir from the 1920's done in the best possible taste!

As the night progressed it was full to the doors of people with only one thing on their minds…having a bloody good time!

The drink was flowing like it was going out of fashion. They met lots of people that they knew. Analeise met a few clients and Tracey met with a load of business associates. They danced all night. Analeise's feet were starting to get the better of her so sat down until it was coming close to 12.

"Come on you lets get a really good spot on the dance floor. I'm gonna have to find you someone to kiss!!" Tracey trailed Analeise to the very crowded dance floor where they pushed and shoved through sweaty bodies. She came across a very sweaty body trying to snog everything on the dance floor. He was 6ft 6 and was built like a brick shithouse! He shuffled towards Tracey and Analeise and put his very large arms around them both. He leaned over to Analeise "Happy new year!" he shouted into her ear nearly deafening her.

"And you!" she tried to deafen him right back.

"Fancy a fuck?" he romantically screamed in her ear again.

She pretended she didn't hear him even though she had a perforated eardrum!

Four-Three-two-one. HAPPY NEW YEAR!! Everyone shouted and the music played, everyone held hands in a big circle and started singing..

Analeise was getting battered about in the crowd as she tried to find her friends.

Everyone was kissing each other including Tracey and Maurice. Analeise tried to make her way back to the seats. "Happy New Year you big tart!" Maurice shouted and gave her a big kiss closely followed by Tracey.

"Happy New Year to you too" she said sincerely and hugged them both.

"I'm going to go now before I have taxi problems later!" She said.

"Don't go!" they pleaded. "Its only 12 o'clock! Have you found a new friend?"

They all looked around at the 'Honey Monster' who was stuck up Analeise's back.

"He's just looking to get 'his end away'." Analeise said as if dismissing him. "I've had my fair share of guys like that!"

"Please don't go" Tracey slurred and put her arms around Analeise's neck.

" I'm going to have major problems getting taxi's later on"

"Stay with us!" Tracey said.

But Analeise really wanted to go home. She had a good night up until then and didn't want to spoil it. Her feet were really starting to bother her now and didn't want to spend the rest of the evening sitting down.

She said goodbye to Tracey and Maurice (and the drunken Rugby Player trying to get into her knickers!) and made her way to the front door.

As she stepped outside in search of a vacant taxi the street was crammed with people with the same idea as her!

Analeise walked up and down the street hailing anything with four wheels. As she turned the corner of the street it was just as busy.

She looked around for a bit and at the other side of the street seen a tall blonde haired man with a very attractive blonde with very large breasts standing hailing a taxi.

"It couldn't be?" she thought to herself. She wasn't sure if it was because she was a bit pissed on champagne or just pissed off. She walked straight over to the loving couple and realised it was Chris Drummond with a piece of arm candy.

He looked in her direction but pretended not to see her.

She pretended not to see him either. She was embarrassed because she was alone and would hate him thinking that she was a lonely pint for the night.

He didn't speak.

She walked away knowing that he was probably telling the poor

Mare that Analeise was some kind of a psychopath! She didn't care.

She kept on walking, and then she started to run. Her feet were so sore. She tripped on a little stone and fell flat on her face in front of loads of people! A young man helped her up from the ground. "Are you ok?" he asked.

"Yes, thank you" she looked at him and couldn't believe her eyes. "Who are you?" she asked.

"Joe" he answered. It meant nothing to her.

"Try not to rush around" he said gently "It doesn't get you any-where!" he then walked away. Analeise stood in amazement for a moment. He made so much sense.

After half an hour a taxi stopped for Analeise. "Can you take me to Lisburn?" she asked

"It'll cost you!" he said chancing his arm.

"I don't care!" Analeise said as she got in. She just wanted to get home.

At 1.30 She finally arrived home safe and sound. She was exhausted.

The next morning she felt the need to go and grab some fresh air so decided to drive to the beach. She wondered about the really nice gentle young man that said those very wise words to her the previous evening. Analeise's head was all over the place and wished she could see things clearer.

As she was walking along the promenade she spotted the little black and white pup running around. She followed it.

It reminded her of herself. It ran around in circles, sniffed around and bounced around the place! She kept walking behind it to see if it would lead her to the stranger she met on the beach a few weeks ago. It kept walking and walking. Then it jumped down onto the sand and bounded towards the sea. Analeise stood and watched it as it ran to-wards a young boy playing with an aeroplane. She looked around to see where the boy's parents were and seen no sign. She was puzzled. He stood and played with the dog and the aeroplane for a few mo-ments then she heard his mother calling him.

"Jack, its time to go now!"

Things became clearer to Analeise All of these messages and weird people speaking to her meant something.

It was divine intervention. It had to be.

"Be careful, stop rushing around, look after yourself." It was as though someone was telling her to start loving herself and looking out for herself.

When she watched the little boy playing with his aeroplane it became clearer to her that she really needed to get away from it all. Take a flight somewhere and work things out. Her life lately had been a whirlwind of running; chasing and suiting other people especially the disastrous men she had came to meet.

Although Analeise had been off work for a few days, she hadn't been anywhere. The last holiday she had was a whirlwind adventure around New York, which was far from relaxing!

She followed her gut feeling and went deep down into her heart for the thing she really desired.

She longed to see San Francisco for many years and it would be such a treat to go. She felt a rush of excitement at the mere thought of it. Analeise rushed back to her car and drove to her Mums house.

"Happy New Year!" she said as she hugged her. "Did you have a good night?"

"Just the usual!" Analeise answered, "I'm going to San Francisco!"

"Who with?" she asked surprised.

"Just me Mum. I've always wanted to go and am fed up with the whole scene here. I just feel I need to get away from it all my head is wrecked." She said quickly.

"You *have* been through a lot lately," her Mum said thoughtfully. "When were you thinking?"

"Two weeks time!" She announced proudly. "For 10 days!"

"TWO WEEKS?"

"What is the point in hanging around? Anyway January is a really quiet month for me in work." Analeise said.

She couldn't contain herself with excitement. At last something she would be doing herself, just to suit herself!

Analeise started back to work the following day and called Kevin to ask him for some time off in January. He was delighted as January was one of the quietest months of the year for the business and Analeise always had problems filling in her time.

"Sounds like a good holiday you have in mind?" He Said.

"I just want to see Alcatraz, go shopping and maybe take a trip out to the wine valleys." She said planning the whole thing in her head.

When she spoke to Penny about it she was very proud of her.

"It's the best decision you have made in a while Ana!" She said.

Whenever she called Pauline and told her she was thrilled. "Just what you need babe! Forget about all those shitty boys that you play with and do something for you! I've been telling you that for ages!"

"I'm only coming to my senses now!" Analeise agreed.

Too much fucking around, chasing people, worrying, working, getting stressed!

In fact everyone was very positive about the whole thing. Daryl offered to lend her all her expensive, designer clothes. Tracey thought it was the bravest thing she had heard any one do. Tara loved the idea and her brother Ben told her that he would look after her house while she was away.

Analeise went to the Travel agency that afternoon to book the trip so there would be no turning back!

CHAPTER FORTY-THREE

She was so excited about this trip, and had the whole thing planned to perfection. She just couldn't wait.

She stayed in her parent's house the night before and slept in her old bed.

They gave her a lift to the airport the following morning and Analeise cried all the way.

"What are you crying about?" Her Dad asked slightly confused. "Are you having second thoughts?"

Her emotions were all over the place at the moment and she had no idea why.

She took a flight to London Heathrow where at 2.00pm would fly to San Francisco Business Class!

She kissed her parents goodbye and went to check-in.

"This is it!" she thought to herself proudly.

Her flight arrived in London on schedule and Analeise had plenty of time to go somewhere nice for a spot of brunch after she checked in. She took her time over her very large coffee and went to the nearest bookseller.

She bought a map of California, the latest James Patterson novel, a large bottle of water and an even larger bar of her favourite chocolate!

She walked around a few more shops and then headed to her boarding gate.

At 1.15pm everyone travelling on The British Airways flight to San

Francisco were called to gate 27 where they would wait to board. Ana-leise was already there waiting in anticipation!

She looked all around her and wondered what business all of these people had in California. There were old people, young families and even young children travelling on their own obviously going to meet family when they get to the other side. Did they live there? Were they on holiday? Were they visiting relatives?

The seat numbers where Analeise was sitting were called and Ana-leise couldn't wait to be seated.

She was in Row number 14. Seat A. Wow, it was great. She had loads of legroom and her very own TV screen with a wild array of movie choices.

As of yet there was nobody in Seat B.

Meanwhile in the main Terminal Mr James Davenport was being called to go to Gate number 27 where his flight was now boarding.

On the other side of the Terminal a Young Man by the name of Jack Houston walked up to the British Airways ticket desk and asked for a ticket on the next flight to San Francisco.

"I'm sorry sir, but the next flight leaves in 40 minutes, it's full and it will soon be boarding." The girl said as she batted her eyelids flirting at the handsome guy in front of her. "The next one is at 9.30 tomorrow morning."

"I will pay whatever you want if you let me travel on the next flight?" He pleaded very politely in his American Accent. "I am a law-yer and I need to be in court with a very important client tomorrow. I don't have to check anything in, I'm only carrying hand luggage."

"WOULD A MR JAMES DAVENPORT TRAVELLING ON BRIT-ISH AIRWAYS FLIGHT BA237TO SAN FRANCISCO PLEASE GO TO GATE 27 AS THIS FLIGHT IS NOW BOARDING!" Was the second an-nouncement made for this mysterious man.

"Just hold on sir" The British Airways assistant said to a tall distinguished, tanned Jack Houston.

He stood and looked at his very elegant wristwatch and brushed down his creaseless black woollen Jacket. His dark blond hair was very tousled as he kept putting his hands through it in anticipation.

"There is someone supposed to be on that flight, but they seem to have disappeared." The kind girl said, "if he doesn't show up in the next couple of minutes I can sell you his seat is that alright sir?"

"That would be great!" He said smiling, showing off his perfect teeth as she reached for the telephone.

"Strange?" she said to her colleague at the end of the phone as she was staring admiringly at the man before her.

"Ok sir, you are a very lucky man!" She said as she put the phone down. "Can I have your passport please?"

Analeise was sitting on the plane playing around with the radio, television and the incredible reclining seats as she patiently waited for the flight to leave.

Jack Houston was running towards gate 27 as if his life depended on it.

"Can I see your boarding card sir?" The steward asked as he finally arrived a little bit shaken. "You are the last to board Mr Eh?" he looked puzzled.

"Oh yes of course. You were very lucky to get this flight. The passenger who was supposed to board has just disappeared. Lucky enough he didn't check in any luggage! Enjoy your flight!"

The steward scratched his head and watched Jack Houston boarding the flight.

With just minutes to go Jack looked at his boarding card for his seat number.

Row 14. Seat B.

Analeise had opened her water to take a drink whenever he arrived.

He fumbled in the overhead locker, sat down and looked at Analeise.

She was so shaken she spilled some of her water on to her lap.

"Careful" He said. The familiar eyes burning into Analeise's "Are you ok?" He asked with a knowing, gorgeous smile. He smelt of Lemons and Cinnamon. His eyes were piercing blue.

"Oh yes!" said Analeise. "I most certainly am!" She looked at him and it all made sense.

"My name is Jack!" He said with the kindest eyes she had seen.

'Of course!' she thought to herself.

"Analeise" she said and held out her hand. They smiled at each other knowingly. It was like they had known each other forever.

Jack was so glad he was able to catch the flight for more than one reason.

Analeise knew she would be alright.

For a very long time.

EPILOGUE

*O*f course things do happen for a reason.
The mysterious Men with messages for Analeise all made sense to her in the end. At the time though they meant nothing.

Penny told her how she would 'know' whenever the right person comes around.

This was the journey that she was on and no matter what. She would meet with Jack Houston whatever way it took.

So all that chasing and fussing was over nothing and yes, Analeise was behaving just like the little black and white pup on the beach.

Her Angels had to give the message to her in whatever way she would understand.

Who was Mr. James Davenport anyway?
Without him Jack Houston would not have boarded that plane.
Isn't it a funny old world?

ISBN 141208677-9

9 781412 086776